A LOST PEOPLE'S ARCHIVE

Also by Rimli Sengupta

Karno's Daughter: The Lives of an Indian Maid

A LOST PEOPLE'S ARCHIVE

a novel

RIMLI SENGUPTA

ALEPH

ALEPH

ALEPH BOOK COMPANY
An independent publishing firm
promoted by *Rupa Publications India*

First published in India in 2023
by Aleph Book Company
7/16 Ansari Road, Daryaganj
New Delhi 110 002

Copyright © Rimli Sengupta 2023

The author has asserted her moral rights.

All rights reserved.

This is a work of fiction. Names, characters, places, and incidents are either the product of the author's imagination or are used fictitiously and any resemblance to any actual persons, living or dead, events, or locales is entirely coincidental.

No part of this publication may be reproduced, transmitted, or stored in a retrieval system, in any form or by any means, without permission in writing from Aleph Book Company.

ISBN: 978-93-93852-70-0

1 3 5 7 9 10 8 6 4 2

Printed in India.

This book is sold subject to the condition that it shall not, by way of trade or otherwise, be lent, resold, hired out, or otherwise circulated without the publisher's prior consent in any form of binding or cover other than that in which it is published.

For Ma

I want you to know that I am hiding something from you.

—Roland Barthes

CONTENTS

Author's Note	ix
Prologue: The Notebook	xi
Act 1: Kindling	1
Act 2: Fire	59
Act 3: Embers	145
Act 4: Ash	223

AUTHOR'S NOTE

This work, sparked by a found notebook, is based on the true story of a woman and a man. She was close family; him I've never met.

PROLOGUE
THE NOTEBOOK

You know none of this—so don't;
All my songs are still meant for you.

—Jibanananda Das

5 June 1991
New Alipore, Calcutta

SHISHU WAS HAVING TROUBLE FINDING the house. He felt exhausted yet strangely awake. How odd, he thought, that some people insist real life lacks plot. Here he was at seventy-seven, about to see the one who had brought him to poetry at fourteen. And held him there. She was called Noni—cream. Just as his nickname was Shishu—baby. 'Ramesh Chandra Chatterji,' Noni-di would tease him in a mock drawl, 'you'll be a shishu forever!' He heard her infectious giggle and smiled. Giggle and smile, call and response. An intact capsule defying space and time. That's what happens when you're ten, he thought, your days are sealed in amber. Especially your Noni-di days. She was three years older. Noni-di eighty! One of those things you know but really don't, Shishu mused, like the Russian revolution. She was sixteen when he last saw her. All those years, they felt spongy today, like a pillow accordion. Very unlike the dank tunnels they were when lived. He had been looking for her like he'd been breathing. He wasn't expecting anything to happen. Then it did. There's the plot. Had he died without finding her, would that not count as plot?

Lately, Shishu had conjured a reason for his search: he would give Noni-di his notebook. Not that he needed a reason. This was largely a sleight of mind, something that gets you out of bed. Over the past six years he had carefully collected his best poems into a handsome notebook, most composed in jail. Yes, the early ones were coloured by his youthful obsession with her, but that mattered little. His had been a lifelong practice. It was how he had survived. None of his poems had been published, though not for lack of trying. But Noni-di would understand. He would find her, hand her his life's work, and say: here it is, this is what you wrought, the life raft I gripped to get ashore. Shishu slid his hand into his cotton tote bag and touched the notebook.

Technically, he hadn't found her yet. The address he received from Noni-di had a garbled digit. The '4' in Bangla script looks like '8'. Noni-di had written the address twice in her letter, once in each script, but with an '8' in both. The house number, therefore, could be 143/1 or 183/1. Shishu walked the leafy streets. This was only a couple of miles from the jail that had been his home for over a decade, he noticed. More real-life plot. The shade helped but the late morning was already steamy. He felt his thin kurta cling to his back. Wide sidewalks, stately three-storey homes with deep balconies. Noni-di's son had done well. Sweat slid his heavy glasses down his nose. Ah, these dog days before the monsoons. How unfair that it had taken him deep into old age to find her. So old that he couldn't even savour the search for her home. Caught in summer's dragon breath, off by a digit, Shishu felt a belly laugh bubble up at this injustice. He straightened his aching back and approached the local post office for help.

∽

What I want to tell you is that all of this is true. The woman Shishu is about to meet is my grandmother, Dida. At this time, she is mother to eleven, grandmother to twenty-two, and great-grandmother to two. She lives with the family of her eldest son, my Baba. The home Shishu is searching for on this sultry morning is mine. I have never met him. Growing up we had heard of Dida's friend, the freedom fighter who had served time as a political prisoner. Not much more. But the notebook Shishu is carrying for her today has recently come to me. That is how I found out that my Dida was once called Noni. And that she had lived other lives.

The notebook is black, its hard cover bound in faux leather, a typical diary that midsize businesses used to hand out in the New Year. This one, from 1985, was issued by Modi Steels Ltd. Head office: Swallow Lane, Calcutta 700001. It came within a hair's breadth of becoming scrap and has seen some rough weather. Its edges have water damage. The covers are warped. The binding is partly off the spine, pushing the pages out like old teeth. But the contents are intact. The pages are covered in a neat hand, dense in places. Fountain pen ink, not ballpoint. And it gives off that rich musk all you used-book lovers know. I can smell it even without cracking it open.

It is filled with poems, but not just. Opening epigraphs are followed by a long preface, then 108 poems composed between 1928 and 1981, each tagged with a date and place. That number is not an accident; 108 signifies a devotional offering. Interleaved with the poems are memoir entries, footnotes, newspaper clippings pasted and neatly bordered, letters copied, and more—all in a deliberate arrangement. This is evidently a highly meticulous mind, Teutonic in texture, borderline obsessive even. He seems confident that his work is worth preserving, worth tracing the evolution of. The collection is like an immersive cyclorama of a long and improbable life. A life tattooed with his Noni-di, my Dida. Its peculiar effect on me has been one of phantom memory. I'm remembering things I didn't know I knew. For instance, this meeting in June 1991. The notebook doesn't describe it. And I had already left home. Why, then, should you believe me?

∽

With his own ninth decade approaching, Shishu had grown increasingly sure that his Noni-di had passed on. And then, just like that, in February 1991, a chance encounter: he found out that she was living and that someone knew where. The common acquaintance didn't have her address but could arrange to deliver a letter. This knowledge did not bring the electricity Shishu had long expected. Instead he felt something like the fatigued relief of a salmon reaching its spawning ground, its flesh mostly digested, its skin in tatters, eager to lay eggs. Then, a practical problem. Her last letter to him had been in 1945, just after he'd stepped out of jail. What should he, what could he, write her now? He stewed on this for weeks. With mid-April nearing, he found an innocuous excuse: he would write her with wishes for the Bengali New Year. He tried to keep the tone even, wordsmithed endlessly, then handed the letter over for delivery.

A month went by, then another. His contact probably didn't act right away. Why would he? Shishu hadn't said his letter was urgent. The idea of urgency, after all these years, didn't fit. Yet this wait for a reply that may not come felt surprisingly heavy. And then it came, Noni-di's reply. That was two days ago, 3 June, in the afternoon. A brief letter, even-toned like his but the effort not showing. Shishu read and re-read it, the lines and in between. She had written that his letter had taken over a month to reach her. That he should come to the provided address by 15 June. That 'I remember Patuakhali. So much water has since flown down the rivers. There's a deep awareness in the human subconscious. It stirs to life, then hides again. Don't you think?' Shishu marvelled at this rounded adult voice, circumspect yet vulnerable. And then there was this: 'Perhaps you'll be curious to know all the news of the intervening years. But is knowing that really possible?' Ah, that is masterful, thought Shishu. Noni-di always went straight to the heart of the matter.

Shishu had waited a day simply to savour all of this. Last evening he went for his usual walk near the Serampore flagstaff, his favourite stretch along the Hooghly. Afterwards, he sat on the parapet at nightfall and watched the river change from silver to dark glass. His thoughts veered to other rivers, to the water world of Barisal, across an international border.

This morning he could've easily taken the 5 a.m. train but he didn't want to arrive at an unseemly hour. He caught the 8.45 a.m. Serampore Local instead and reached Howrah station at 9.15 a.m. Weekday, rush hour. Platform 13 was a roiling sea of humanity. He hugged his cotton tote close. Precious cargo. The official purpose of his visit, he had declared to himself, was to give Noni-di his notebook.

Yes, he had a purpose, just like all these officegoers. Swarm into the subway with them and up the steps to the station's bus bay. Then a whole hour on bus number 37. And another fifteen minutes on foot in the scorching heat to find her home.

∽

It was my mother who answered the doorbell. She saw a tall man, weathered but wiry, with flared ears and kind eyes. An uncertain, buck-toothed smile. He was drenched in sweat and looked sapped. She noticed his crumpled clothes, his white cotton dhuti far from white—here was an elder not well-looked after. Ma sat him down under the fan, got him a drink, and went in to inform Dida. Shishu cooled down soon enough but was starting to quake within. This, that which was about to happen, was a runnel in his brain sculpted by a million dry runs. Which version would play now? Ma came back to take him to the balcony where his Noni-di was waiting.

There she stood, a few feet away. Not an apparition like those that sometimes used to cut through his tar nights in jail. This spacious balcony was real. That bleached sky beyond, the chequered mosaic underfoot—all real. She, rail thin, in a plain cotton sari. Widow's whites. He knew this from her letter. She was sixteen when they parted, eighty now. All this he knew. But knowing is not seeing. And yearning, waiting, working to make something happen is not the same as being ready when it does. He had been calmer on death row. Why was this so much harder? He felt trussed in a straitjacket. Then she held out her quiet, bare hands and some dam broke somewhere and maybe he lunged or maybe she fell towards him and his arms engulfed her and she was so tiny and how could so much feel like such a wisp. Tears now, like the season's first rains. They stood there, fused. Space fused, time fused. Washed by waves upon waves of something like song memory.

After they had collected themselves, Ma brought them in and sat them on Dida's bed. She then went about arranging an elaborate lunch for Dida's special guest. She gave them some privacy. They had so much catching-up to do.

∽

But they don't speak. There's too much to say. The two old friends sit silently on that bed like bookends. A contented silence. Not empty, not angry, not hurt. Minutes tick by. She reaches under her pillow and brings out a gift: a book, with a small sticky-note on the wrap bearing a brief poem. It is a stiff paean to Shishu. Do remember this sticky-note, it may come up again. Shishu has placed it prominently in the notebook, you see. It is neon green, covered with my Dida's looping scrawl. She has dated it: 5 June 1991.

As he receives her gift Shishu remembers his: the notebook. He pulls it out and delivers his practised speech: 'Here it is, Noni-di, this is what your words inspired me into. Your 1928 letter, remember?' Then he goes on: 'There's plenty of room in it. Won't you add some of your poems here? We could leave an *us* in poetry,' he adds earnestly, 'for posterity.' Even as the words leave him Shishu thinks he has perhaps said too much. Noni-di accepts the notebook with an enigmatic smile.

∽

They won't speak. They care too much about what has happened in the in-between years. An imperfect sharing is the only choice and they seem to not want it. Perhaps we should leave them be. But one of Shishu's poems has this line: *Will my fervent songs find room in any heart?* And one of his notebook's epigraphs poses another dare: *Don't write anything until you feel a child kicking inside you, impatient to be born.* He seems to be egging me on to root at the in-between.

Shishu's notebook is the gist, the crust left behind on the pan. The cooks are long gone. I can taste the intense flavours in the pan's scrapings. From this I'm going to try and reconstitute the dish. There are bound to be errors. If you quit trusting me, I'll understand.

Act 1
Kindling

chapter 1

10 March 1929
Kali Bari Road, Barisal town
Barisal district
British India

THE LANKY BOY RAN LIKE the wind. It was his legs that ran; his brain was crumpled paper. He didn't know what he was running from. The blood? But that was splattered all over his face. And his right hand. He tried to wipe it off his cheeks with his left and found tears. Why was he crying? In his head two lines played in a loop: *jini tilo phulo, nashika awtulo*—like a sesame blossom, that matchless nose. Over and over and over. An absurd metronome. Please. Not Noni-di in his head now, not near all this blood. Something must have brought this on. The man, he had a nose like Noni-di's. A fine ridge dipping to a point, flanked by flared nostrils. Flared in horror. That image broke through the fog in his head. That and the warmth of the blood. The warm spray that had hit him in the face. His mouth must've been open, some of it had got in. That taste now lay coiled on his tongue. He couldn't spit it out, his mouth was too dry. He sucked in great gulps of air. He could hear the clamour of his pursuers. They were closing in on him, the boys of B. M. School. Last week he'd played football on the school grounds with some of them. He wished they would speed up and snare his legs. The blood was bothering him. Need a rinse, need a rinse. He saw the arched gate coming up on the left: the ancient Pashanmoyee Kali temple. Ah, Ma Kali, I've also had some blood today, like you! He swerved into the compound. The temple pond looked inviting in the dusk, like a well-made bed. The plunge broke his delirium. He snapped awake. As the waters closed over him, Shishu knew. He had pulled off the plan. He had punctured through, into another kingdom entirely.

§

The plan was quite simple. Sub-inspector Jyotish Chandra Roy, the officer-in-charge of Barisal's Kotwali police station, usually went on his evening patrol only during the week. But since the big flare-up at the end of January, he had taken to doing a solo round on Sunday evenings as well. The city was amidst an uneasy truce, with sporadic incidents but nothing serious. Roy usually finished his round by sundown and cycled along Kali Bari Road back to the kotwali. The decision had been to target him at a quiet stretch of this road, along the park adjoining B. M. School. That spot at dusk on Sunday offered the best chance at eliminating witnesses. There would be two lookouts, Nitai and Srimanta, posted at the intersection where Kali Bari Road meets the Bogra Road arterial. Both were known to the police: they had arrest records. A fresh face was needed for this mission and Shishu was it. Once Roy passed the intersection and entered Kali Bari Road, the lookouts would let out two long whistles. That would be Shishu's 'get set' signal. Near the park, Shishu would see Roy come into view and call out while rushing towards him, as if to anxiously report a problem. Roy would slow down and come to a stop to ask what the matter was. Shishu would get close, talking all the while, then whip out his dagger and stab Roy to death.

Except it's hard to stab someone to death. Roy was a burly figure. Shishu would only have a split second for the first strike, and depending on how that went, maybe time for another. The group worked on this all through February at Batakrishna Misra's gymnasium, where they trained in baton and dagger play. This was really a hidden cell of Tarun Sangha, a revolutionary outfit headed by Satindranath Sen, Barisal's firebrand Congress leader. The boys had set up a hemp effigy of Roy, about the right girth, draped in a police uniform shirt. All of this was new. The cell had a slew of other actions under its belt but had never attempted murder before. Shishu kept up the drill: first a hard stab in the midriff, then as the man lurches a quick stab at the heart. The tough fabric of the uniform posed a challenge, even for Chawkbajar market's meanest dagger. Exposed skin was a much better bet. But practising on animals was out, the squeals would attract too much attention. Shishu was encouraged to hang out with the Chawkbajar butchers, maybe pick up a few ideas. But the idea came to him in biology class. Shishu was in the ninth standard at B. M. School. After literature, biology was his favourite. The teacher had hung up on the wall a graphic poster of a skinned human neck: veins blue, arteries red, muscles beige. He was surprised to learn that the jugular vein is practically skin deep. With a visual clue, he could slash it open with no trouble at all. But the goal would be to go a bit deeper and at least nick the carotid artery. Arterial pressure would do the rest.

Later, at his trial, the crack lawyer from Calcutta defending Shishu would say to the judge: 'In our experience, Your Honour, for it to be someone's first time, and with a dagger, that's rare. And for this slip of a boy to overpower a man thrice his heft. Injure perhaps, but kill? Stabbing someone to death is hard. There's a certain amount of...have you ever slaughtered a pig?'

In the actual moment, Shishu remembers to take his time. He keeps jabbering in response to Roy's questions as to what the matter is. They now are a couple feet apart. Roy's face, still seated on his bicycle, is about level with Shishu's. He has set his right foot on the road, the left is on the pedal; his ample paunch spills over his belt. He begins to bark at Shishu's incoherence. This brings out a bulge on the left side of Roy's neck. Shishu notices. Hand–eye. His right arm swings out as if on its own, and whips back. One strike. The warm spurt still catches him by surprise. Then the next one. A pulsating spray. He has hit the artery. That is Shishu's final lucid thought before shock takes over. Roy grasps his neck and lets out a piercing shriek that thins to a gurgle. He then slumps, his bicycle toppling with him. Shishu, trembling and bloodied, is briefly glued to the spot. His training is to yell 'Bande Mataram!' He tries, it comes out in a croak. He drops the bloody dagger and his legs begin to run. That's the training. Bhagat Singh escaped too and hasn't been caught yet. There are pedestrians about, they've heard Roy scream.

They see a man down in a pool of blood, a boy running. They yell, 'Stop, stop him! Thief!' The boys wrapping up their Sunday afternoon football at the B. M. School hear the alarm. A half-dozen or so dash out in hot pursuit. The chase lasts less than five minutes. Shishu dives into the temple pond. His pursuers fish him out. The Kotwali station is a short walk. The police arrive. Shishu is roughed up, arrested, and thrown in jail.

∽

With nightfall, the word fanned out through town like the spring breeze coming up from the Kirtankhola River: Sub-inspector Roy had bled to death within minutes of being stabbed by Shishu. The news eddied along the riverbank, where Shishu's winded friends had gathered; it swirled through the warrens of Chawkbajar, thickening at Shishu's favourite kite shop, at the carpentry kiosk that lathed his prized tops, and at the blacksmith's where he'd bought the dagger; it shuttered Batakrishna Misra's gym, where light-headed party members swung between jubilation and envy. It hushed Shishu's home, where his father, a government pleader in Barisal District Court, sat in a heap on a darkened balcony overlooking the river's sweep. Shishu heard it, too, inside the top security cell of Barisal District Jail. The guards told him. Their words were intended as threat but came out as fear, Shishu could tell. Manacled to the floor, on his first night ever away from home, Shishu wanted to feel heroic but could not. Something crept up him like ice on a lake freezing over. A dark lack of purpose. He couldn't stop shivering.

Barisal was no stranger to political unrest, but murder? Of a top cop? In the heart of town, on Kali Bari Road! Tongues clucked into the night. These things happened far away, usually in Calcutta or Lahore. Not in provincial Barisal. Moreover, Bengal had not seen a political murder in nearly three years. And by a fourteen-year-old? Was he the youngest ever, the townsfolk wondered. An ace student at B. M. School, no less. And a pleader's son! Did you know that he also sketches well? Such a promising boy. The pervasive shock was laced with admiration: this was a daring and unprecedented strike.

Law enforcement had been hit, they would pay back with interest. The town braced for a blitz.

∽

When Shishu was produced in Barisal's criminal court three days later, he had a swollen black eye. His other eye was vacant. Much of his scalp was exposed and scabby, his hair had been ripped out in handfuls. He was charged with first-degree murder. A swift trial ensued. The government furnished witnesses who undid the defence lawyer's case that the person who had stabbed the Sub-inspector was different from the boy found swimming in the Kali temple pond. The Sub-inspector's inconsolable widow was in attendance. The court found Shishu guilty. The sentence: death by hanging. Shishu was to be transported to Calcutta's Presidency Jail and await his execution.

chapter 2

The past is a country that issues no visas.
We can only enter it illegally.

—Janet Malcolm

SHISHU DID NOT HANG AT fourteen. You would have heard of him if he had. He would be calendar art, like Khudiram Bose or Bhagat Singh. No, he lived. We have met him at seventy-seven. But before we get to the whys and hows of the murder, there is something you should know: Shishu's notebook is silent about it. He does say that he got the death penalty that was later commuted to life. It is clear that he saw himself as a freedom fighter. A poem he wrote while still on death row has these lines: *they'll hang me, Ma / for loving freedom*. But he mentions nowhere that he had killed a man. Given his fussy attention to detail throughout the notebook, this omission can't be an accident. But what is it saying? We all want a shot at being remembered as we wish to be. This is getting much harder with the digital contrails we shed now. But Shishu left contrails too, his crime did. Clenched facts in the government's intelligence and court documents, flowery homage on the other side. And Shishu must have known this. He was seventy-two when he began curating his notebook. I wish I could ask him why he left the murder out. But he's been gone over twenty-five years now.

Maybe what Shishu is saying with the omission in his notebook is that he had lived with that murder-shaped hole all his life. I have stepped into that hole: a portal into a time, a place, a people. These are my people, but I still feel like I may be trespassing.

∽

Here is one text in which Shishu makes an appearance: 'Terrorism in India: 1917–1936', published in 1937 by the Intelligence Bureau,

Home Department, Government of India. This internal report bears Britain's imperial coat of arms—lion and unicorn, tongues lolling—and is marked 'Confidential'. It is the colonial administration's assessment of India's nationalist revolution over those two decades. The first, and by far the fattest, chapter is on Bengal. For 1929, the report on Bengal says:

> The year opened with the murder in March of a Sub-inspector of Police, Jyotish Chandra Roy, who was stabbed to death in Barisal by Ramesh Chandra Chatterji. The murderer fled, but was captured by students, and was sentenced to death, although the High Court later commuted the sentence to transportation for life. This murder was the first committed by terrorists since the murder in May 1926 within Alipore Central Jail.

Then there's the 'Bengal Green List', a document marked 'Secret', published internally in March 1930 by the Intelligence Branch, Criminal Investigation Department, Government of Bengal. In the preface, F. P. McKinty, Special Superintendent of Police, writes:

> This volume contains the names of persons who have been warned or detained under the Defence of India Act (1915), Regulation III (1818), Ingress into India Ordinance (1914), Bengal Ordinance (1924), the Bengal Criminal Law Amendment Act (1925), and the members of the revolutionary and anarchical movement who have been convicted under the Indian Penal Code and the Arms and Explosives Substances Act, or bound down under the preventative sections of the Criminal Procedure Code. It supersedes the 'Blue List' issued in 1924. It is correct up to the end of 1929.

This alphabetical list of 1833 profiles was the British government's roster of bad actors in Bengal. Shishu shows up as entry number 517:

> **Chatterji, Ramesh Chandra**: son of Durga Kumar, of Kirtipasha, Jhalokathi, district Barisal. Year of birth: 1914. Prosecuted in the case of murder of Sub-inspector Jyotish Roy,

Officer in charge, Kotwali, Barisal, committed on 10 March, 1929. Convicted and sentenced under section 302 of the Indian Penal Code, to death. On appeal to High Court, the sentence was, on 26 July 1929, commuted to transportation for life.

There are other names on this list of interest. At number 295:

> **Bhattacharji, Srimanta**: son of Haraprasanna, of Chandshi, Gournadi, district Barisal. Year of birth: 1914. A member of Satin Sen's party. Bound down under section 110, Criminal Procedure Code, to furnish a bond of Rs. 1000 with one surety to be of good behaviour for three years, in default to suffer rigorous imprisonment for that period. Judgement delivered on 29 October 1929.

Shishu says in the notebook that Srimanta was a dear friend: a classmate in school, and a comrade-in-arms in the party. They also shared a budding enthusiasm for poetry. One of Shishu's early poems was inspired by one of Srimanta's entitled 'Blow it all up!' Srimanta was one of the lookouts on the day of the murder, although Shishu does not mention that. Here's the other lookout, at number 515:

> **Chatterji, Phani Lal**: alias Nitai, son of Surjya Kumar, of 53, Hari Ghosh Street, Calcutta. Year of birth: 1904. A member of Satin Sen's party. Bound down under section 110, Criminal Procedure Code, to furnish a bond of Rs. 1000 with one surety to be of good behaviour for three years, in default to suffer rigorous imprisonment for that period. Judgement delivered on 29 October 1929.

Both lookouts were arrested and spent about seven months in jail as undertrials, before getting out on bond. As did the man, number 1246, who ran the gymnasium where Shishu trained with Srimanta and Nitai:

> **Misra, Batakrishna**: son of late Rajendra of Dacca town. Year of birth, 1905. A member of Satin Sen's party. Bound down under section 110, Criminal Procedure Code, to execute a

bond of Rs. 1000 with one surety to be of good behaviour for three years, in default to suffer rigorous imprisonment for that period. Judgement delivered 29 October 1929.

We're seeing Satin Sen's name a lot. Curiously, however, his profile is absent from the Bengal Green list. This despite the fact that he was in jail when the list was prepared. Satin or Satindranath Sen is at this time a prominent leader of the Congress Party in Barisal. He's in jail along with fourteen members of his underground revolutionary outfit, Tarun Sangha, whose names show up on the list. They were all swept up in the aftermath of Shishu's arrest in March 1929. Sen was not freed until July 1930. The corresponding verdict from the Calcutta High Court had this to say about a speech he gave on 1 February 1929 at Barisal's Town Hall:

> One can easily imagine the effect of such speeches on the impressionable minds of Satin Sen's young followers who looked up to him as a hero, and it was one of them, Ramesh Chandra Chatterji, who less than six weeks later murdered the Sub-inspector Jyotish Chandra Roy who had arrested Satin Sen under Section 107, Criminal Procedure Code, on 30 January. Two of the other appellants, Srimanta and Nitai, were seen in Ramesh's company loitering in suspicious circumstances on the road just before Ramesh stabbed the Sub-inspector with a dagger very similar to one that came from a local shop. Dagger play was taught at a local gymnasium by the appellant Batakrishna Misra to Srimanta and Nitai as well as to Ramesh Chatterji. There is evidence that Satin Sen was interested in this gymnasium, and there can be little doubt that it was there that Ramesh learnt the skill in the use of the dagger that he displayed in the murder of the Sub-inspector.

There are other sources that shed various bits of light on this murder. The location and the time of day, for instance. But it'll get tedious. I wanted you to have a glimpse under the hood. Shishu doesn't want to talk about it, but he did kill a man. That act forever changed his life.

chapter 3

Oh wail no more, you kite of golden wings
It reminds me of her eyes, pale like rattan fruit

—Jibanananda Das

1927, Patuakhali town
Barisal district
British India

THE JANUARY EVENING IS CHILLY but Shishu has worked up a sweat. He is dashing home from the Tarun Sangha library. Clasped to his chest is his prize: a copy of *Pather Dabi*, Sarat-babu's latest. He'd been keeping an eye on the library's hidden stash of books banned by the government. But he can barely believe that he's managed to grab it before anyone else. The book is quite a brick. He pictures Noni-di's face lighting up when he hands it to her. The two of them have been dying to read this novel ever since it came out. Shishu is bursting from the run and the thrill. Who's going to have the first go, he grins to himself. Why, Noni-di, of course.

∽

Patuakhali at this time is an urban speck, deep in the delta where the mammoth Meghna breaks up to meet the sea. The town is encircled on three sides by water—two rivers and a canal—and the land beyond further dissolves into a filigree of water. Shishu will turn thirteen this year; he's in the seventh standard at the city's premier Jubilee High School. Noni turned sixteen in January. They've been next-door neighbours for five years now. Their fathers, both government pleaders, are colleagues at the Patuakhali Sessions Court. The two families are close. Since Noni's mother passed away four years ago, Shishu's has become the surrogate. The brood of children—five siblings in Noni's case and three in Shishu's—have grown up as one, swarming seamlessly through the two homes. But Shishu and Noni share a special bond. She no longer goes to school, too unseemly for a girl of marriageable age. Yet she has a life of the mind: a poetry practice that only a few know about, Shishu being one, and an insatiable appetite for reading. Shishu, also a bookworm but with library access, keeps her supplied. Together they read serious literature, both canon and contraband. But they also devour *Mouchak*, a popular literary monthly for the youth. They love the adventure novels of Hemen Ray, *Jakher Dhan* is a favourite. The treasure hunt in it infuses the land around them, a verdant water world, with exciting possibilities.

They used to have adventures of their own, Shishu remembers ruefully. Up until a couple years ago, when Noni-di could still move about freely, she was always the lead, he the sidekick. They would take a slim dinghy out into the surrounding beels—vast shallow seasonal waterbodies, the water so clear you can see the mossy bottom. In the filtered light the moss takes on magical hues. Schools of fish flit about, some translucent, some streaked with neon colours. Water lilies bob in clusters on the surface. The electric blue ones were Noni-di's favourite, with their yellow centres. She would pull them out, stem and all, and with some deft fingering but no threads fashion intact garlands out of them, the flower a dangling pendant. One for him and one for her. She would then break into song, her voice ringing out full-throated over the open water. Or recite long poems by Rabindranath. On Shishu's prodding she would occasionally say one of her own, maybe her latest. Shishu marvelled at how Noni-di could bend words at will.

Not just words, her voice itself had a special timbre. Particularly when she sang. Shishu recalled the marathon choral sessions at their courtyard in the thick of the monsoons. His mother in the lead, singing songs of Manosha, the patron goddess of snakes. This being the season when Manosha's wards emerged from their flooded homes, the songs sought her benediction to protect against bites. Women and girls from the neighbourhood gathered to take part,

Noni-di amongst them. Even in a chorus Shishu could easily pick out her voice, like a gold thread in dull tapestry.

In the spring, he and Noni-di often rode into shady canals lined with rattan thickets, hunting the ripe fruits. The women scrubbing dishes with mud at the water's edge would chuckle while calling out warnings about the dagger-like thorns. Noni-di flashed a grin at them, whipped the end of her sari around her waist to make a pocket for their harvest, and plunged the bamboo pole deep into the mud to nose the dinghy ashore. Then the game was on: pick the most fruit with the least scratches. Shishu always won, or maybe Noni-di let him. She got busy washing the blood off of her cuts. After getting back, they would peel the scaly skins off the ripe rattan, each the size of a human eyeball, sprinkle rock salt, give it a shake, and pop them into their mouths. Mostly pit, with a lucent layer of sweet-tart flesh, the fruits were not the main pay-off. The fun was really in the hunt. Shishu wanted those afternoons to never end.

But end they did. Noni-di was now largely homebound, busy with embroidery projects: tablecloths, pillowcases, handkerchiefs. Shishu likes to draw, so she commissions him to make patterns for her. He makes a sketch, then traces the outline on her fabric with carbon paper. Noni-di always has high praise for his art, which thrills him no end. She fixes the marked fabric in a bamboo embroidery hoop and fills the pattern in with a variety of stitches, in various shades. Some of these projects stretch into weeks. Shishu watches her as she works: collected, eyes lowered, humming a tune. Something has shifted in Noni-di, Shishu can't put a finger on it. She has always been pretty but now she seems magnetic. And condensed somehow, like milk cooked down. Maybe she's really turning into noni, Shishu thinks. A titter escapes him. Noni-di hears it and looks up from her work. Her gaze dazzles him; he has to look away. Is it she who's changing or is it me, Shishu wonders.

∽

He knows he's changing, too. Just in the past year an entirely new world has opened up for him. It was Noni-di's elder brother,

Shankar-da, who first took him to Tarun Sangha and introduced him to Satin Sen. Shishu had seen him once before, Patuakhali's most famous son. Jubilee High was Satin-da's alma mater and he had come to talk about Tarun Sangha, on a recruitment drive. Shishu remembers being utterly struck: Satin-da looked like a mountain, towering and broad-chested, with a faraway gaze. Hearing him speak Shishu had felt a tingle come up his spine, as if straightening it. Dozens of boys got fired up and joined in. Shishu wanted to sign up too, but one look at his own skinny arms had wilted his resolve. Shankar-da was already active in the party. He was nineteen, practically a grown-up. Shishu admired him, his rippling biceps, but also felt intimidated. One time, when he had come by with books for Noni-di, Shankar-da pulled him aside. 'You like to read,' he said, handing him a few books, 'read these.'

Shishu was thrilled with Shankar-da's attention and wanted to live up to it. But try as he did, he couldn't get into the books. One was a dry manual called *Bartaman Rananiti* (Modern Warfare) sprinkled with religious quotes from the Gita and the Chandi. Shishu dipped into it and had to give up. The book on the Italians, Garibaldi and Mazzini, and the military exploits of their valiant band of 'red shirt' volunteers, was better, but too far away and too long ago. Then there was *Anandamath* (Abbey of Bliss) that he had really looked forward to reading. He had heard that this novel from 1882, banned since 1905, had birthed Bande Mataram, the clarion cry against the British. But he found the book strange. India in it is imagined as a Hindu goddess. And in her name, a band of militant Hindu monks repeatedly kill Muslims just for being Muslims, loot and burn their villages, even mutilate their corpses. They mob pedestrians and force them to say Bande Mataram under the threat of bodily harm. Shishu didn't like the taste of this at all. The book spoke of a thing called Hindutva—the monks seek a Hindu nation. Is that what we want, Shankar-da?

Many long sessions followed. Shankar-da explained that the book was set at a different time, but had valuable lessons for the current: discipline, loyalty, sacrifice. That there was a real abbey in Barisal town modelled on *Anandamath* called Shankar Math. Even Satin-da had trained there. He said the country was still in chains, like in the book, and needed Shishu to pick up arms if necessary. What kind of son stands by and watches his mother get degraded? A weak son. That's what Hindus had become. Shishu glanced at his own form and had to agree. My friend Latif is skinny, too, he wanted to say, but felt tongue-tied. Shankar-da pronounced a prescription for Shishu: twenty push-ups and twenty sit-ups every morning, followed by a fistful of Bengal gram soaked overnight. There were exercises for the mind as well: take a mouthful of the most delicious rabri, hold it without swallowing, then spit it out. Shishu would inevitably swallow, then dissolve in embarrassed coughs. One new moon night, Shankar-da took Shishu to the cremation ground at the edge of town on the Golachipa River, and left him there: Shishu was to stare down his fears. Steeped in a treacly darkness, with his heart in his mouth, Shishu managed to stay put for twenty minutes before fleeing. But it was a start.

Around this time, Patuakhali became abuzz with news that Barisal's itinerant bard Mukunda Das was coming to perform. A strapping figure with a thunderous voice, Das's witty and caustic anti-British songs were wildly popular. But his best hit by far was a quiet ballad—'Say goodbye, Ma, I'll be back'—an elegy to the eighteen-year-old revolutionary, Khudiram Bose, who had been hanged for murdering two British women in 1908. Every man, woman, and child, even in Bengal's deepest rural recesses, knew this song by heart. Out after serving time for sedition, Das was now crisscrossing Barisal district with renewed vigour and new material: songs of Nazrul Islam, a fresh name on the rise. The 'rebel poet', they called him. Shishu and Noni were beside themselves with excitement. They had loved Islam's recent book of poems, *Bisher Banshi* (Poison Flute) that was banned immediately upon publication in 1924 and went viral underground. And to hear those poems in Mukunda Das's voice!

The event was at the spacious grounds of Jubilee High School. Townsfolk came out in droves, especially women, defying social taboos. There was Mukunda Das on the dais, in saffron robes, his wild curls in a nimbus, his eyes flashing, on his chest a gleaming array of medals he'd been awarded. He opened not with a song, but a poem by Nazrul Islam. He spoke slowly, like a sermon, in a sonorous tone:

> bawlo bir
> bawlo: unnato mawmo shir
> shir nehari amar nawtoshir oi shikhawr himadrir

> O valiant, speak
> Say: my head is high
> So high, it shames the mountain peak

The crowd was transfixed, some in tears. Shishu felt something course through him and fill him out, as if he'd been inflatable all along and had just found his source of air. He looked over at Noni-di. They shared a smile. She was feeling it too. Then came the songs, like repeated strikes of lightning.

> karar oi louho kawpat
> bhenge phyal, kawr re lopat
> rakto-jawmat shikawl pujar pashan-bedi
> ...
> mar hnak, haydari hnak
> kandhe ne dundubhi dhak
> dak ore dak mrityuke dak jeebon pane!

> That steel jail gate
> Smash it, wipe out
> The bloodied altar of chains
> ...
> Go on, roar
> Pick up the war drums
> Call, o call death towards life!

As they walked back home, some of the charge from that night got stowed within Shishu. He felt more hefty somehow. Shortly thereafter, he signed up with Tarun Sangha and began working out at their gym. He joined classes on wrestling and dagger play. And he began noticing things, like he had put on glasses he didn't know he needed. For instance, one of Nazrul Islam's songs, which he had enjoyed before for its catchy tune, now revealed itself as a whip:

> *jaater naame bojjati shawb jaat jaliyat khelcho juwa!*
> *chnulei tor jaat jabe? jaat cheler hater noyto mowa.*
>
> *All this evil in the name of caste, you swindling rascals!*
> *You lose caste at a touch? It's not kid's candy.*

It pried loose a memory from a recent vacation at Goila, his mother's village in north Barisal. The homestead there was spacious. The main gateway in the boundary wall opened onto an outer courtyard, which then led to an inner courtyard surrounded by several thatched huts: living quarters and kitchen. A narrow alley between the kitchen and the adjoining hut went out to a tree-filled backyard and steps to the river. A gaunt man used to chop firewood in that backyard. Shishu never found out his name. A Muslim, he remembers, beard and skullcap. A tattered lungi. He would heave his load up, ribs showing, walk all the way around to the main gate, pass through the outer courtyard, then into the inner, and finally unload, panting, near the kitchen. One blistering morning, he took the shortcut—the alley from the backyard to the kitchen. The reaction was instant. Shishu's uncle, Chotomama, pounced on him.

'You son of a bitch, you just touched the kitchen! There goes all the food!'

The man tried to explain: 'Didn't touch it, kawrta, I walked down the middle of the alley. I didn't touch the wall!' But this only inflamed matters.

'Don't the two adjoining thatches touch above the alley? Didn't you therefore trample the kitchen's shadow, you numbskull? And you're giving me lip? How dare you!' Chotomama tore off his slipper and began slapping the man with it on his bare back.

The man mumbled through tears, 'Kawrta, even your pet dog

passes through that alley, do you throw out all the food then? And I am a man, kawrta!' Logic, from one who should be silent, was the last straw.

Chotomama now charged at him with a bamboo rod. The man fled. Without his wages.

The final glance he had flashed before fleeing was seared in Shishu's brain. The blue fury in it. At the time it had scared him. Now, he began to burrow into it. He had seen variations of Chotomama's behaviour countless times. Shishu knew he was a Brahmin; he couldn't eat with Muslims or low-castes. Some in his family even avoided contact with their shadow. He had grown up with these things. They seemed natural, like breathing. But he now began to wonder. Were they? He tried talking to Shankar-da about this but didn't get very far. Shankar-da said once freedom comes the rest will get worked out. What about until then? Shishu wondered if the Muslims and low-castes around him—in the fields, on the fishing boats—were all like that woodcutter. Violated and bottled up. Very different from Nazrul Islam in faraway Calcutta. And he could see Hindus who admired Islam's poetry and yet continued to be his 'swindling rascals' in real life. Shishu couldn't figure any of this out.

Then, in late July 1926, Tarun Sangha informed him that he was ready for his formal initiation. On a rainy new moon night, he was taken to the ancient Dakatiya Kali—Bandit Kali—temple, atop a knoll on the south bank of the Laukati River. The temple was a short walk from Shishu's school. The story went that back in the day, this area teemed with bandits who terrorized the river traffic. Before any major attack, they would come here to seek Kali's blessing. The association was not lost on Shishu; the setting both thrilled and unnerved him. Satin-da had been called away on urgent business, but three senior leaders were present. All were solemn. The temple was closed for the night, but Kali was visible through the locked iron grille. Light from a lone oil lamp glistened on Kali's lolling tongue. Like it was wet with blood, thought Shishu, alive with goosebumps. The group sat on the porch, Shishu facing the goddess. He was read a set of vows and asked to repeat them aloud, eyes on Kali. First vow: I will not leave the sangha until its object is fulfilled. Second: I will not let ties of affection distract me. Third: I will, without excuse, perform the work assigned to me by the leader. And so on. The penalty for any breach: Kali's wrath.

After the vows, he was given a brief primer on the Gita: that he was to practise the idea of being a nimitta matra—a mere implement of divine will; that Krishna tells Arjuna 'those men whom you shrink from slaying are already slain'; that the sin was not in the killing but in the attachment to it. He was then handed a copy of the Gita and asked to read the marked passages from it each morning.

Shishu had gone through the ceremony wanting to be present. He felt honour and heft in being part of something big. It excited him. But there were these gnawing questions. He decided to let it be for now. He had pledged to follow the leader. Surely, Satin-da couldn't be wrong.

3

Barisal district at this time was over 70 per cent Muslim; for Patuakhali subdivision within it, the figure was 86 per cent. Nearly half the district's Hindus were Dalit Namasudras. The economy was agrarian; peasant masses worked the land and water under a handful of landlords, who were overwhelmingly upper-caste Hindu. This slim minority also dominated the professional class—government jobs, hospitals, schools, colleges—to which both Shishu's and Noni's families belonged. Muslim participation in Western-style education had begun ramping up only in the 1910s, over seventy years after the Hindus. In Barisal, the anti-colonial movement was largely an elite Hindu endeavour.

The movement's leadership was aware of this and tried to build mass support through outreach. Ashwini Kumar Dutta's Swadesh Bandhab Samiti had 175 branches all over Barisal district. Through these, committed cadres brought relief to the deep rural interior during floods and cholera outbreaks, both of which were common. They also helped with legal arbitration in land disputes, an immense help for the illiterate peasantry. The cadre were thus armed revolutionaries on the one hand and social activists on the other. But the literature and techniques used to train them, the iconography used in propaganda, were overwhelmingly Hindu. This slim upper crust tried to recruit the masses to the fight to free India using slogans and symbols that often alienated them.

Mass support came easier when the pocketbook was involved. Such as in April 1926, when Satin Sen, then the district secretary of the Congress Party, led a successful campaign to resist a steep tax hike imposed by the Raj. Over eight thousand Muslim and Dalit peasants, across ten villages in Patuakhali subdivision, stood to benefit. This success was replicated over the next few months in dozens of villages throughout Barisal district, winning Satin Sen and his followers wide support amongst the overwhelmingly Muslim masses. Banking on this, Sen launched another campaign in August 1926 that would end up undoing it all.

∽

Within days of his initiation, Shishu found the Tarun Sangha gym in a flutter: Satin-da was planning something big. This had been brewing since February, when the government had banned their immersion procession on Saraswati puja. Jubilee High School always held the biggest puja, after which the idol was taken out in a raucous procession weaving through town, with music and dance, before immersing her in the Laukati River. This year, the district administration had prohibited it, saying the noise would disturb the two mosques on the procession's route. The Tarun Sangha youth were livid. Satin-da had advised patience then. The green light had now been issued.

By mid-August, volunteers in all branches of Tarun Sangha had received alerts—Patuakhali, Barisal town, Jhalokathi, Madhobpasha, and elsewhere. On 29 August, the day of Janmashtami, volunteers feasted on jackfruit fritters at the Patuakhali Tarun Sangha clubhouse. That afternoon, a procession singing kirtans, accompanied by khol drums and cymbals, walked the same route past the mosques that had been prohibited in February. The police barricaded it. Every subsequent day, four Tarun Sangha volunteers showed up, with drums and cymbals, to attempt the procession and court arrest.

Patuakhali was agog. On the cusp of his first political action, Shishu felt giddy. As a new recruit, he wasn't picked for the first wave. He was secretly glad, because the plan confused him. Why harass the Muslims when our fight is with the British? As the campaign continued, Satin-da came to the clubhouse to boost his volunteers. He explained: this protest wasn't anti-Muslim but anti-British, because it was the British who had issued the unfair order that they were defying. Besides, this was training for Patuakhali's minuscule Hindu minority to build confidence and capacity to hit out directly at the British. Someone asked: will the Muslims understand that this is really anti-British? Will we retain their support? Satin-da was certain of that, because they were doing exactly as in the tax campaign that had brought huge benefits for the Muslims—non-violently defying British law. He said, this is a satyagraha, just as Gandhiji has taught us.

As the Patuakhali satyagraha wore on, draining manpower and finances, Satin Sen approached the Congress Party for assistance. He presented his case at the party's annual session in December at Guwahati. When grilled about the sectarian nature of his campaign, Sen responded along lines similar to what he had told his volunteers. The Congress high command, satisfied, approved financial and manpower support. Volunteers began arriving at Patuakhali from all over the country to fill the dwindling ranks. Fundraising drives were initiated throughout Bengal. Lawyers were retained to represent the satyagrahis in jail. Top Congress leaders such as Lala Lajpat Rai, Madan Mohan Malaviya, Rajendra Prasad, and Srinivas Iyengar publicly pledged their support for Satin Sen's campaign.

By December 1926, Shishu had walked for the satyagraha quite a few times, playing the cymbal. The police were no longer making arrests since the jails were overflowing. They had taken to dispersing the protesters with batons. Shishu came away every time with deeply mixed feelings. Satin-da had explained it and it made sense. The part about defying the law excited him. And yet, he kept seeing the eyes of the woodcutter at Goila. At his home there was broad support for the campaign. Some of the city's Hindus had initially joined it. Shishu's father was in favour of upholding Hindu rights. He just wanted his son to stay out of trouble. Shishu was torn and had no one he could share this with. Except Noni-di. She understood him, but what was to be done? What was the right path? They talked about *Pather Dabi*. It was being serialized in the *Bangabaani* magazine. They had read only a few episodes. But even in that limited view there had been a glimmer of a new approach. Apparently, it had just come out as a book in Calcutta. But when would copies arrive at Patuakhali?

∽

Pather Dabi by Sarat Chandra Chattopadhyay was published on 31 August 1926. It is the story of a secret society led by women—called Pather Dabi or Right of Way—that aims to free India from colonial rule through a socialist revolution. Unusual for its time, the novel considered the question of India's self-determination in its fullness. It attacked British imperialism with the same intensity as India's entrenched religious orthodoxy, its horrors of both caste and class, and the wretched state of its women. Chattopadhyay was already a household name in Bengal. This novel was a runaway hit also because it came at a major inflection point in India's nationalist revolution.

After a police massacre of hundreds of unarmed civilians at Jallianwala Bagh in April 1919, Gandhi gave a call in September 1920 for non-violent defiance of British rule as a path to autonomy. A mass insurrection ensued nationwide. Hundreds of thousands poured onto the streets, in towns and villages, courting arrest and sustaining injuries at the hands of law enforcement. They boycotted and burnt British goods, resigned en masse from government offices, and picketed those offices to disable them. A repressed and indignant population put its life on the line for the cause of self-rule. In February 1922, with the movement at its peak and the British on the back foot, a violent clash at Chauri Chaura killed twenty-two policemen and three protesters. Gandhi abruptly called the movement off, saying that it had veered away from nonviolence, that the nation was not ready.

His move was met with shock. It winded the nationalist revolution, which did not fully regroup until the end of that decade. Bengal, in particular, seethed with resentment. Several of its Congress leaders broke away from the party; some launched their own. Organized resistance was thrown into disarray. The British administration imposed in 1924 a harsh anti-terror law in Bengal and used it to virtually break the backs of the two major armed revolutionary groups—Anushilan Samiti and Jugantar. This spawned numerous secret societies all over Bengal that employed political terror as a mode of resistance. Some of them used the Congress Party as a front, as the only party with a national footprint. Satin Sen's Tarun Sangha, formed in 1924, belonged in this category.

Pather Dabi, at the time it came out, spoke to this widely felt yearning for action. The colonial administration was swift in its response. They considered arresting Chattopadhyay but eventually decided against it, considering the potential fallout given his high profile. In mid-December, the Bengal government filed a case of sedition against the novel at the Calcutta High Court. On 13 January 1927, the government announced its ban citing 'strongly seditious material on practically every page'. By this time, more than 3,000 copies had already been sold. The ban ensured that the book became a must-have for every secret society in Bengal.

The protest against the ban was immediate. Calcutta's literary elite spoke as one, demanding that it be scrapped. There was one prominent exception—Rabindranath Tagore refused to join in that demand. On 10 February 1927, he wrote in a letter to Chattopadhyay that he didn't support the ban, but that he understood it. He said:

> Had you written an anti-Raj piece in a newspaper, the effect would be short-lived. But when a writer of your calibre airs ideas as a story, their impact defies space and time. It is recurrent and permanent. And it touches all, from immature boys and girls, to the elderly. Given this, if the British didn't ban your book that would only establish their sheer ignorance of and disdain for your literary strength and your national stature.

Banned or not, *Pather Dabi* fuelled revolutionary dreams in an entire generation—'immature boys and girls' like Shishu and Noni among them.

∽

On the same evening that Rabindranath writes to Sarat Chandra about *Pather Dabi* in Calcutta, in faraway provincial Patuakhali, two teenagers, swathed in shawls against the February chill, pore over the book by the light of a hurricane lamp. The flickering shadow on the wall is one shape, not two. The novel is over 400 pages but Noni, electrified, has devoured it within days of Shishu bringing it to her. After Shishu had his turn, they have sought out a quiet corner on the porch to compare notes on their favourite bits and reread them.

Shishu loves the part where the male protagonist—a defining force in the book—says:

> The farmer or the factory worker cannot spare their life for freedom. They seek peace and stability. The idea of freedom is far too abstract. Only the educated youth can afford to die for an idea.

Only the educated youth. That's him! Shishu feels breathless even rereading this. Noni's favourite is the scene where a new male recruit to Pather Dabi witnesses a young woman's initiation and asks why women should come out and crowd men's work. The party's leader, a woman, says:

> That's an empty complaint, the view of one who's never worked for the nation. There's not a whit of substance to it. When you get to do the work, you'll realize that which you call 'women's crowding', if that ever happens, only then will the nation's true work get done. Otherwise, with a crowd of men alone, all will crumble like so much dry sand, never congealing.

Noni doesn't know this yet: she will see a lot of that crumbling sand over her long life. But at this moment she feels a swell of force. 'I feel like I'm Durga,' she tells Shishu with a giggle, 'with ten empty hands, itching to work!' Shishu has never doubted his Nonidi's strength; it delights him that she sees it too.

∽

By February 1927, Patuakhali was in the throes of virulent unrest. As the satyagraha pressed on for months, things had slowly spun out of control. The Hindu and Muslim sides had exchanged heated words in the press. Sporadic violence had broken out throughout Barisal district, in escalating rounds of tit and tat. Desecration of Hindu deities, damage to mosques, a Muslim slum set aflame, a Hindu trader robbed. When a Muslim judge was attacked and injured in Patuakhali, a full-blown communal riot seemed imminent. The authorities beefed up law enforcement. Satin Sen split his volunteer force in two: one half kept up the daily procession, the other was a defence corps to deal with attacks on Hindus.

The climax came on 2 March 1927 on Shivratri. Not in Patuakhali, but in a village called Ponabalia near Barisal town, home to an ancient Shiva temple. In the ever-worsening sectarian air, and with the prohibition on playing music in front of mosques in force throughout the district, Muslims had begun setting up mosques at locations strategically close to temples. One such mosque had come up a few months before on the approach road to the Shiva temple in Ponabalia. On Shivratri, a stream of devotees came to the temple to bathe their god. Satin Sen dispatched a band of his boys from Barisal town to mingle with them and make music. The District Magistrate, sensing the potential for trouble, sent in a police contingent. As the devotees neared the mosque en route to the temple, the tinderbox was lit.

There are competing versions of what happened next, but no dispute about this: the police opened fire and nineteen men, all Muslims, were killed.

As riots broke out in Patuakhali, the administration cracked down on the satyagraha. Satin Sen was arrested in mid-March. Over the following month, numerous Tarun Sangha volunteers were arrested and roughed up in jail. Shishu's Shankar-da was picked up at Patuakhali; Srimanta Bhattacharya, who would befriend Shishu later that year, was picked up at Barisal. Shishu was brought in for questioning but not arrested. The police proceeded to ransack Tarun Sangha's clubhouses and seal them. The town's businesses were warned against providing food or shelter to volunteers coming in for the satyagraha. Police surveilled the ferry terminal and smaller boat docks, screening visitors for likely participants. Armed riot police patrolled the streets at night.

In the fullness of time, this would all be chalked up as the struggle for freedom. Against British rule.

∽

In mid-1927, Patuakhali was shrouded in an uneasy quiet. Its small Hindu community felt besieged. With a son in jail and a daughter marriageable, Noni's father felt that the city was no longer safe for his family. He had decided to move them to his village, Mahilara, in the far north of Barisal district. Shishu's father, equally unnerved, was also making arrangements. Once his transfer to the Barisal district court came through, he would move with his family to Barisal town. Meanwhile, school was out for the summer and Shishu had strict orders to stay indoors.

Shishu felt limp; he didn't mind being grounded. He wanted to figure out these seismic times. Why did the men in Ponabalia have to die? Yes, it was the police who killed them, but it was clear to Shishu that Tarun Sangha had played a role. His Tarun Sangha. What did that make him? He understood the need to kill. He had been reading the Gita; he'd heard Satin-da speak. Even *Pather Dabi* makes a case for it. But you kill with deliberation, for a cause. Not this. These deaths had added nothing to the push for freedom. In fact, with them something had ended, something big. Shishu felt it but couldn't spell it out. He knew Latif had stopped talking to him, even before school got out. He felt feverish.

And then there was Noni-di, who no longer smiled. She had fallen silent. They were leaving for Mahilara in mid-June. With all the violence around, and maybe more brewing, her wedding had been finalized in a rush. It was set for July. The groom was a college student in Barisal. Noni-di would live in her in-laws' village near Jhalokathi. Shishu would never run to her with a book again, never hear her sing on the open waters of a beel. Each time he looked at her he felt as he did on the day of Durga's immersion—a dry heave of grief, for something you knew would end all along. He tried to camouflage things by teasing her: 'A village bride! What's that going to be like, Noni-di?' She shot him one of her fiery glances that could make even a grown-up wince. One time he broke his curfew and snuck out to pick a few partly ripe mangoes that she loved crushed with hot mustard. That only brought on wan thanks. He couldn't fathom her mind. It was as if an utterly familiar beel had overnight turned into the vast Meghna.

As summer thickened the air became laden with moisture. One sultry afternoon he found her at their favourite nook on the porch. The household was still, steeped in sweaty siesta. Noni-di sat hunched over a notebook, writing. He crept up from behind and peeked over her shoulder. A poem. He glimpsed the title—'Shackled'—before a drop of water smudged it. Then another. 'Noni-di, are you crying?' She looked up with a start, eyes brimming. Then calmer, she folded the notebook, held his gaze and said, 'You don't understand a thing.' As she walked away, Shishu felt that maybe he finally did understand. That smudged word would keep coming back to him for decades afterwards.

The monsoons broke the following week. Their two families had a tradition: the children greeted the season's first shower by getting drenched. As the parched earth released the sweet petrichor and all got cleansed of summer dust, they hopped about the courtyard squealing with delight. And the elders stood beaming, in the swell of their own memories of first showers. This year there was no Shankar-da. But Shishu dragged Noni-di out. One last time, he insisted, for old times' sake. She didn't hop about this time, neither did he. He watched her as she stood there, her face upturned as the skies opened up, eyes closed. The rain was a convenient cover for his tears. If she was crying, too, he couldn't tell.

The next day, she was gone. He would not see her again for sixty-four years.

chapter 4

1928, Barisal town
Barisal district
British India

'BAG-AH-REE-ZAY...BAG-AH-REE-ZAY...BAG-AH-REE-ZAYYHH!'

    Sunday morning at the Kirtankhola River. Shishu sat with his sketchbook watching the quay come to life. The overnight ferry from Khulna to Barisal was docking. The steamer's mammoth dual paddles churned the water to froth. Flocks of gulls rooted in the wake for prey. From the deck, a sailor tossed a coil of fat rope at a dockworker, who caught it in his cradled arms and slung its noose around a mooring post. One smooth arc, like a dance move. As the vessel inched towards the shore, voices repeatedly rang out: 'Bag-ah-ree-zay!' Back her easy. That's what they were saying, Shishu had recently learned from his English teacher. That a ship can be a 'she'. Bag-ah-ree-zay. That sailors brimmed with such Hobson-Jobson words. He rolled this one around in his mouth. It tasted better in this, his own Borishailya dialect, all honey and muscle. He looked up at the steamer's chimney, painted black with two white stripes; on the hull in large ornamental type was its name: *Florican*. Other vessels plied this route but Shishu liked *Florican* the best. She was massive yet pretty, with dainty railings. The passengers now expectantly crowded her decks, impatient to get off. Shishu found it stirring, their eagerness to get to where he already was.

    He glanced back, following their gaze. Bell's Park to the south, shady with rain trees around a lake. Then a row of fancy brick bungalows: homes for the sahibs of the shipping companies. The broad foreshore road neatly laid with red brick chips. And lined with kerosene street lamps—a complete novelty, Shishu remembers, when he first arrived. Beyond, a copse of spindly jhau, their lacy leaves quivering this spring morning. On full moon nights, there was magic here, Shishu knew. The moonlit river, the red-brick road, the breeze raising a murmur in the jhau trees. The promenade didn't empty before ten. Even women were out. Barisal had begun to grow on Shishu, this leafy big town with its street lights, its libraries, its shops. He had initially missed Patuakhali like he would his liver. His school, the playground, his friends, his Tarun Sangha world. And Noni-di, of course. Although in that regard the move had been a relief. The two months they had stayed on beyond Noni-di's departure had been brutal. At least this place wasn't sticky with memories. Besides, Noni-di had begun writing to him. Even demanding patterns for her embroidery, thought Shishu happily, as he put finishing touches on the wings of the gulls he had sketched.

∽

The *Florican* had docked; the passengers were streaming out. Most were headed north on the foreshore road, towards Chawkbajar. If you followed them, you would turn away from the river at the post office, pass by the spacious compound of the District Collectorate and come into a thicket of office buildings including the District Board's office and the District Courthouse. The Barisal Bar library is to the right. In its reading room, free to all, Shishu gets to read excellent magazines like *The Strand*. Keep going, because at the next intersection is Mihilal's mishti shop—Barisal's best sweets. The display case heaves with trays of sandesh, rasogolla, pantua, and terracotta pots of mishti doi. Just thinking about it makes Shishu's mouth water. Across the street is Barisal's famed sari store: Brajamohan Bastralay. The road now narrows and winds, and is lined with shops on either side. You've walked for about ten minutes since leaving the ferry and are already in Chawkbajar. If you kept going, you'd see Gouri Stores to your right—this is where Shishu buys four hard candies for a paisa. Opposite Gouri Stores, between two shops, a hair-thin cul-de-sac leads to a spacious home with sweeping views of the river that Shishu's father has rented. But Shishu isn't going home. He'd continue further ahead as the road climbs a bridge across a canal lined with boats—both vendors and buyers park here.

He'd turn before the bridge though, because at its foot, on the left, is a kite store. This is where he gets his winning petkati and chandiyal kites, a paisa each. Then he'd stop to chat with his friend Bacchu, whose father runs the opium store next door.

Shishu had found a clutch of playmates since moving to Barisal—Bacchu, Mointa, Lawkha, and others. They teamed up flying kites, played football, and had fierce contests in the lanes with tops and marbles. But he had only one real friend: Srimanta. He was a classmate in school, lived close by in Chawkbajar, and was also active in the local chapter of Tarun Sangha. Shishu's father had explicitly barred him from Tarun Sangha after the spate of arrests last April. The police chief in Patuakhali had taken him aside and grilled him: did he, a government pleader, keep track of his son? Does he realize that by not arresting Shishu they'd given him a last chance to reform? That Shankar-da was the opposite of a role model? Shishu had broken his vows to Tarun Sangha and stopped being involved—his father's humiliation on his account seemed worse than the Dakatiya Kali's wrath. And he'd been fine with the break due to his own conflicts over Ponabalia. But now, the more he talked to Srimanta, the more he felt the pull once again. He was struck by how experienced Srimanta was, even though they were exactly the same age. Srimanta had been at Ponabalia! He was one of the Tarun Sangha volunteers that day. And he said what happened was not Tarun Sangha's fault. That a hard-line Muslim cleric from Noakhali had brought a band of outsiders to rile up the crowd at the mosque. And that one of them had lobbed a spear at the police. Why else would they start shooting? This made some sense to Shishu. But it was Srimanta being at Ponabalia that really impressed him.

With Srimanta, Shishu always felt a thrill, like something unexpected was right around the corner. Unlike him, Srimanta was taut and sinewy—a coiled whip ready to strike. And he was from here, a big-town boy. Quick with words and a throaty laugh. There was an ease about him. It was he who had cracked Barisal open for Shishu: shown him the kite shop, the mishti shops, the shop with the most lethal tops, the moonlit river. Shishu had told him about his father's ban. But that hadn't stopped Srimanta from taking him on a surreptitious visit to Batakrishna Misra's gym, which now served as the Tarun Sangha clubhouse since the crackdown last April. Shishu met the chapter head, Hiralal Dasgupta, and his deputy, Phani Lal Chatterji, also called Nitai. They told Shishu that the Patuakhali satyagraha was still on, and that Satin-da—his Satin-da—was still in jail, on a hunger strike. How could he, a Patuakhali boy, stand idly by? Afterwards, Srimanta led Shishu to the well-stocked library at Shankar Math and picked out two books: Ashwini Kumar Dutta's *Bhaktijog* and Aurobindo Ghosh's *Bhabani Mondir*. 'Read these,' he said, urgently. Shishu tried and felt the same unease he'd had while reading *Anandamath*. These books had a pronounced Hindu flavour.

'Why does this have to be about being Hindu?' Shishu confronted Srimanta.

'Why, aren't you a Hindu? You're a Brahmin, just like me.' Srimanta shot back.

'I am. But isn't our fight to free the land for everyone? And Bengalis are majority Muslim. What do we gain by alienating them?'

'Muslims are behind,' Srimanta said matter-of-factly, 'they are largely peasants. We are not intentionally alienating them. The British are strong. We need to become their equals to attack and eventually evict them. We are simply reviving our heritage to acquire the necessary physical and spiritual force. When we win, everyone will benefit. Including Muslims.'

'And what about until then? Aren't we harassing them at Patuakhali? The satyagraha is now in its eighteenth month!'

'That is exactly what the British want you to think. That is how they divide and rule. All we are doing is defying British law.'

Shishu found Srimanta's calm logic rather attractive. He began to come around. But he couldn't help notice the separate Hindu and Muslim drinking water taps in his school, the Hindu and Muslim hostels for out-of-town students. And that the Muslim boarders had begun to say that they wouldn't eat food cooked or touched by Hindus. Would these hard borders disappear when freedom came, like Srimanta said? That seemed like magical thinking. But so did freedom. If you didn't believe, Srimanta said, you could never make it happen.

One evening Srimanta took Shishu to the Town Hall and pointed out a row of bamboo-rattan sheds across the street, bearing various banners: Congress Party, Communist Party, Swaraj Party, Hindu Mahasabha, Muslim League. Young men milled about, reading by the light of the streetlamps, or arguing. 'See those party offices,' Srimanta said, 'each one has a mini library, backing up their ideology. Anyone is free to walk in and read. Congress, Swaraj, and Hindu Mahasabha have large overlaps in their collections. For variety, try the Communists or the Muslims. But the Communists have to follow the line from Moscow; our freedom is not their priority. You'll find everything: Gandhi-ism, Marxism, Socialism, histories of various revolutions worldwide. Sometimes party workers hold classes in the evening. I attended one but didn't get much out of it. You should give it a try. If you're not convinced about our path, find your own. But don't just stand by.'

The more time Shishu spent with Srimanta, the more sure he became that above all else, he wanted Srimanta's comradeship. He wanted to fight, yes, but mainly beside Srimanta.

∽

On 20 March 1928, within weeks of his Town Hall outing with Shishu, Srimanta was arrested. So were Hiralal, Nitai, and other Tarun Sangha members close to Satin Sen. A devastated Shishu rushed over to Misra's gym to learn what had happened. Barisal's new district magistrate, Donovan, had decided to forcibly break the Patuakhali satyagraha by arresting Satin Sen's followers across the district. Sen, who was serving time in Calcutta's Presidency Jail since the Ponabalia incident the year before, had been slapped with fresh charges. Shishu heard that Srimanta, Nitai-da, and Hiralal-da were thrilled about being arrested. Why? Because they hadn't seen Satin-da in a year and now the government was bringing him to Barisal District Jail. They would all be together! What could be better?

The following week, Shishu stood with a crowd outside the

District Courthouse. Satin-da was being brought in to be charged. As the police van arrived, the tension was palpable. Satin-da emerged, gaunt, his feet shackled, his arms tied behind his back, his prison rags hanging like dry bark on a tree. He looked half his normal size, the skin on his cheeks hung in folds. The crowd gasped in horror, then collectively let out a volley: 'Bande Mataram! Bande Mataram! Bande Mataram!' Shishu had known that Satin-da had been on a hunger strike protesting the treatment of political prisoners. But knowing is not seeing. He could not look away. Satin-da walked upright, his gaze distant as usual. But his eyes had a special light, one that warmed Shishu up from within. Here was a man, thought Shishu, who had nothing he called his own: no property, no family, no time. Every waking moment was spent for the greater common good. Yes, Shishu had questions, but this, unquestionably, was his captain. This is who he would aspire to be. Shishu struggled to contain his tears. The other prisoners were being brought in. Srimanta, grinning ear to ear, gave Shishu a jaunty wave. Shishu felt bereft, gripped by a yearning he could not name.

That evening, he went to Misra's gym and renewed his commitment to Tarun Sangha. This time, he kept it hidden from his family. He began working out again. When his comrades came out of jail, he would be ready.

∽

After World War I, to allay India's persistent demands for self-rule, the British administration had instituted a limited dyarchy in 1919, with a provision for further reforms based on a ten-year review. The Simon Commission, charged with this review, arrived in Bombay on 3 February 1928. They were a group of seven British MPs, led by John Simon, who were to travel through India for a year, investigate the state of the dyarchy, and submit a report with recommendations upon return. That the Commission was an all-British business with no Indian representation provoked fierce outrage. Every major political party in India boycotted it. Wherever the Commission went, massive crowds waving black flags roared: 'Simon, go back!'

The police took to violent methods of crowd control, the resultant injuries only adding further fuel to the protests. Such clashes took place throughout 1928, all over India. Barisal was no exception.

As the Simon protests spread, District Magistrate Donovan, fighting fire on several fronts, decided to back down on the Patuakhali satyagraha. On 7 July 1928, he presided over a session with representatives from the satyagrahis and the Muslim leadership, in which it was resolved that all public thoroughfares in Barisal district would be open to all processions at all times. In effect, nearly two years after it began, Satin Sen's satyagraha had achieved its objective. Sen immediately called off the satyagraha, at which the charges against his followers were dropped. The charges against Sen himself were cancelled on the technical ground that on the date they were drawn up he was in a Calcutta jail, beyond the jurisdiction of the Barisal District Court. Satin Sen and his followers were released from Barisal District Jail.

∽

There was jubilation all around. Srimanta, Nitai-da, Hiralal-da, and others were amidst a raucous celebration at Misra's gym. It had taken two years, but they won! Shishu basked in their glory, feeling a little off-centre, but very much a part of this. The group was abuzz with the strategies Satin-da had outlined in jail to deal with the Simon Commission. Srimanta, in particular, was boiling over. Now they would show the British! Shishu had waited two and a half months for this. He was ready for the plunge. After the meeting, he and Srimanta walked home, hand-in-hand. As certainty set in, Shishu felt a weight lift and relief washed over him.

As if his cup of happiness wasn't full enough, he received a striking letter from Noni-di in late August 1928. They had been writing to each other for about a year. She would commission drawings from him on occasion. Even if she didn't, Shishu would send her one with each letter anyway. With this letter, Noni-di made such a deep impression on Shishu that he wrote about it with graphic recall in his notebook, over fifty years later. He wrote this before he had reconnected with her, or even known that he ever would:

> I always liked to sketch, even as a child. But the thought of writing poetry had never occurred to me. With just a few lines in that letter, Noni-di opened a portal to entirely new horizons in my life. The letter is lost to time, but her words are seared in my mind and I'll try to express them. To be honest, as I sit writing this, it is as if she's speaking them in my ear. She wrote: 'You are an artist. I've heard artists have tender and empathetic minds. I've also heard that poets have those same virtues. So it is my dearest wish that you write poetry. The insight that you bring to life with brush and paint, use the same insight to paint your mind's pictures in words. And do send me your poems! You'll see, when you grow old, you'll look back and find your youthful mind etched in these poems, in all its colours.'
>
> I was so charged and inspired by this letter that on the very day I received it, I sat down and wrote my first poem. It was a banal expression of my political thoughts at the time, and naturally immature. But because it was my first, and because it is inextricably tied to Noni-di, I can't help mention the opening:
>
> **Freedom**
>
> Will we ever be free, Ma
> Rid you of hurt and misery?
> With your blessings upon us
> We'll give our life trying.
>
> Up until my arrest in March 1929, I had written quite a few poems. Most were political. They are an invaluable treasure for me. And it is my lasting fortune that having weathered so many storms, my little poetry notebook from that time is still with me today.

Shishu shared his first poem with Srimanta, who in turn got enthused. Poems poured forth as they prodded each other. In addition to all else they were doing together, the two were now comrades in poetry, in the hunt for words. Meanwhile, in September, the Barisal District Board convened to discuss an address that they would present to the Simon Commission. Tarun Sangha, with Satin Sen in the lead, decided to picket the meeting. Shishu and Srimanta joined others in lying down as a body in front of the District Board office. They kept this up until the Board chairman agreed to drop the address.

More jubilation ensued. An ecstatic Srimanta wrote a poem called 'Blow it all up!'. This inspired Shishu to write a rejoinder. Throughout, he kept sending his poetic efforts to Noni-di, who responded with her own poems, echoing his revolutionary timbre. Ever since re-entering Tarun Sangha, Shishu had shared his secret life with her. And unlike anyone else he knew, she had given him unstinted encouragement in this work, calling it virtuous. Shishu felt both anchored by and bloated with pride for his unusually illuminated Noni-di. He urged her to share her light with the rural women around her. To him, the time felt charmed, as if the universe had become aligned.

∽

Shishu had no way of knowing this, but all was not well with Noni. She had been married for over a year now and throughout had been shunned by her husband. That would be my grandfather, Hira. A sensitive and artistic man, tall and angular. Like many of Barisal's youth of his time, he'd been drawn to the idea of armed revolution and by 1927 became increasingly swept up in the surrounding fervour. When his family got wind of this, they decided a pretty bride would be a suitable antidote and had forcibly married him off. He was deeply resentful of this and as retaliation, had shut Noni out. He held her striking good looks against her and avoided all physical contact with her on his visits to the village. Learning of Hira's poetry practice, Noni had tried to share hers with him. He ignored her poems, chalking them up to airy feminine fancy. He would confess this to Noni later, in a state of mortification. But at the time, stranded in an unfamiliar rural household, Noni was gravely alone. Her invitation to Shishu in the letter that he so lovingly quotes from memory, one that transformed his life, was perhaps not the selfless gift from on high that it was received as. Maybe it was a camouflaged cry, of a mind fertile and marooned, seeking companionship in poetry.

∽

On 30 October 1928, the Simon Commission arrived in Lahore, where it was met with the usual crowd of protestors waving black flags. At the head of the crowd was Lala Lajpat Rai, sixty-three, a top Congress leader. Under orders from their superintendent, James Scott, the police force attempted to disperse the protestors by flogging them with batons. Many were hurt in the ensuing melee. Rai, directly assaulted by Scott, was badly wounded and on 17 November, died of his injuries. The news sent shock waves through the country. A band of young revolutionaries in Punjab vowed to exact revenge. On 17 December, Bhagat Singh and his comrades shot and killed Assistant Superintendent of Police John Saunders, mistaking him for his boss, Superintendent of Police James Scott. The group escaped and Bhagat Singh was not arrested until 8 April 1929.

∽

As 1928 drew to a close, Tarun Sangha seethed over the events in Lahore. The loss of Lajpat Rai felt personal. They remembered the crucial support Rai had extended for their Patuakhali satyagraha, without which it would've been impossible to sustain. But their hubbub, in the main, was over the whiplash revenge. Shishu listened in.

'Within a month! A lightning strike! How about that?' Srimanta struck his left palm with a balled right fist.

'What a tiger that Bhagat Singh is!' Nitai-da agreed heartily. 'When he threw dust in their eyes and escaped, he apparently came our way, to Calcutta. Wish I could meet him!'

'Let's not get carried away,' Hiralal-da tried to tone the group down, 'Singh got the wrong man. Scott is still walking, scot-free.'

'But he got a white man!' Srimanta shot back heatedly, 'That is the language the British understand.'

'No, I'm sorry,' Hiralal-da was firm, 'I'm tired of this. This is like Khudiram all over again. And that was twenty years ago. Two white women there, one white man here. Won't we ever grow up and learn to call a mistake what it is?'

'But Saunders is still police, Hiralal-da,' Srimanta wasn't giving up.

'Yes, but a junior, still on probation. And more importantly, not the target. What did Bhagat Singh and his comrades do after escaping? They put up posters declaring they've avenged Lala's death. Except the posters say that Saunders was the target all along. That is a lie!'

The last words came out in a bark. This burst of emotion, utterly out of character for placid Hiralal, subdued the group immediately. In the ensuing quiet, he continued in his usual monotone: 'Listen to me, all of you. I am not taking Gandhiji's line. Satin-da is now tipping that way, but I never have and never will. I believe the current conditions require violence. And I believe revenge is necessary. But when we pick a target, we must learn to hit it. And we cannot, ever, resort to lies in this fight.'

Talking about this lesson warmed Shishu and Srimanta up on their walk home that chilly evening. It had found a deep resonance within them. Little did Shishu know how soon he would need to use it.

∽

The Barisal Agricultural Exhibition was inaugurated by District Magistrate Donovan on 23 January 1929. The weeklong event, held in an open pavilion on the river, was to showcase the district's plentiful agricultural bounty to the city folk. The winter light was sweet, the temperatures mild. There were food stalls and entertainment, a dance troupe all the way from Calcutta. Throwing a lavish fiesta was perhaps an attempt on the part of the British administration to win the city's hearts and minds. But in the backdrop of the raging Simon Commission protests, the idea was tone-deaf at best. The nationalist resistance in Barisal was livid;

Tarun Sangha vowed to scuttle the event. With Satin Sen away in Calcutta, Hiralal Dasgupta decided to follow their successful picketing strategy at the District Board back in September. Accordingly, volunteers began lying down in a body on the ground, blocking the entrance to the exhibition. The protest quickly gathered wider support in the city. Sarat Kumar Ghosh, a senior Congress leader, joined in. As did apolitical figures such as Rasa Ranjan Sen, a prominent educationist and headmaster at Shishu's and Srimanta's school, who had found the idea of scantily clad dancing girls morally repugnant.

On 26 January, Donovan walked through the picket into the exhibition, in an effort to encourage attendance. As he gingerly stepped over the picketers on the ground, he issued them a stern warning. Police Superintendent Colson followed suit. Bringing up the rear was Sub-inspector Jyotish Chandra Roy, the officer-in-charge of Barisal's main police station. As he passed through, one of the Tarun Sangha boys catcalled: 'Hondolkutkut!'—a cutting slur, calling one fat and dark and savage. Roy wheeled around and kicked the boy, supine on the ground, hard in his midriff. At this, the youth collectively reared up in protest. Roy now began to rain blows on them with his baton, injuring several. Shishu took a knock to his left jaw. SP Colson called up forces and ordered them to disperse the picket. In the brutal crackdown that followed, Shishu saw Roy repeatedly hit his headmaster with a baton until the old man slumped in a bloodied heap.

Satin Sen rushed over from Calcutta. On 29 January, he addressed government pleaders at the Bar Library telling them that the exhibition was a farce, that the attendees were being cheated of their money, that the government had no intention of benefitting the farmers. He called for an immediate end to police brutality, but said that the picketers would not be cowed—they were prepared to wash the streets of Barisal with blood from their injuries. The following day, a crowd of nearly 300 gathered in front of Town Hall. As Sen proceeded to lead them to picket the exhibition, he was arrested by SI Jyotish Roy and released on 31 January after the exhibition had ended. On 1 February, back in front of the Town Hall, Sen gave a fiery speech to a crowd even larger than two days before. He then had to leave for urgent work in Patuakhali.

Tarun Sangha was seething, many of them wounded. Shishu was personally in flames. Not so much for his swollen jaw. He wanted to but could not unsee his mild-mannered headmaster bleeding from the head, a stain spreading on his pristine white kurta. Each time he went over that image, he felt an upswell of rage, like a mad elephant. And as if it was not enough to brutalize non-violent picketers, Roy had dared to arrest Satin-da. Shishu remembered what Satin-da had said in his post-release speech: the time had come to do or die. Maybe even do and die, thought Shishu.

When Hiralal-da called a meeting within days, Shishu was surprised that there were only three others in attendance: him, Srimanta, and Nitai-da.

'This is a core committee for a specific action,' Hiralal-da explained, 'no one else must have an inkling of this plan. Least of all Satin-da—he will immediately pull the plug. Is that understood?'

'Yes, yes. We have to act, Hiralal-da,' Srimanta clamoured. 'Please!'

'I want to avenge the attack on our headmaster,' Shishu found himself saying.

'Hear me out, please,' Hiralal-da shushed them. 'Both Colson and Roy are now marked men. Colson ordered the baton charge that hurt so many. And Roy personally assaulted us. But Colson will be a difficult target, because he always moves in a posse. And I want no collateral damage. Roy often goes on solo rounds. We will need to study his patterns. We will be patient. I want no false moves. Jyotish Roy is our target. And only Jyotish Roy must die.'

'Please let me do it, Hiralal-da!' Srimanta begged, 'I want to finish off that hondolkutkut!'

'The action will be at close range,' Hiralal-da continued calmly, as if Srimanta hadn't spoken, 'we will pull him into a ruse and then stab him. So it needs to be someone he won't recognize. Nitai, Srimanta, and I are all known faces, since we've just served time until July. It will have to be you, Shishu.'

Shishu remembers Srimanta's groan and his own euphoria. He remembers feeling unclouded. No big thoughts of India or freedom or jail or hanging. Not a wisp of his obsessions—not Noni-di, not the Goila woodcutter. All he could see was that wet red blotch creeping across crisp white cotton. He felt like a perfectly ripe fruit, swollen with the certainty that he would get revenge.

For decades afterwards, Shishu would look back and marvel at this moment of crystalline certainty, a rare exception in a long life of not being particularly sure.

chapter 5

I'll be back
Maybe as a duck—a girl's pet,
Jingles on my red feet.
To these moist wistful shores
I'll be back.

—Jibanananda Das

Late March, 1929
Barisal–Calcutta
British India

THE PADDLE STEAMER LET OUT a sombre *bhawwnnnmm*, the last call for stragglers to board. To Shishu it sounded like someone was blowing a giant conch. Like the conch his mother blew at nightfall, to greet the impending dark and ward off evil. It must be some other dark now, some other evil, because it was still light out. Late afternoon gold glinted off the river, mussed by the paddles' churn. The sharp light made Shishu's eyes water. At least that's what he told himself, and put on a determined squint. He was fettered in a fixed crouch, next to the steamer's engine room. Three armed guards watched over him. But his eyes were free and they had a job to do. No time for blurriness. He would take a good look and burn everything into his brain. He was leaving home, leaving Barisal, forever. Good to be carried away by *Florican*, his favourite. He had gazed up at her so many times from shore, and now he was aboard. The flag fluttering atop the ferry terminal was white—black would have forecast storms. Good to sail away in fair weather. The world looked happy. Bell's Park crackled with football, the red foreshore road crunched underfoot, the breeze through the jhau trees whispered *sheee-shooo*. These things he could see and hear. What of those he couldn't? What of the kubo birds, with their unnatural red eyes? Or the mongoose, its golden fur catching the light. The mauve wildflowers mobbing the grass each winter. The turtle eggs tucked in the river's sandy shore. The fruits on that wild vine that gave a satisfying pop when pressed. His sister's pet duck wriggling in his arms. What of friends and books and first rains and a soaring kite's tug? No, no, there were far too many things. What would happen to these, his memories? Shishu felt the brush of an unearthly void and began to shiver. People at the pier were waving at those they had come to see off. He scanned their faces, powerless to stop making more memories. A sailor cranked the anchor up. The rope was tossed back on board. And the *Florican* was off. Shishu craned his neck for a last glimpse of his town as it slid behind a bend in the river.

The steamer's churning wake was magnetic. Dual paddles clawed the river and waves radiated out in two diagonal lines, lapping at the green shores. All that emotion in the water. It had a calming effect on Shishu. The spume hitting him felt good. The ship was settling in for the long sail. Liveried waiters carried snacks and beverages up the stairs to the upper deck, meant for first- and second-class passengers. The floor of the engine deck was for the third class. A few feet from Shishu, these passengers were setting up their mats and opening their bedrolls. They looked over at him, words forming in their eyes, then they glanced at the guns on his guards and averted their gaze. The ship followed the meandering Kirtankhola, its shores dense with rain trees, their enormous canopies nearly touching the water, with blossoms like crimson pompoms. The land was crisscrossed with smaller rivers and canals, dotted with beels. They passed a village at dusk, boys splashing in the river, setting off sparks of molten gold. The sun set in a brazen swirl of oranges and pinks. Shishu watched until all had faded to pale blue. How many more sunsets would he see? Ten more? Twenty? The moon rose. On the dappled waters, a lone fishing dinghy lit its oil lamp.

At nightfall, the steamer docked at Jhalokathi to pick up more passengers. Noni-di's village was a thirty-minute walk away, Shishu knew. Had she heard that he was leaving today? He peered at the dimly lit terminal hoping for the impossible. But soon they were moving again. There would be no further stops until Khulna in the morning. The wooded shores turned claustrophobic after dark and took on a tinge of menace. For a boy from river country, this shift in mood was as familiar as in one's mother. And yet it never failed to excite Shishu. He remembered reading Hemen Ray's adventure stories with Noni-di, when these night shores mutated into Africa's hermetic jungles, teeming with lions. They felt certain that you couldn't possibly get the fullest kick out of Hemen Ray if you'd never travelled Barisal's rivers at night. Was that only two years ago? Do all the stories you know really disappear when you die? All the songs?

Dinner time now. Shishu saw some of his co-passengers crack open their food carriers. Others trooped into the dining room. He knew what they were going to eat: chicken curry and rice, a famed specialty of sailor cooks plying these lower Gangetic waters. He'd grown up with the East Bengali maxim: to never taste steamer curry is to not fully live. Shishu had eaten this once on a Patuakhali–Barisal ferry and could not agree more. It was sublime. And a forbidden pleasure. Unlike fish or goat, chicken was taboo in Hindu homes. Moreover, the sailor cooks were uniformly Muslim. Yet, even his rigidly Brahminical father had eaten up with gusto. When asked he had waved the wand of 'big wood'—how eating on or inside a large wooden structure absolves all contact violations. Shishu watched the sated diners return, batch after batch. All he could smell now was the curry. This was a special grade of torture. He'd heard that the night before hanging they feed you anything you wish. This would be it for him. Shishu's guards had taken turns eating. One of them now slid a plate of lentils and rice towards him. Not such a bad second best, Shishu told himself, Barisal's own balam rice and fine mushur lentils. The only thing missing, he thought ruefully, was a piece of Kirtankhola ilish! As if on cue, a green chilli materialized right next to his plate. A kind passenger had tossed it over when the guards were not looking. Shishu's eyes stung at this gesture. Only a fellow Borishailya would understand how much a green chilli improves any meal.

Sleep soon took over, the engine deck became a symphony of snores. Shishu dozed off a couple times but was jolted awake by blasts of heat from the engine. It was a blessing, he thought. He didn't want to miss even a moment. He took deep drags of the river's night breath. He studied the engine room: the wiry men bathed in soot and sweat, shovelling coal into the furnace; the giant boiler making steam; massive instruments coaxing the steam to move the paddles; the shiny brass pistons moving back and forth, back and forth. He listened to the rhythmic whoosh-splash of the dual paddles cutting water. He gazed out on the moonlit waters and the sleeping shores, now near, now far. In his head he wrote a farewell poem to this, to all of this. And he thought of the one question whose answer he really cared about: what did Noni-di think of what he had done?

∽

On the day Shishu killed Sub-inspector Jyotish Roy, Satin Sen was in Patuakhali. He arrived in Barisal the day after—11 March 1929—to a town bracing for a harsh response. That afternoon he walked about town to boost mass morale and was promptly arrested. Over the next week, fourteen Tarun Sangha members were picked up, including Hiralal, Nitai, Srimanta, and Batakrishna. With the resistance jailed, Barisal went into a defensive crouch. The police proceeded to raid homes of Tarun Sangha members. They incentivized false witnesses to pin blame, then dragged such suspects to police stations to elicit confessions under torture. The town was in the vise of intense police pressure. To protest this indiscriminate crackdown, Satin Sen began a hunger strike on 24 May 1929 inside Barisal District Jail.

As the epicentre, Shishu's home was naturally ransacked. The police seized all his books and papers, including letters he had received. That is how they found the address of Noni's marital home. And raided it.

Surprise raids are hard to pull off in rural Barisal. Water being the only option, all arrivals are slow. And if you're an outsider, you only know of a handful of landings. At those, there are eyes everywhere.

A little boy comes running, breathless with news: a police posse had landed at Jhalokathi. There's a white man in the team, with a face pockmarked and red. They were asking for directions to a home in Bikna village. They have Noni-boudi's name. They're in a skiff now, going up the Bashonda canal.

Noni's home erupts in a cocktail of panic and blame and gossip. Her mother-in-law wails, 'I had repeatedly said, please, not a looker! Those are always trouble! What has she gone and done now?'

The neighbours flood in. Even before this, Noni has given them much grist for the rumour mill: she's been married eighteen months and is not pregnant yet. 'Tsk, tsk, such a pretty bride,' they cluck, 'but barren, you know. Whatever will she do with her time?' Noni will deal with them later. Right now, she needs to focus on the job at hand.

She knows what the police will want. They are at the Bashonda canal? She then has ten minutes to hide Shishu's letters. In the cattle shed, maybe in the stack of hay. Too obvious? How about in the eaves of the back porch, tucked into the thatch. This is trickier than expected: the bundle refuses to go in fully, a tell-tale bit sticks out. Running out of time now. The rice drum, of course! They would never dare touch the rice, least of all red-face—contact taboos stood in the way. Noni dashes into the kitchen, tears the conical lid off the massive wicker drum that can hold a quintal of rice. Hers is a big family, and in these parts you eat rice three times a day. She burrows with both hands through the fragrant grains, going halfway to the bottom before placing the bundle of letters. She makes sure the grains are level. Fastens the lid back on. Straightens her sari and covers her head with its end so that barely her chin shows. Like a rural bride. Just as she emerges from the kitchen, the police walk in.

With her family watching huddled in one corner of the courtyard,

Noni is pulled aside. Through the thin cotton of her veil, she can see that red-face has sent a few of his men into the cattle shed, they are poking about in the hay. But no one steps into the kitchen. With the help of an interpreter, red-face questions Noni. She answers in barely audible monosyllables, as a rural bride would. Yes, she knew Shishu, they had been neighbours, their fathers were colleagues. No, she doesn't know much about his life since she got married. Yes, she'd written him a few letters, as any older sister would. No, she couldn't keep any of his, they were lost in the chaos of a rural household. No, she hadn't heard any of those other names.

An hour later the police leave, empty-handed. The household is abuzz: who had ever heard of a red-face policeman in a village home interrogating a bride! But Noni isn't listening. She rushes out the back door towards the pond. Outside, she slows down, her bare feet cool on the moist path slick with snail tracks. She steps into the gloom of the bamboo grove. In the stillness her tears come. It starts with relief, then swells into a vortex of things that are and are not, until she is wracked with sobs. By the time she comes back in, her family has figured out that the questioning had to do with a freedom fighter. They look at her mottled face with a mix of incomprehension and awe. Noni has decided she won't speak to any of them. She will wait for her husband to come home.

∽

Noni would later see this raid as a watershed.

Hira's attitude towards her had shifted since Shishu's murder and arrest. He had known of Shishu, Noni's almost-brother who wrote her letters, but that didn't carry any meaning for him. This changed radically in March 1929. His own revolutionary aspirations thwarted, Hira felt enormous admiration for the much younger Shishu. And he began to view Noni in a fresh light, as Shishu's associate. But it was the police raid on their village home that served as the crucial catalyst. It drew Hira to Noni, broke his embargo on her. He soon came to see that his wife had an inner life of substance. He realized the brutal effect of shunning her, for no fault of hers. On top of being lonely, she had been putting up with vicious taunts of infertility. He was mortified.

In trying to save India, Shishu had inadvertently saved his Noni-di's marriage. Hira became a devoted husband and the couple went on to have eleven children. His dreams of being a revolutionary, however, remained unfulfilled.

∽

The raid had further dividends downstream for Noni.

It began with questions from Binti, Hira's precocious eleven-year-old niece. Binti admired Noni and trailed her like a pet through household chores: in the cattle shed as she chopped hay, in the kitchen as she cooked, at the holy basil in the courtyard as she lit an oil lamp each dusk. Her chief obsession was Noni's splendour: her features, her gait, her voice. Given the slightest chance she would undo Noni's chignon just to see her hair cascade like a waterfall. But Binti's focus had shifted since the raid. She wanted—needed—to know what had caused the police to come and bring such ignominy on her idol. And Noni decided to tell her.

She spoke of the shackled land where they lived. Of those fighting to free it. Of the distortion in seeing these fighters, and those who aid them, as nothing but trouble. Of the role women had in this fight, if only they were unshackled. Binti, transfixed, was utterly convinced. With the urgency of a fresh convert, she brought her friends home for Noni to talk to. Her friends in turn wanted Noni to talk to their mothers. Word soon spread and caused a stir. The village folk were aggrieved. Who was this two-bit city bride, barren to boot, stuffing their womenfolk with dangerous notions? Hira, by now, had *seen* Noni and was squarely in her corner. He stepped in to publicly proclaim his role as Noni's rock. A man of few words, what he said silenced the wagging tongues: that Noni spoke the truth, was raising awareness, and not forcing it upon anyone. That all were free to ignore her, but none were free to harass her.

Noni thus went about her outreach among rural women, with the full weight of Hira's support. She held small meetings upon invitation, where she spoke and sometimes read her poems. She soon initiated a literacy drive for adult women in her village. While doing this work, she saw what Shishu had meant when he had urged her to spread her light. The darkness was pervasive. Her heartache in not being able to share all of this with him she kept buried deep within.

∽

Khulna was a bustling terminus connecting the ferry and railway systems. The *Florican* had docked here at daybreak. But Shishu had to wait, he would be escorted off last. He sat watching the enormous ferry terminal, so much bigger than Barisal's. The passengers streamed off the ship. Some headed towards the row of food stalls. Some settled down on the benches to wait for their connection. Where were they going, he wondered. A whole subcontinent to the west to choose from! He knew he was getting on a train to Calcutta. The tracks were not far. He was goose-stepped there, his fetters jangling. Being from waterlocked Barisal, Shishu had never seen a train before. The first sight sent a shock through his system. So that's the steam engine, that huge, hissing, hot monster! And look at how many cars were hitched to it, the first few glossier than the rest. He wanted to shout: look Noni-di, look Srimanta, Mointa, Bacchu, Lawkha! None of them had ever seen a train either. He would be the first to ride one. But what was the point if you couldn't share?

The train headed west. Shishu sat sandwiched between two guards, handcuffed to both. The three guards from Barisal had handed him over to these two at Khulna. They spoke a different Bangla, Shishu noticed. No 'z' in their speech, only 'j'. Didn't have the satisfying chew of his own. And they were calling him a 'Bangal'. He'd heard that people in Calcutta used this word for East Bengalis, but it felt like these two were using it to mock him. Like when his jaw had dropped at the first sight of the steam engine. So Shishu tried to keep his maiden train ride to himself. When the train juddered like it had skipped the tracks, he tried hard not to jump out of his skin. He gazed out the window at the new land. Within two hours, the palette had faded from effusive green laced with water to patches of dun and little water. As they crossed the Ichamoti River, his guards said that they were now in the western half of Bengal. The land looked awfully dry to Shishu. Were the people dry, too?

The train reached Calcutta's Sealdah station late morning. The ride from Khulna had taken four hours. Shishu could not believe this. Just four hours, for intergalactic travel? That's how alien Sealdah station felt. Look at this mammoth space with sky-high ceilings! He had never seen so many people in one place, all in motion. If people were ants, this looked like a raging infestation after a giant had tipped over a jar of date syrup. And the din, ah, the din! Someone kept saying something over and over and over, it echoed in the cavernous halls and gave Shishu a headache. His guards kept up their tutorial: those were train announcements, there were thirteen tracks, over a hundred trains daily, innumerable passengers. Shishu didn't care. He wanted to leave but was stuck because the paperwork for his transfer took time. The wait wore on. And then, as dusk fell, something magical happened. He could see twilight in a patch of sky above one of the tracks. But where he was sitting, inside the arrival hall, it was still as light as day! This so baffled Shishu that he had to ask the guards. They exploded in hoots, laughing so hard that they had to wipe their tears before enlightening him: electric lights. Shishu was dumbstruck. He had learned about electricity in school, he knew of light bulbs in theory, but had never seen one in practice. And this scale was unimaginable! The train ride in the morning, and now this. How many more firsts would there be today?

The police van wove through Calcutta's evening traffic. Sitting in the back, peering through the barred windows, Shishu got his first taste of Calcutta: the empire's second city. The firsts kept coming. Cars, he'd never seen those before. He was now riding in one. Buses. The street lights, he could tell now, were electric. They were driving on a road ten times wider than any he'd seen. Lined with shops, all lit, some with neon signs. People milling about. So many people, many were white. Some of the brown ones wore clothes like the white. So here it was, mused Shishu, the empire he had tried to strike. His action now seemed woefully paltry, a mere bug bite on a giant. Could they really bring it down someday? Wait, what was that? A small train trundled by, going the opposite direction. Two cars, no engine, but a rod connected to a line above, and light from its lone eye glinting off its own tracks. Electric tram, his guards intoned, bored by now with Shishu's firsts. The van veered into a leafy neighbourhood with big bungalows. Alipore, the guards said, where the sahibs live. They soon passed through the high walls of Presidency Jail. The metal gate slammed shut.

For Shishu this day had been unlike any in his life. He knew there would be at least one more first: his first night on death row.

∞

Within Calcutta's maximum-security Presidency Jail was the infamous '44 decree' barrack: a row of forty-four solitary cells for those decreed with especially harsh terms of incarceration. Each cell was 6' x 9', its grating opening onto a 6' x 6' walled patio. Each patio, open to the sky, had a single-leaf wooden door to the outside, with a glass-paned eyelet through which the sentry looked in during their rounds. Outside the wooden doors, a long yard ran along the barrack, bound by blank walls 20 feet high and manned with watchtowers. Unless otherwise decreed, the cell's grating stayed unlocked between 5 a.m. and 5.30 p.m. when the inmate could be in his patio, and would be surveilled from the watchtowers; the remaining time he was confined to the cell. The first four cells of this barrack comprised the death row, meant for political prisoners. Other inmates were allowed walks in the yard, and had daily tasks assigned. Those on death row were condemned to be alone with their thoughts, in their cell or patio.

Shishu occupied the barrack's first cell; the rest of the death row was currently empty. The last political murder in Bengal had been committed nearly three years before, on 28 May 1926, inside Alipore Central Jail. Bhupendra Nath Chatterjee, Special Superintendent of Police, Intelligence Branch, was battered to death with a crowbar by five revolutionaries incarcerated in a bomb-making case. They called him a tiktiki—a gecko—on the hunt for snitches. Two of the assailants were hanged shortly thereafter, the rest transported for life. This had been the only political murder since the imposition of the anti-terror Bengal Criminal Ordinance in 1924. In the entire decade since the passage of the harsh Rowlatt Act on 10 March 1919—enabling the internment of suspects without trial—until Shishu's crime on 10 March 1929, the total number of political murders in Bengal was eight. And this was the province with the highest incidence of anti-colonial violence. What Shishu had done was exceedingly rare.

The inmates of this barrack in Presidency Jail fondly called it '44 degree', in a wry reference to life there. For Shishu, this term would also become literal. This is where he was to spend an entire summer.

∽

Summer 1929
Death Row, Presidency Jail
Alipore, Calcutta
British India

Midday, mid-April. Shishu sat cross-legged on the floor. His cell was a furnace. The sleeping alcove was too hot to sit in, even after rolling up the coarse blanket. The floor felt marginally cooler. Or maybe it was the contact with his own sweat on cement. His grating was unlocked, but the patio looked sun-blasted, its flagstones white-hot. Probably enough to fry an egg. When had he last eaten an egg? Would there ever be another? From the patio at daybreak, he had seen a striking dawn, like a punctured yolk spreading on pale blue marble. And peering above the high walls beyond, the tops of mango and jackfruit trees, painted by that crimson light. And birdsong, who knew this city had so many birds! But the sun was short-tempered, the sky quickly got bleached, and he'd scurried into his cell like a rat. At least out of sight of the watchtower, where a red-faced guard, blue-eyed, kilted and helmeted, paced with a gun. Was he red from the heat? Shishu felt sorry for him. From inside his cell, he could still see the treetops. Which was worse? Seeing a tree and knowing its shade was forever out of reach, or not seeing one at all. These trees were laden with fruit. Look at those rounded mangoes, on the cusp of ripe.

You keep circling back to food, so let's talk about food. Rice gruel at 5.30 a.m.: some variation there—plain or with lentils or with jaggery. Lunch at 11 a.m.: rice, lentils, lump of greens. Dinner at 5 p.m.: same as lunch. No, no, don't get into the grit and bugs and hair in the rice or the dishwater lentils. You are a political prisoner on death row, what did you expect? I didn't expect they'd make me shit in the same bowl I eat the gruel or lentils from. I didn't, Hiralal-da. The same bowl for rinsing my mouth or as a scoop for bathing, that's still fine. But shitting? They did that for the first week. I came very close to cracking, maybe that was their intention. Then they gave me this tar-lined basket. There, it's parked in that corner of the cell, can't you smell it? The janitor picks it up once a day. What if I have to go more than once, like today? This has been happening, must be the greens. When that happens, with lunch at 11, and the courtyard like a hotplate, I will eat in here within sight and smell of my shit. And see that tin jug for drinking water, that water is already warm. It will practically boil by the day's end. It does nothing to slake my thirst, Hiralal-da, I get so thirsty. You're right, I sound pathetic. But I'm not a wimp. When they were tearing out clumps of my hair in Barisal jail last month, did I make a sound? Did I name any names? Yes, it's all about mind control, isn't it. All about figuring out what to think of, every hour of the day. They won't allow me books. But I won't let them get to me, you'll see. I have all these poems wriggling in my brain. Just wish I had some paper and pencil.

Shishu kept up an internal chatter with various people, depending on need. When he wanted a whip cracked, he summoned Hiralal-da; when he felt playful, it was Srimanta; when he found beauty, it was Noni-di. And so on.

Filling the blank hours was his biggest challenge. Looking around his cell he found a movement of large black ants emerging out of a hole and proceeded to follow their activity. A line of tiny red fire ants soon entered the scene. A fight broke out between the two clans, with the black tearing the red to bits. Look look, Srimanta, the blacks are killing off the reds, we have to help them! Let's drive the black ones off. Careful, their bite is lethal. Here, maybe we can trap them with this bowl. The ants kept him occupied until lunch. Since they were moving to stay out of the heat, Shishu had plenty of fodder.

Late afternoon, a mad gust kicked up swirls of dust. Shishu rushed out onto the patio. A Kalboishakhi, Noni-di! Yes, of course, how did he forget? Today was Poila Boishakh—the first day of the Bengali New Year. The sky had darkened with heavy, scudding clouds, treetops swayed wildly, the light had taken on an underwater tone. Soon, a furious storm blew in. Crashing thunder, lightning. Shishu sang at the top of his voice—*My heart dances like a peacock*! Then slanting ropes of rain, ah, sweet rain. He stood there singing and getting drenched, like he and Noni-di used to, and imagined rushing out later to pick the mangoes littering the ground after the storm. He noticed that the rain had flooded the floor of his cell. No matter. Things had cooled down considerably, maybe he'd be able to sleep in the alcove tonight. A bit of rain, a song or two. Shishu felt renewed.

When the rain had stopped, he noticed an eye peering through the pane in the wooden door. He walked over jauntily, still singing. He had seen this guard before, a towering Sikh.

'You sing pretty well,' the guard said.

'I don't, sipai-ji. It's just the rain,' Shishu grinned. 'Rain makes me happy!'

'Happy? Tu to Bangal da sher nikla, puttar!'

He had spoken in Punjabi; Shishu couldn't follow what he said. But from his tone and the twinkle in his eye, it sounded like he had paid Shishu a compliment. He then dropped his voice: 'Don't speak, just listen. My shift ends at six. When I come in to lock your cell grating at 5.30, we'll talk for a bit.' He paused, and with a heavy sigh, added: 'They've arrested our Bhagat Singh in Delhi last week.' Then he walked away, leaving Shishu stunned.

During the post-dinner chat, he served up another surprise for Shishu: the jail was abuzz with what he had done; everyone wanted to set their eyes on Shishu. At fourteen, he was the youngest they'd ever heard of. 'We are guards on death row,' he said, eyes shining, 'we should know. And you hit your target, beta, shabash! I have a son your age, in Gurdaspur. Anything you need, just ask. If it's within my power, you'll get it.'

Shishu couldn't sleep that night. Not due to the stench from his wet blanket, or the basket of night soil. He sat up replaying the guard's kind words. He realized how much he had needed them. Was he being self-indulgent? But he finally felt human again, and whole. They could hang him now.

Over the next weeks, the guard smuggled him priceless gifts. A narrow-necked terracotta pitcher that kept his drinking water cool. A few sheets of paper and a pencil. Shishu's vacant hours were now spent in the hunt for words, and a yearning to share them with Noni-di. As the poems poured out, he took to composing them in his head and during holes in his surveillance he furiously jotted them down in a miniature scribble to conserve space. In late May, he was informed that a case appealing his death sentence had been filed at the Calcutta High Court. He was now an undertrial, entitled to a monthly visit from family. He was also allowed his school books. Shishu kept his poetry sheets carefully tucked inside the protective cover of a textbook.

His cousin, Rohini Chatterji, lived nearby and came for visits. Starved for human contact and outside news, Shishu would count the days to this each month. Rohini-da soon became acquainted with Shishu's guard-friend, to whom Shishu made a request: could he please ensure that his poetry sheets reached Rohini-da after his hanging?

This was unnecessary in the event. On 26 July, the Calcutta High Court found Shishu to be a minor and commuted his death sentence to transportation for life. In September, he was moved to Alipore Central Jail for the next phase of his incarceration.

∽

Shishu writes in his notebook that he had been in the throes of poetry while on death row. Sadly, none of those poems made the cut for his curated set. Perhaps the writing had been too close to the feeling. We'll never know. He had saved them from oblivion with great care, but in the end hadn't found them worth sharing. Except one that he calls a song, set to the tune of Mukunda Das's classic elegy to Khudiram Bose: 'Say goodbye, Ma, I'll be back'. Shishu wrote this—his own farewell ballad—in early July 1929, while still slated to hang. Here is the opening and the finish:

> I'm off to a new land, Ma
> Let me touch your feet
> With a smile.
>
> I won't be late, Ma
> I'll come back to your lap
> In new clothes.
>
> ...
>
> They'll hang me, Ma
> For loving freedom
> Hope that's still my garb
> In the next birth.
>
> Let me say as I leave—
> On return, I wish to see
> Flags of freedom, Ma
> Rippling on every land.

Act 2
Fire

chapter 1

I WISH SHISHU'S NOTEBOOK WAS a poetic masterpiece. There is romance in a sacrificial boy, blooming behind bars into a man, feverishly bleeding poetic gems. But his notes suggest that Shishu read a lot of poetry and knew that he was not a good poet. This did not deter his practice, however. And its dividends are visible over time: the imagery gets crisp, the words more bracing, their fit more snug on the meter. Yes, only metered poems; Shishu had no patience for free verse. He even has a poem about this, with the line: *rhythm shattered, like a pelted pane*. At sixty-five, after fifty years of practice, he made his first submission: a single poem to the Sunday supplement of a leading Bangla daily in Calcutta. In the accompanying cover letter, copied into the notebook, he says: 'If you publish this, that will be the most memorable event of my life.' A remarkable claim about a life dense with events. 'Because it would be my debut, no doubt a brazen trespass, into the elusive world of poetry. But should this end up in your waste basket, I won't complain. I'll accept that it has found its correct address.' He includes his submission in the notebook: a tinny poem on love, with such lines as *the fullest love burns eternal*. He never heard back. Under the letter is a wry postscript: 'After waiting quite a while, it appears that they did send it to the "correct" address.'

His jail poems—over three-quarters of the corpus—I find striking for two reasons. One, that he wrote them at all: the why, the where, the how of it. Two, that they are marbled with Noni: the sixteen-year-old he last saw on the eve of her wedding, forever fixed under the slip cover of his mind-scope. I'll get to the second one first because I have more skin in it. This Noni, who would much later become my Dida, I knew nothing about before the notebook. Here is an excerpt from a poem Shishu wrote in Alipore Central Jail on

10 April 1931 that portrays him gazing at a photograph of her:[1]

> Will I only get to talk to you
> When I'm a photograph too?
>
> Your crimson lips cling to silence
> As if words are so much cheaper.
> Your eyes dart, your braid swings
> Your feet skip on a victory path.
>
> There, your lips just moved
> Melting away my vain pique!

Did he spirit a photograph of her into jail? There are other poems that suggest he may have. But photograph or memory, it matters little. The images are vivid enough. And recorded nowhere else. By the time Noni became my Dida, her lips were a clamped brown line, her eyes were still, her hair had thinned, her feet had done some tortured travel. She must have packed Noni away somewhere within, but I had no news of it. That our elders had lived lives before us is like saying Jupiter has massive vortices. You know, but do you really? Then one day you get to do a fly-by. Shishu's poems were written close to the living. They are capsules of time I can parachute into. The effect is heady and disconcerting. For example, an earlier poem written on 26 November 1929 in Alipore Central Jail, ends thus:

> My eyes beg: 'Sleep!'
> But I can't.
> When I think
> Of not thinking of her
> I still really am.

Shishu at this time is fifteen; Noni, far away, is eighteen. Had she been a stranger, or better yet, a public figure, I'll bet my thrill in this time travel would be pure, free of these tendrils of panic. What else

---

[1] Shishu's poems are in Bangla. The translations are mine.

didn't I know? Who else, close to me, do I not know? How much can you really know?

∽

Dida always arose before first light. In the pre-dawn blue, her slender form in widow's whites moved soundlessly through the household steeped in sleep. She would bathe, wake her gods with prayer. Her radio turned on low, she'd make herself a cup of tea. The station's signature tune played in a loop: a shrill violin phrase riding atop a plush drone, like a toddler's whine over his mother's attempts to soothe. Over and over. This is the soundtrack of stress from my youth, of pre-exam cram sessions, the only times I'd be up at daybreak. It is also the sound of my clearest Dida memories. My desk lamp aglow, I am bleary from an all-nighter. Dida brings me tea along with hers. The angled light glints off her wire-rimmed glasses, deepens the creases in her sunken cheeks. A cool hand on my shoulder. She crisp, me wasted, we move to the balcony with tea. She sings maybe, her granular voice slightly nasal with age. Together we savour the stillness and promise of dawn, on the cusp of cracking open into the bedlam of day. Just the two of us, a rarity in the bustling home I grew up in.

This home was ruled by my Baba, ever the patriarch. But even as children we sensed that Dida was another power centre. When pitted against him, she usually got her way. As grandmothers go, she wasn't the soft-toy type. No kiss and cuddle. At most a head sniff, as is the old custom. But we shared a special bond, Dida and I. Together we'd devour novels, recite poetry, burst into song. At eighteen, when I proceeded to break Baba's house rules, Dida was my advocate. She was also a kitchen wizard, producing a stream of daily magic from the most pedestrian ingredients. Such as bawkphul bhaja: a fritter of the flamingo bill flower. Or kochu bata: a velvety taro mash with a lick of mustard oil. Or thorer chnechki: the spongy trunk of the banana plant, rid of its pesky fibres, shredded and sauteed with coconut. And so much more. But through all of this ran a seam of distance, a bit she kept for herself. Maybe for her writing life. We got handwritten poems on birthdays and special occasions, in her distinctive looped scrawl. She never had a desk, but wrote daily. I see her now, on a low wicker stool, her thin back upright, left hand steadying the notebook on her lap.

As kids, Dida used to tell us that Barisal was our desh—a chameleon word that in context can shape-shift from land to home to simply a state of mind. She would say: in Barisal district, past Jhalokathi town, is a village called Bikna. As these names rolled off her tongue, her angular face would soften with a mix of pain and pleasure. To us those words bore a mythical aura; they were central to our family's origin story. But what did those words do to her? Were they buttons wired to her Noni fossil within? I never thought to find out. Tracing Noni in Shishu's poetry now feels a bit like forensic archaeology: reading an old fire by studying the burn.

∽

Alipore Central Jail has a yard shaped like a teardrop, with twelve spokes of varying length radiating from a high central watchtower. The spokes are the wards. Shishu was placed in number 11, which he shared with about a hundred inmates. The jail could hold two thousand. Between the spokes, a few smaller squat buildings housed the death row, other solitary cells, and those for elite inmates such as Jawaharlal Nehru and Subhas Chandra Bose. The generous grounds—about twenty heavily treed acres, with the Adi Ganga River as the eastern boundary—stand in the heart of tony south Calcutta. Alipore, once home to the British elite, now houses Calcutta's rich. The jail was in continuous service from 1906 until 21 February 2019, when the inmates were moved to a new facility outside the city limits. The compound being prime real estate, the government was inclined to treat it as trapped capital but stalled under pushback from civil society. It stood abandoned for a few years, overrun with feral cats that once were jail pets, until it was converted into a state-run museum and opened to the public on 21 September 2022.

Shishu began his sentence here in September 1929 and was

transported to Cellular Jail in the Andaman Islands in August 1932. He returned here from Cellular in January 1938 and stayed until his release in September 1945. Over half the poems in the notebook—57 of 108—were composed during his first stint at Alipore Central, in a furious burst that began in April 1931. A large majority from that first flush are love poems. Here are two samples in full:

Attraction
16 April 1931

Your lithe body sways,
You speak, I lose my words;
Your sari's fleeting graze
And all my world is hushed.

Only you do I seek
And wish to wrap up in my heart;
I thirst for a glimpse
Yet quake to call you close.

Those dark eyes of yours
Hide lightning at their edge.

Fathomless
24 April 1931

Who says your lake of love
Rains peace on my scorched soul?

To love you is to wring out
My nightingale heart,
And be drenched in
Separation song.

Those dark eyes of yours
Never let me look at you;
Your silence drains me.

> Sleep well, you, I'll stay up
> Hoping for a glimpse;
> Push me away in the light of day
> I'll love you in the quiet of night.

> Each time I steal a glance
> You stay unfathomed,
> And I drown.

There are dozens of poems like these. This period is close to the start of Shishu's life sentence. His suffering often gets unbearable. He pines, old enough to be wracked by carnal love but not old enough to finesse it. Many of these poems are therefore downright nasal, peppered with such bits as:

> Will I have to immerse her
> My soul-deity,
> In these hot tears?

Or,

> My dusk is now come
> And you still not here.
> Without you I'm a raft
> Adrift on high seas.

Other than their high sap content, what is notable about these poems is their suggestion about Shishu's state of being. He seems to be occupying a different rung than what one would expect of a political convict in a British colonial jail. Imagine being half-starved, your back an open wound from your last whipping, your neighbour down the ward roaring in pain, and you writing a poem about being a wilted sunflower yearning for light. Perhaps Shishu was getting enough food and sleep? Maybe there was no hard labour? No torture?

These questions are answered, emphatically in the negative, in a parody poem Shishu wrote describing the dire conditions in Alipore Central Jail. This poem, from 3 March 1932, is the only one in which he lets us zoom out and observe his setting: the place where he writes, the place he won't write about. The poem—a song, really—is a witty spoof of a popular nationalistic ballad, 'Our flowering land, heaving with grain and gold' by Dwijendra Lal Ray that extols the virtues of the motherland. Shishu twists this into a vicious roast of Alipore Central and its administration. And he does this while being an inmate. This song is, sadly, inaccessible to those unfamiliar with the Bangla original it cleverly parodies. But not so the intriguing glossary that Shishu attached to it, of the terms he uses in the song, common to prison life. They show a keen reporter's eye and form a dispassionate account of the horrors he was amidst:

1. Bara Saab: Jail Superintendent, always a red-faced Brit, who, along with the Jailer, led a reign of terror.
2. Case table: Desk and chair, seating the Jailer or the Superintendent, where a stream of inmates are presented daily to be read out punishments for transgressions, many fictional.
3. Sarkar Salaam: Whenever the Jailer or the Superintendent visits a ward, or the jail hospital, or the labour sites such as the oil and legume mills, the head constable barks out these two words. The instruction is to display allegiance to British rule. All inmates within earshot must line up, salute like soldiers with their right hand and in their left hold up the leather ticket stamped with their prison roll number. When the constable says 'aaiz bor'—that is, 'as you were'—you bring your hands down.
4. Lopsi and ghyant: Thin rice gruel and vegetable mash. A standard meal, one that frequently causes the runs.
5. Jolap: Laxative. This, and quinine, are the first line of treatment, regardless of symptoms.
6. Chakki: Circular grindstones with which inmates mill by hand legumes, such as lentils or gram. Usual workday is ten hours. There are daily quotas to meet.
7. Ghani: Mustard or coconut oil presses. Inmates are hitched

to a central pole and walk in a circle to press oil. Ten-hour workday and daily quotas here as well.

8. Danda beri: Bar fetters. An iron rod, 18 inches long, fixed between two rings around the ankles. This forces the legs apart. Makes walking very difficult and running impossible.
9. Shikli beri: Cross fetters. Two iron rods, attached to ankle rings, come up to the waist and are shackled. Precludes bending the knees. The cross and bar fetters are often applied together.
10. Night cuffs: For certain violations you sleep handcuffed. Makes continuous sleep impossible.
11. Tiktiki: Gecko. A wooden contraption for easy caning. When affixed to this, the inmate resembles a gecko stuck to an angled wall, hence the name. Face down, arms splayed and cuffed, body propped at an angle, buttocks level with the caning hand. Fifteen to twenty lashes are standard.
12. Gunny sack: For certain violations you wear pants and a tunic made of burlap, for weeks. No underwear. Only those with experience know what class of agony this is.

Shishu was a meticulous curator. These notes on physical horror—an outlier to the rest of the notebook—therefore seem like a deliberately planted clue. That his poetry *was* the resistance. Trussed in burlap, he would write romantic poems heaving with birdsong and fragrance and full moons. He would conjure the poetic sap, tend to it, keep it alive in these surroundings, against these odds. That was the work he had set for himself. When the horrors got dialled up, as in his next phase at Cellular Jail, he would simply ratchet up the moonlight. But that comes later. For now, there's something else to nut out.

From his first stay at Alipore Central, the notebook has only one poem each from 1929 and 1930. Then a rash of over fifty poems starting April 1931 until he was shipped out to Cellular in August 1932. What had triggered this outburst?

I find that Shishu's notebook reads like a seismogram. His poems, in their frequency and tone, form a temporal record of shocks. Shocks of big Time: history breaking at his door, and of small: his heart breaking within. Then there are those braided shocks, most lethal, where the personal and the political bleed into each other.

⌇

As a militant in India's nationalist revolution, Shishu's path was star-crossed. He got drawn in, signed up, killed someone, and was jailed—all within a relative lull. The movement had suffered a setback in 1922 when Gandhi had pulled the plug on his nationwide campaign of resistance. By 1929, it had regrouped and was at the cusp of explosive activity, but Shishu was already behind bars. As he spent his first year at Alipore Central, the country outside its walls was being convulsed by seismic events.

At its annual session in Lahore on 19 December 1929, the Congress Party passed a resolution on complete self-rule for India, rejecting all overtures of British colonial dyarchy. A formal declaration of India's sovereignty followed on 26 January 1930. On 12 March 1930, Gandhi began his historic Salt March, where he would walk 240 miles to the coast to make salt from seawater, against the law. He led, by example, a nationwide movement of non-violent civil disobedience: breaking British laws, defying British taxes, and enduring police violence without retaliation. Millions hit the streets in a brazen challenge to colonial rule.

Amidst Gandhi's landmark display of non-violent defiance on the coast of Gujarat came an equally historic militant action on the opposite coast, in Bengal: the Chittagong Armoury Raid. On 18 April 1930, Surya Sen led coordinated raids on the armouries of the police and auxiliary forces in Chittagong. Over 100 revolutionaries, acting in cells, struck simultaneously at multiple locations. They killed British officers, captured a huge cache of arms, derailed a goods train, destroyed a telephone exchange, snapped telegraph wires, and briefly cut Chittagong off from India.

The British Intelligence Bureau's report on this operation concedes its stunning success, calling it a 'daring coup, meticulous in planning and execution'. Its effect on Bengal's militant resistance was electric. Recruitments surged, with women joining the armed fight for the first time, both in killing and being killed. Bengal erupted in a conflagration of militant actions, 'an orgy of violence' is how the IB report puts it, with 'the most widespread activity that had yet occurred in the history of terrorism in India' and 'terrorist crimes far exceeding anything that had been known before.' Not just the cities, even the districts—Barisal, Chittagong, Khulna, Midnapore, Mymensingh—were inflamed. The British administration hit back with ever harsher anti-terrorism laws and virulent crackdowns, which in turn attracted retaliation. This feverish cycle raged for the next three years.

Alipore Central was not sealed from news of the outside world. But Shishu's notebook bears no trace of these titanic events. His sole entry from 1930 is a paean to poetry, in an elaborate meter, full of clever wordplay. He was not someone immune to the heft of capital-T time, many of his later poems are marked by its claws. But this is not where his mind was then. The build-up for that first poetic outburst in April 1931 was elsewhere. The shock that triggered it had something of that lethal personal–political nature.

In the aftermath of Shishu's action, his political idol, Satin Sen, had been jailed along with fourteen members of Tarun Sangha. Shortly after his release on 23 February 1930, Sen spent a week with Gandhi at Sabarmati Ashram, on the eve of the Salt March. He came back alloyed by this visit and plunged into Gandhian civil disobedience. Throughout 1930, with Bengal's militant resistance in spate, Sen spearheaded Gandhian campaigns, courted arrest, and went in and out of jail like other Congress leaders. In March 1931, he called his Tarun Sangha members to a meeting in Barisal and declared that henceforth they were to abandon all forms of violence against colonial rule and resort only to non-violent methods. His congregation was stunned; this radical shift did not go down well with many. In particular, Hiralal Dasgupta—Sen's close lieutenant and Shishu's direct mentor—was vigorously opposed. With Sen unyielding, Dasgupta broke away, taking with him a large fraction of the membership, and joined the Communist Party then ascendant in Barisal. This effectively disbanded Tarun Sangha.

It couldn't have taken long for this news to trickle into Alipore Central Jail, the firestorm outside was generating a steady stream of inmates. How did Shishu feel when he heard it? He doesn't say. I imagine it was akin to the rug being pulled out from under him. He was marooned, high and dry.

Satin-da has turned Gandhian. Hiralal-da has joined the Communists, whose focus is not on India's freedom. At least that's what Srimanta used to say. But I'm sure he's followed Hiralal-da. So what does that make me? Who did I kill for? And why? What am I a part of now? This is just the start of my life sentence. How am I supposed to survive, Noni-di?

Will I only get to talk to you
When I'm a photograph too?

∽

Shishu's response appears to have been a dive inwards. He seized poetry as a life raft, with both hands. Later he would view this as a defining moment, one that forever linked his survival to Noni. He clung to the words in her letter inviting him to poetry, urging him to trust it as a candid record of his heart. He would let it rip, no more holding back. The notebook has over fifty poems from the following months. He says that he had written many more, but these he chose to share. A majority were love poems and we have seen some of those. But there were others too, some with hints of the work he was doing to cope with being politically stranded. He fought his inner demons using poetry both as baton and crutch. Here's one from 22 April 1931:

Looking back I see how small I am
So far behind in the war of life
My fight now is with me alone.

A shooting star I never sought to be
The pale lotus is all I wanted
But vicious thorns got in the way.

> Only he who fights in raging storms
> Deserves a place in the world's breast.

This is an excerpt of a poem from 13 June 1931, a plea for his poetic imagination to stay unfurled, to keep him afloat:

> You stub out affront and taunts,
> Bring hope in all dejection,
> Stealing into the prison dark
> In the poet's soul you stir creation.
>
> Oh, touch me with your radiant wand,
> I'll cling to you and retreat into my heart.

But this didn't always work. In a series of eight poems, written over six consecutive days in March 1932, Shishu essentially says: I quit. He is not yet eighteen. Notably, this is less than two weeks after his parody on Alipore Central, with the journalistic notes. Did a guard hear him sing it and get him punished? Suicidal thoughts were not uncommon amongst political prisoners in British colonial jails—death by one's own hand or via a revenge strike on a detested jail official. We won't know what had brought on Shishu's bout. But we do know that the revolutionary eruption raging in Bengal at the time had worsened the already grim conditions inside the prisons. Inmates faced increased brutality, floggings, the occasional gunfire, and the torture of witnessing their comrades being hanged. Here's a poem from Shishu's 'I quit' series in full:

Farewell
15 March 1932

> I could've been a poet
> I could've practised art
> The notes from my flute
> Could've scattered far apart.
>
> But my words they never came
> My paint did never gel,

> My flute it didn't play
> At the grievous night farewell.
>
> I'll go, I'm not unhappy
> A wayfaring buffoon,
> Quietly lighting up my life:
> This wild paper balloon.
>
> When all of you look up
> And see my light on high,
> There'll be no sorrow, none at all,
> No better time to die.

In two poems both written on 17 March 1932, Shishu separately bids his parents goodbye. In another, from 19 March, he takes leave of a beloved sister-in-law. The remaining four, likely meant for Noni, have such lines as:

> To the one I have pined for
> Night and day,
> I now say farewell.

Or,

> What use staying up
> To weave a wreath of pain?
> With her mark on my forehead,
> I'm ready to say goodbye;
> Let the light now go out.

But he didn't let the light go out. The act of tending to it, in fact, became the fuel. And a torrent of poems, all blood and sap, poured forth.

∽

Shishu sent exactly one poem to Noni from Alipore Central. Titled 'Offering', this is the poem his notebook opens with. In a preface, he mentions his choice in giving it the inaugural spot. Addressed directly to Noni, this is a long letter in verse, written on 27 July 1932. By now he's been writing poems intensively for over a year, most have been about her. This is the first one intended for her eyes. Somewhat guarded relative to his private poems, it still reveals much. In my quest for the Noni seam in Shishu's poetry, this is the Rosetta stone. It traces the arc of their time together, the winds that had buffeted him, and where he'd been deposited. But in the main, the poem is about her. Here are some excerpts:

> You are still chiselled in me, not a trace erased
> When did I see you last, that faded jot of time?
> Since Patuakhali, I've sworn you as my goddess
> The lamp you lit in me, I shall never let out.

Later, a tribute, for her gift of poetry:

> It is you who has built my poetry realm
> Imagine, if I had missed your letter
> And the gates to this land were forever locked!
> Today, alone with words is how I pass my time
> I play, I fight, I hunt—they keep trouble at bay.

Then, an intriguingly open declaration:

> I left you, like an impotent, that day
> Could you see the helpless pain I bore?

The scene this suggests has no records anywhere. Had Noni sought an initiative from him as they were about to part, her marriage impending? We'll never know. There are other bits of candour:

> Will I ever see you again?
> I think of you night and day.

Or,

> Maybe you've forgotten me
> Or one day you will;
> Don't know if I ever shall,

I can't forget you still.

And then the finish:

> With the poetry gems you gave me
> Look Noni-di, I've strung a necklace
> Take this, the only offering of
> Your captive: Shishu-Ramesh.

∽

Within three weeks of sending Noni this letter, Shishu would be on a ship bound for Cellular Jail in the Andaman Islands, the harshest prison in British India. An offshore site of state atrocities since 1858, Cellular was designed to be hidden from scrutiny. But news of its heinous practices had been trickling out for years. By 1921, even the British Indian Jail Commission had internally concluded that transportation to Cellular was 'demoralizing and unreasonable'. Under intense public pressure, the British government suspended deportations to Cellular in 1922. But following the Chittagong Armoury Raid, as the Bengal firestorm raged unabated—armed revolutionaries had inflicted more damage in one year than in the previous ten—deportation was back on the table. On 13 July 1932, Sir Samuel Hoare, secretary of state of India, announced in the British House of Commons that political prisoners were once again to be transported to Cellular. The first batch of inmates were shipped soon after. The S. S. *Maharaja* steamed off Calcutta's Takta Ghat dock on 17 August 1932. Shishu was on it.

He must have heard the stories. Since news broke of their transport to Cellular, the halls of Alipore Central must have been abuzz. Not merely with the stigma of crossing the 'black waters', but real stories. Of the brutal jail superintendent who puffed on a cigar while inspecting inmates yoked to the oil press, ready with blows if one slumped. Of the sadistic jail doctor who certified malarial inmates fit for flogging. Of inmates drowned by force-feeding, or driven insane by torture. Of inmates killed in secret drug trials. Cellular sounded like a black hole. Perhaps Shishu was convinced he'd never make it back alive. And that is how he had brought himself to send this letter to Noni—his first since the murder. There were things he didn't want to leave unsaid.

∽

Weeks later, far away in her kitchen in rural Barisal, Noni read and re-read the letter by the stove's flickering firelight. Freshly out of her 'barren' status, her year-old firstborn was latched at her breast. A vat of rice bubbled on the stove. It was the thick of the monsoons. The rain fell in a steady hiss, pouring from the thatched eaves, whipping the inner courtyard into mud. Her baby sensed something and began to whimper. When her mother-in-law walked in, Noni pretended it was the firewood smoke that was tearing her up.

The season, after all, was of damp wood.

chapter 2

Put out your skiff to sea, comrade
See the east sky limned with crimson
Sleep no more now, oh rise!

—Pratul Mukhopadhyay

AS SLEEP GREW ELUSIVE IN his later years, Shishu would often hear the sound in the dead of night. It welled up in the fatigued crevices of his brain. A distant hum at first, then progressively louder. Soon a deafening roar, up close. Wing 5, Cellular Jail; well past midnight. Over a hundred men, across all three floors, hollering in unison to the toll of their manacles slammed against their cell's bars: 'Inqilaab zindabaad!' Long live revolution! Over and over. The staccato chorus reverberates off the brick walls, fills the long corridors, escapes its barred arches, snakes up the central tower. Then the thunder of running boots. The warders, their batons. Clang of cells being yanked open. Thwack of wood hitting muscle and bone. Animal shrieks. Split skin, blood. But the chant keeps going. Even fifty years on, it would soak Shishu with adrenaline. And dread. Yet another life pivot, he would muse, now wide awake. Perhaps no less than the one on Barisal's Kalibari Road. But this time, he was not alone. He had felt not alone right from the start, even on the voyage that had carried him to Cellular, into what had been widely called the jaws of death.

∽

18 August 1932
At sea aboard the S. S. *Maharaja*
Calcutta to Port Blair

The crossing was rough. It was day two; a grey dawn. Shishu looked around the hold. A wan light trickled through the portholes to reveal a pitiful scene. Men in exhausted heaps, some in their own vomit, finally asleep after a harrowing night. The monsoons in full flow had whipped up the seas, which toyed mercilessly with the ship. With each pitch and roll, it had tossed about the fifty men locked within a cage in the hold. When lightning cracked the sky, they saw fat ropes of rain lash the portholes. Shishu was terrified. Then the retching began. The stench from one led more to vomit, like dominoes. And not just the vomit. The open cask in the corner, for night soil, had toppled. Amidst this horror, one man began to laugh, and then broke into song:

> Who are we afraid of:
> These doddering robbers?
> Whatever else they snatch,
> They can't steal our madness!
> Rise or fall, we dance;
> Win or lose, we play.

The men all knew this song by Tagore. Those not actively retching joined in. First in ones and twos, then in dozens, whether they could carry a tune or not. Soon the hold was an uproar of song and guffaws. The absurd had broken through the carapace of tragedy and glued the men together. Their ruckus drew a posse of guards to the hold, who were taken aback by the merriment. The song leader held the sergeant in a cool gaze: 'If you give us hammocks, we won't puke. And won't keep you up.'

His name was Kedar but everyone called him Doityo—giant. Shishu felt it wasn't just because of his physique. But also the air about him, like a king in exile, a sort of furious solitude. And an uncanny eye for the ludicrous. Shishu had first noticed him yesterday. It was barely daybreak. Alipore Central was geared up for its first batch of Cellular transports. Fifty inmates had been lined up at the jail gate. A convoy of police vans were to take them to the jetty, before the city awoke. The men stood in a drizzle, their feet fettered, their hands shackled. Their shirts hung rumpled over short sarongs. Around each neck was an iron ring, with a wooden ticket dangling from it, like a bell on a bullock. Shishu noticed Doityo's strapping form quiver, his face mottled. He sucked in deep breaths, cleared his throat and appeared to calm down, before another fit of shakes hit him and this time infected his neighbours. It was laughter they were trying to contain, Shishu realized. And immediately felt the mirth tickle his own belly, as he stepped out of himself and saw what they did: the bedraggled row, the ridiculous bullock rings, that outfit, the hairy legs with fetters. They would be rolling on the ground but for the guards strutting about with batons. Once bundled into vans, the suppressed laughter and jokes fizzed forth like soda bottles sealed for too long. Doityo didn't lead, he just was; the rest was contagion.

On the half-hour drive to the river, Shishu brimmed with an incongruous joy. Doityo had picked the seat next to him and fondled his neck ticket. Everyone else's was circular, meant for usual political prisoners. Shishu's was rectangular: he had committed political murder. This always brought him extra attention. It turned out, Doityo was a Bangal—an East Bengali—like Shishu. Since the Chittagong Armoury Raid there had been a steady inflow of Bangals into Alipore Central, much to Shishu's relief. When speaking to them he could relax into familiar inflections, with the muscular chew and no hiding the sibilant 'z's. Here in the van, for example, were Satish-da from Dhaka, Niranjan-da from Mymensingh, Sushil-da from his own Barisal—deep in conversation. Bangals all, and senior to him in age, though not in jail time. Doityo was from Rajshahi. 'Call me Doityo,' he insisted, 'not Doityo-da.' Shishu felt as if he was going on vacation, cocooned amidst friends old and new. They were off on a voyage! He would see the ocean for the first time since Patuakhali. Since that family outing at Kuakata beach, where the sun both rises and sets. Oh, a lifetime ago.

Shishu's buzz remained even at Takta Ghat—plank jetty—where, their fetters jangling, the men walked the sagging gangplank to board the S. S. *Maharaja*. It didn't fully flatten even when they were corralled into a barred section of the hold and the gate slammed shut. The portholes were much higher than the men. Some jumped up to catch a glimpse of a magnificent white pavilion on shore, catching the early light. Satish-da said it was a memorial to James Prinsep, whoever that was. It wasn't until departure, when the ship had sounded its horn and began to judder, and a few men desperately clung to the portholes, that Shishu felt a twinge. Would he ever be back?

∽

The next three nights were not much better than the first. Shishu saw a lot of ocean and found that shoreless it held no appeal. An unexpected lesson. At daybreak on 21 August, a sliver of land appeared on the horizon. The hold erupted in cheer, trading a known misery for the unknown. Mid-morning, as the ship approached shore, the prisoners were brought out and lined up on the deck. Ah, fresh salt air, after days in the dank hold. But it tasted ominous. Was this the proverbial last meal? Shishu looked around, savouring every morsel. 'Look, Sushil-da,' he cried, 'this land resembles our Barisal!' It was that familiar unbridled green. Every bit gleaming, cleansed with rain. Above, a tentative sun had broken through heavy clouds. Behind, the ocean stretched endless and inscrutable. To the right rose Mount Harriet, the highest point in the Andamans. Clad in dense woods it resembled a shaggy bear, asleep with its muzzle tucked in its paws. A palm-lined shore arced to the left, the treed upper slopes tinted blue-green. Straight ahead was the bustle of Aberdeen jetty, at the foot of a hill. Atop its dark rise loomed an imposing structure, its lofty walls crenellated: Cellular Jail. Shishu tried to perk himself up. 'Look at you,' he wanted to say, 'only eighteen but so scary that they'll lock you away in a high fortress on an island in the middle of the ocean forever!' But his mouth had run dry.

∽

Despite the upheaval, Shishu found out a way to quickly resume his poetry practice. His first poem at Cellular Jail is from 29 August 1932—a mere week after arrival:

> Who are you at my door
> On this rainy night?

> Your dark hair a nimbus
> On your lips a flash of lightning
> The drip drip of your wet sari
> Like the tinkle of anklets.

His door was really the grating of his narrow cell. Claustrophobic walls of exposed brick. At the back a vent, tiny and barred, far above his head. Not much natural light, therefore. The grating opened onto a deep veranda running along thirty or so identical cells, with barred arches overlooking the jail yard. If the rain slanted enough, Shishu would see it on the veranda. Maybe even hear its music? His cell was on Level 2, Wing 5. There were seven such wings, three levels in each, for a total of 698 cells. These wings radiated from a three-storey central watchtower, with a metal gate to each of the twenty-one verandas: the only possible access, in or out. A vision of ferocious symmetry. If Shishu stood at his grating, he could catch a sliver of the yard's green through the arches. And beyond, he'd see the back of the adjacent wing: blank rows of vents. No faces. Cellular Jail meant to isolate its inmates. The intention, as conceived, was 'a fate more dreadful than the hangman's noose'.

Shishu was not new to solitary confinement. He'd been on death row at Presidency Jail. The narrow, slatted bed, next to the tarred pot for night soil—all of this was familiar. But there he had the patio. No sky here at all. Besides, he had become accustomed to ward life at Alipore Central. To company. To the sound of normal voices, which helped cope with the sergeant's frenzied barks when those hitched to the oil mill didn't move fast enough. But here you were whipped if caught talking. It was hard to keep despondence at bay.

1 September 1932

> Go ahead, take it all
> All that you gave me at dawn
> Take back at dusk.
>
> This wilted morning flower
> I place at your feet.

> What I get by giving you,
> In this darkness, please
> Take that too.

Shishu thought Alipore Central had cauterized him. The meagre meals, the crushing labour, the floggings. But within a few months at Cellular, he began to look back at it as a cushy place. The miseries here were not unfamiliar: hunger and torture, in the main. With isolation being the new, and harshest, component. But the real difference lay in tenor. Untethered from the mainland, everything about Cellular had a brazen edge. The rice in Alipore often had stones; here, it also crawled with worms. The vegetable mash here was not merely repetitious, but largely inedible weeds and mouse pellets. As a result, dysentery was rife. So was malaria. At the coconut oil press, inmates were to meet an inhuman daily quota of thirty pounds, or be flogged. And if the jail doctor—aptly named Dr Edge—found you too malarial for flogging, you might instead get 'standing handcuffs': hung from a peg on the wall by handcuffs, face pressed against the bricks, feet barely brushing the floor, for days. And the warders here also brutalized the mind. Humiliation was their chief currency. But there was more. When you're starving and bloodied, a bit of sugar can snuff out your sense of self. Make you snitch on your friends. Even barter your body. No, Shishu wouldn't go there. He would fall back on his training. Steeped in the unspeakable, he would squirrel away bits of paper and write a poem on spring:

> 19 April 1933
>
> On the flowered bough
> The cuckoo calls
> The humming bees
> The robin swings
> Oleander blossoms
> In a leafy fringe.

Love blooms like a rose
The east sky is gold
A lover reaches out,
To draw his lover close.

∽

By now, a rupture had become imminent. Malnourished and malarial, the prisoners had begun to die, the corpses slid down a chute into the sea. The hospital was a farce, with little by way of treatment. Matters came to a head in early May when a hospitalized inmate, feverish and desperate, threw a shoe at Dr Edge. He was dragged out, trussed to the tiktiki in the yard, flogged until bloody, then fitted with cross-bar fetters, and tossed back into his cell. Whispers started making the rounds. Shishu heard them too. Snatched words when the warders were not looking. Sushil-da was one the planners. They were calling for a hunger strike.

Shishu felt torn. He too was past his limits of endurance and shared the outrage of his fellow inmates. But the rules were clear: if you hunger strike, you forfeit all letters for the year. Cellular's inmates were entitled to send and receive letters three times a year. In his verse letter to Noni on the eve of being shipped to Cellular, Shishu had asked her to write him: *if you can, do write me a letter/ all paths are blocked now but this*. He hadn't received any yet. But what if she had written and it was in the next mail? If he severed this link, could he still remain human? His decision to sit this one out would haunt Shishu later. He wasn't proud of it, but he forgave himself when, with age, he could no longer muster a motive so pure.

On 12 May 1933, twenty-eight inmates on Level 3 of Wing 5 went on hunger strike. The men were punished with the usual arsenal but held their ground. They got organized, tapping out messages with handcuffs on their cell's bars. Their demands were proper food and medicines, first and foremost, and release from harsh labour. They were political prisoners, they argued, not indentured slaves. They should have the freedom to associate and study. History was repeating itself at Cellular: fourteen political prisoners underwent hunger strike with similar demands nearly twenty years before. The lesson the Empire appeared to have retained—with Cellular shut down for a decade over egregious practices—was that the optics had been poorly managed. This time, the Government of India's Home Department, in its Orders to Provincial Governors and Chief Commissioners, wrote: 'Very Secret: Regarding security of prisoners who hunger strike, every effort should be made to prevent incidents from being reported. No concessions to be given to the prisoners, who must be kept alive. Manual methods of restraint are best, then mechanical when the patient resists'. That slip, from prisoner to patient, was portentous.

Five days later, on the morning of 17 May, warders trooped into Level 3 of Wing 5 with equipment and extra personnel: the force-feeding squad. As Dr Edge followed them up the central tower, past Level 2, Shishu heard his voice boom: 'Teach the terrorists a lesson!' The squad would follow the official recommendation 24/1629/1: 'A rubber catheter should be inserted through the nostril and into the gullet and so to the stomach. A solution of milk, eggs, and sugar should be poured via a funnel. In certain cases rectal feeding should be tried.' The inmate would be immobilized by four men pinning his forearms and thighs, an extra warder riding his chest in case of strong resistance.

The chilling soundtrack seeped out the veranda down to Level 2. Shishu heard it all: bolts being slammed open, scuffles, cussing, whack of batons, muffled shrieks, retching coughs, coaxed gurgles. It went on for hours. In the medley of screams, one stood out: a piercing wail, more pain than terror. It dimmed to a wheeze but didn't let up. Then the heavy tread of boots down the tower—the wheezing inmate being carried out. Finally, a pallid silence, broken with whimpers. It was late evening by the time the news filtered through. The inmate was Mahavir Singh, the man who had driven Bhagat Singh's getaway car in Lahore back in December 1928. Instead of his gullet, the feeding tube had gone into his lungs, filling them with milk. He was in the hospital, drowning. The doctors were trying to revive him.

The chant erupted spontaneously: 'Inquilab Zindabad! Inquilab Zindabad!' Starting on Level 3 of Wing 5, it caught on at Level 2 and then 1. Warders rushed out of the central tower, batons drawn. One cocked a gun. A few inmates were beaten up. But the chant went on. Around midnight came the news: Mahavir Singh was dead. The collective gasp gave way to a chant of renewed vigour. The men stood at their locked gratings, beating manacles on the bars, in a synchronized din of metal on metal. 'Inquilab Zindabad!' Shishu was hoarse from screaming, tears streamed down his face. But he had never felt so alive. Something had shifted in him. Yes, he would be human, part of a collective whole, with his brothers forged by the same fire. And if the fire took him, it would burn brighter. No fear. This moment, this night of the chant, would be forever seared in his brain. Long after the glow had faded.

Shishu now joined the strike. Satish-da, Sushil-da, Niranjan-da, and Doityo were already in. That night ended with twenty-six men from Levels 1 and 2 joining the twenty-seven remaining strikers on Level 3.

∽

One morning soon after, Shishu found that his drinking water pot had been quietly refilled with milk. 'What should we do, Narayan-da?' he asked a neighbour, also on strike. 'What kind of question is that from a Bengali boy? Haven't you played football?' came the reply, 'Give it a hard kick, go on!' Shishu did. As did the others. Soon, milk coursed down the veranda of Level 2. Warders and batons followed. And standing handcuffs, which Shishu had learned to tackle. Strung up for days, he composed long poems in his head, repeating aloud until time turned spherical and exuded a glow of cogent busyness. Being pressed close to the brick wall, he told himself, gave his voice a nice ring.

The feeding squad came for him, too. Even Dr Edge showed up once: pot-bellied, his pink face misshapen like a chalta fruit. Shishu tried to not resist as they pinned him down, lest they rammed the tube down the wrong path. But the squad just kept pushing harder. And he'd eventually feel the cool gush of liquid. Defeat and nourishment made a tense couple, Shishu learned.

As the strikers dug in their heels, bad news kept coming. On 26 May, Mohan Kishore Namadas was killed—drowned in milk, like Mahavir Singh. On 28 May, a third striker—Mohit Moitra—was killed the same way. Three deaths by aspiration pneumonia, in eleven days. Dr Edge had become a liability and was recalled to the mainland. His replacement, Dr Barker, arrived mid-June, determined to play the good cop with the strikers. They were unaware of his sinister memo to the Government of India's Secretary on 20 June 1933: 'If the medical authorities can be assured of immunity, they should be given absolutely a free hand.'

The hunger strike, with over fifty inmates, had now lasted over a month. Its news had begun to trickle out.

∽

Amidst all of this, Shishu wrote poems. He includes three in the notebook. One from 1 June 1933—within days of the third striker death—is filled with such lines as: *When will you return/ to love me/ I can bear no more/ these lonely leaden nights*. In another, written on 2 June 1933, the monsoons have arrived and the poet imagines himself drenched and unloved, lost on the street one evening, walking and crying in the rain. The third, from 5 June 1933, is a dreamscape of someone's nocturnal visits:

> You slid in on moonbeams
> Through my window,
> Playing Holi with the stars
> You came that spring night
> Sitting at my head, you gazed down
> And kissed my sleeping lips.
>
> You sat on my heart
> All night, like dew,
> And vanished
> With the rising sun.

Shishu by now has been on hunger strike for nearly twenty days. He does not have a window; his barred vent is too high to look out of. Did it ever let in a shaft of moonlight? He imagines this magical spring night while writing on a monsoon day—he couldn't have written it at night, no lights in the cells. And he imagines an actual kiss, the only one in the entire notebook teeming with love poems.

I will admit that when I had first read these poems I scoffed at them, almost hard enough to overpower the shock and thrill in finding that my Dida, that muted figure in widow's whites, had once inspired love poems in a dank cell on a penal island a thousand miles from shore. Reading verse after saccharine verse had taken its toll. It turns out, I had missed the dates. Only later did I realize that Shishu wrote these poems while on that historic hunger strike, one that would radically alter the lives of political prisoners in Cellular Jail. Not before or after. During. He had tuned out unspeakable horror and imagined a moonlit kiss. He had then held on to these poems for over fifty years, cupped like a flame against time, before placing them in the notebook. But he chose to mute the context in which they were written. Except the date and place. But with that alone one could reconstruct the rest. So who was this hint for? Not Noni, surely. At eighty she wouldn't dig around archives for pieces and solve a jigsaw. Who then? I was starting to feel like Shishu was watching me put his life together: prying loose his carefully planted clues, holding them up against the light, unravelling the attached ball of lint. Perhaps a pursed smile, seeing a mortified me reverse my initial disdain for his florid love poetry.

∽

July 1935
Attic, Central Tower
Cellular Jail
British India

Shishu looked up from his book and gazed out over the rooftops. Another monsoon. A flabby grey sky rudely jabbed by the jail's symmetrical spokes. A sliver of green below: the yard he helps keep, trimming grass or planting flowers. But this was a Sunday morning, and he was in the library. Sitting here still occasionally felt out-of-body, even though it had been months since they had set this up: a meeting space in the attic of the central tower, with a few bookcases. Look around, he thought. Here we are, twenty or so inmates, reading, some chatting with each other, waiting for Satish-da's class to begin. Two years ago, each of these acts would have separately attracted lashes. He hadn't been flogged in a while and didn't want to remember. His memory was even starting to lose bits from the hunger strike, like peeling paint. It's hard to fully recall a toothache you no longer have. The strike had ended on 26 June 1933—forty-five days in all, thirty-nine for Shishu. They had won: edible food, soap, minimal labour. They got lights in their cells, access to books and periodicals, freedom to assemble and talk to one another. And the prison officials were now better behaved. The two warders over there, guarding the stairwell? They could still punish, and did, but there was little of that wanton humiliation. In fact, when the inmates lobbied for a library—with the embargo lifted, book parcels flooded Cellular's mail—they had provided material for bookcases, which the inmates then built in the carpentry workshop.

Speaking of books, Shishu could barely put down the one he was reading now—*Ten Days that Shook the World*. America was the enemy but this American, the author John Reed, was a hero. Imagine being in Petrograd when it happened, the great Bolshevik Revolution of 1917. Such an incandescent read! Shishu found Reed's ringside account breathtaking. Not dry at all like Lenin's *What Is to Be Done?* Or Marx's *Das Kapital*, which he'd hardly been able to make a dent in. Satish-da had recommended these to those who joined the study circle. In fact, he had handed out a whole list of books that Shishu had been slowly chipping away at. The library was largely socialist and Marxist literature, books that the seniors had written home for after winning the strike. They now took turns leading the study circle: Satish-da, Niranjan-da, Narayan-da, Batukeshwar-da. And, of course, Ambika-da, Shishu's favourite, and yet another Bangal. He was larger than life, full of hair-raising stories of the Chittagong Armoury Raid—it was he who had led the destruction of the telephone and telegraph systems—his daring escape and eventual capture.

Shishu loved the study circle: the community, the sense of purpose. The dark vacuum in him after Tarun Sangha's dismembering had faded. He read diligently, but had questions. It felt like déjà vu. Nine years before, in Barisal, he'd had questions for Shankar-da when assigned to read *Anandamath* or the story of Mazzini as revolutionary literature. The seniors around him now labelled those books as reactionary. They said Mazzini was a fascist, that the pronounced Hindu flavour in *Anandamath* made it rightist. That the Left is right and the Right is wrong. That socialism was the economic path forward. That communism—as fulfilled by the Soviets—was the political ideal. Shishu wanted to believe, but didn't feel like he fully understood. He kept looping back to the point Srimanta had flagged all those years before: the communists have to follow the line from Moscow, our freedom is not their priority. So, what about us, Satish-da, Shishu asked. Isn't India's freedom our priority? Didn't that fight bring us here, to the middle of nowhere?

Satish-da always opened his classes by taking questions. Shishu's brought on a lopsided smile. 'Good, good,' he nodded, but his eyes were on fire. 'Let's play a game,' he began, 'how many here have witnessed another's oppression?' All hands shot up. Images of the Goila woodcutter came flooding back to Shishu. 'Right. Now let's share some stories,' Satish-da went on, 'must be first-hand accounts, because I'll ask you how it felt. Who'll go first?' Doityo volunteered. 'Ah, Doityo,' Satish-da grinned, 'our sceptic feudal son! No, no, no smirks please. Many of us here are from landowning families. We'll all take turns. Go on, Doityo.'

Doityo leaned back and stretched his long limbs. 'Yes, there certainly is feudal blood in me,' he said, cracking his joints, 'I sometimes feel it even here in jail.' The group tittered. 'Our mansion in Rajshahi is right on the Padma. All you Bangals here know how fickle Padma's banks are. A bank calves here and a sandbar rises there. Only the utterly hapless live on a sandbar. From our front porch the

Padma's far shore was barely a sliver, but a fairly large sandbar was much closer. As boys, it fired our imagination for adventure. It had a clutch of hutments. In one lived Hasan, a handyman who did the heavy work in our garden. He commuted each day in his tattered dinghy. I know how tattered, because a cousin and I had snuck into it once and tried crossing over to the sandbar. Despite constant bailing we almost lost it. And there were two of us. God only knows how Hasan managed to paddle and bail at the same time. His real boss was our head gardener, Saiful. As Hasan quietly went about his work, Saiful, hookah in hand, would spray him with verbal abuse. I don't think we ever gave Hasan anything to eat. There was one exception, and I still remember how his face had lit up that day. After work, he took a dip in the river, then hacking off a banana leaf with his sickle he came near the kitchen. The cook, standing on the kitchen porch—a couple feet above Hasan—poured out the food onto the leaf he cradled. Hasan carefully wriggled about, trying not to miss the torrent. And he had a big smile on. I see many of you nodding. Yes, we've all seen contact taboos in action. But that's not my main story.' Doityo took a breath before continuing.

'The only time I saw emotion in Hasan, other than that smile, was on the day we fired him. A set of metal cookware had gone missing, rather pricey. How did this happen? We had two full-time guards at our front gate. But no one questioned them. Saiful blurted out, "It must be Hasan, the dingbat!" and the household's suspicion had found its focus. Rather than consider the absurdity of Hasan porting heavy utensils in his leaky dinghy, staff members chimed in that the timid tend to be latent criminals. The most vocal ones almost surely had something to do with the theft. A consensus was quickly reached. They ganged up on Hasan and thrashed him. Hasan didn't say a word. He took his dinghy and left for the sandbar. As he pushed away from our ghat, tears streaked his face. I never saw him again. Days later, Saiful said to my father in a gloat: "Did you notice, kawrta? The prick never came back." As if Hasan's non-return had proven his crime.'

'And here's the thing: I could have rowed out to the sandbar to find Hasan. But I never did. Then one morning we found the sandbar gone. Swallowed by the Padma.' Doityo drew up his knees in a hug.

The attic had fallen silent. Shishu was steeped in the parallels between Hasan and the Goila woodcutter, whose name he had never asked. A million injuries, he thought, every day, for centuries. His chest felt tight. Satish-da broke the silence: 'I hope you all noticed the hierarchy. Hasan reports to Saiful who reports to Doiyo's father—the high-caste landlord. That's how power travels, it follows the money. Saiful and Hasan both happen to be Muslim. One or both could have been low caste. The landlord could've been Muslim.'

'But could the victim have been high caste?' Doityo interjected, 'Not likely!'

Satish-da let this pass, as more of the group clamoured to speak. Several stories followed. Each with elements from Doityo's, each fitting a broad pattern. Just as Shishu was starting to wonder what this exercise had to do with his original question, Satish-da posed yet another question: 'Is this what we mean by free India? The freedom to drain the masses of lifeblood?'

Manish-da, quiet thus far, now spoke up: 'Knock the high castes all you want, but aren't we the ones fighting the British? Look around you and take a headcount. I was on munshi duty last week and went through the jail register. Cellular has 385 political prisoners right now. I counted 339 Bengalis, of whom nearly 300 are high caste and not even ten are Muslim!'

'Ah, while we're doing accounts, can we please keep track of the Bangals too?' Ambika-da's baritone boomed out in mock seriousness. 'You'll find that an overwhelming majority of those 339 are Bangals. Three men were killed during the hunger strike, Mahavir Singh and two Bengalis. Mohit Moitra, from Pabna—a Bangal, high caste. And Mohan Kishore Namadas, from Mymensingh—another Bangal, but a Namasudra Dalit. Eh heh, did that mess up your accounting, Manish?'

'You just proved my point,' Manish-da shot back angrily, 'the exception shows that the rule exists! I won't stoop to a broad body count. But if you do, I urge you to go back at least to 1905, to the first explosion. I'd say the high castes have atoned with disproportionate sacrifice!'

A vigorous argument ensued, both for and against Manish-da. Satish-da's voice cut through the hubbub: 'Wait, all of you! I'd like to respond to Manish. Imagine for a moment that you are a Muslim fisherman, or a low-caste farm labourer. Why would you want a free India, where not even the British can reign in your despicable landlord? Wouldn't that be like going from the frying pan into the fire? And now, with the Communal Award in 1932, the British are actively wooing the Muslims and the low castes. Find the cracks and rip them wide. Divide and rule. Our only option in fighting back is to unite, to de-class ourselves. All that retail violence we've been party to that landed us here? That was largely fruitless. So quit your infantile accounting of bodies. What we need is organized mass outreach. Revolution is the goal. And we have a manual. From Russia.'

The session left Shishu invigorated. He thought he understood most of it, but also had a niggling sense that the goalposts were being shifted. Yes, the upper classes in Bengal were overwhelmingly high caste, the masses Muslim and low caste. But class was not the same as caste. There could be classes within a caste, castes within a class. How, then, was the class lens alone enough? As the group broke up, he cornered Doityo, whose sidelong remark about this had gone unaddressed.

'Satish-da can roar all he wants,' Doityo said in his unhurried drawl, 'but I don't believe a Russian revolution will ever come to India.'

'Why not, Doityo?' Shishu was agog.

'Our masses are far too riven. The caste lines run deep, cutting all the way through the lower classes. There is not one mass, hence there cannot be one revolution. Unless the caste system is dismantled.'

'How?'

'Magic! That's the only way I can think of,' Doityo grinned. 'The literature we're studying here speaks of de-classing—it comes from Europe. But what about de-casteing? No European prescriptions for that!' He gave a wry smile, then fell serious. 'Can we, the high castes, truly imagine the lives of the caste-ridden? How then would we imagine their wants? We violate them for centuries, then suddenly wake up, and bathed in guilt forge their revolution and force it down their throats? No!' His voice had briefly swelled. 'They need leaders to rise from their own, marked by their life experiences. Like Ambedkar. Our job, as the forever entitled and therefore illuminated upper crust, is to make such rise possible. And then fiercely support those leaders from the sidelines. We need many more Ambedkars. We need leaders from Bengal's massive Muslim peasantry. Fazlul Huq, from your own Barisal, is a magnificent mass leader who represents peasant interests. But he hasn't risen from peasantry. He's from the literate elite. Just like you and me.'

'Do we have an Ambedkar in Bengal?'

'I'm just starting to hear a name. Also from your Barisal,' Doityo gave Shishu a friendly poke. 'What is with you Borishailyas! Jogendranath Mandal. A Namasudra Dalit from rural poverty. Now a talented lawyer rising in the Barisal High Court. He is someone to watch.'

Shishu filed the name away: Jogen Mandal. A decade would pass before he came across it again.

ო

Several of Shishu's contemporaries in Cellular identified with the political Left even before their transportation; some were members of the fledgling Communist Party of India (CPI). On 26 April 1935, they founded the Communist Consolidation within Cellular Jail. The initial membership of thirty-nine inmates would later swell to 200— over half the political prisoners at the time. The Consolidation held regular study circles; its members managed an ever-growing library. It also published a monthly journal, named *The Call*, complete with an editorial board, which carried articles on communism and socialism. The journal, about 150 pages long, was handwritten and its sole copy was placed in the library.

The Consolidation's anti-imperialist stance could not have been unknown to the jail authorities. But there are no records of them trying to muzzle it, contrary to the administration's ban on the CPI in the mainland. Perhaps it was dismissed as an innocuous study circle on a remote penal island, with none of the disruptive potential of the CPI's trade union strikes. But the Consolidation's hefty membership and network would figure crucially in the success of Cellular's final hunger strike in 1937 that shut down the jail for good. By that time, Cellular had schooled hundreds of communists, Shishu among them.

∽

Other than prison duties, Shishu's time was now spent in study and debate. He was finding little time for poetry. In fact, he had begun to feel like his love poems were...what was the term Ambika-da recently taught him? Ah, yes. Boor-zho-ah. Sounds familiarly Borishailya. He rolled it around in his mouth: boor-zho-ah. A middle-class conformist, a conventionalist. If that's what he was, he would learn to rise above it. To de-class himself. For that he needed contact with the masses. How about the non-political prisoners?

On yard duty one day, Shishu found himself next to Kartik Pramanik and felt a stab of thrill. Here he was, a Brahmin, trimming grass beside Kartik, from the lowly barber caste! The thrill was quickly tainted by a slow recognition of how naturally he had noticed the caste boundary. He thought of Doityo's point. How does one overcome this? But he was working alongside Kartik, wasn't he? That would never happen outside of jail. Shishu found out that Kartik, a poor labourer from rural Nadia, was serving life for killing his cousin in a drunken fit. What was his dearest wish? Most of all, to see his little daughter, who was not little any more. He wanted a fresh mango from a favourite tree in his village. And a dip in the river after a hot day. Kartik's pinched face was suffused with imagined pleasure, his eyes half closed.

'But Kartik, Kartik, don't you want the country to be free?' Shishu urged.

'Free, kawrta?' Kartik drew a blank. 'A cow can be freed. Can a country be freed?'

'What about you, are you free?'

'No, kawrta,' Kartik broke into a toothy grin. This one he knew the answer to, 'I am in jail.'

'Now imagine the country is in jail.'

Kartik's heavy brow became knitted. No, too hard, Shishu thought. He would need to find other ways. He would need to keep trying.

He'd had better luck with Ajmal. Thickset Ajmal, son of a Muslim peasant from Murshidabad, serving life for armed robbery, who had skipped up the ranks for good behaviour, and was now a warder often on duty at Level 2 of Wing 5. Shishu tried to catch him on morning shifts, when he was fresh and loose. Unlike Kartik, Ajmal understood the meaning of free India, but he wasn't sure he cared. His father had worked for the landlord and he worked for the British. What was the difference? And the British police had been nicer to him than the landlord's goons. One time, when they had failed to pay taxes, the goons came, thrashed everybody and broke his father's leg. 'They even hit my sister! And scraped up every last thing in the house.' His eyes flashed, the sting still fresh. 'My mother begged them to leave the pot of date molasses she had saved. But no, they had to take that too!' Why else would he have chosen armed robbery?

'You work for the British, Ajmal,' Shishu ventured one time, 'and I fight the British. Does that make me your enemy?'

'I am only doing my duty,' Ajmal answered, a bit cagey.

'Yes, of course. And you can flog me if I break rules. But would you agree that I, we, fight for you too? For your right to live in a free India? For your children's?'

Shishu watched Ajmal grapple with this. But he had no idea that a breakthrough had occurred until a few days later. It was late, well past 9 p.m. when the cell gratings were locked. Ajmal was starting the night shift. He rushed to Shishu's cell, smuggled him something, and quickly walked away. A warm chapatti, smeared with coconut oil fresh from the press, sprinkled with sugar, rolled up. Shishu felt hot tears spring up. He had been able to reach Ajmal! And when was the last time he ate sugar? A rare treat couched in an even rarer victory!

Having missed out on formal schooling, Shishu always credited

Cellular as his university, as the place that had forced him to live with others whose stories were vastly different from his. He would look back at it wistfully as a natural incubator for an India unhindered by caste and class. An incubator for a revolution that never came.

∽

I have only one direct memory involving Shishu. Dida had spoken of a man she called a brother, a freedom fighter who had been in touch with her even while serving time in Cellular. 'I had encouraged him to write,' Dida had said, 'I had told him that his body may be behind bars, but his mind was not.' She had described his claustrophobic cell, from which he could barely see a sliver of sky. 'I had said, you can touch the sky with words. Not just the sliver you can see. All of it.'

Noni wrote to Shishu in Cellular. And Shishu wrote back. I have not seen those letters but my mother has. Just weeks before Dida's death, Ma had found her brushing off tears while browsing a stack of old letters. A thin stack, maybe five. Ma remembers the letters being marbled with dark redactions of jail censors. In one, Shishu had written: 'It is you who has shown me the light. I now try to write a bit each day. Mostly poetry, some prose. I ride the words and push past the bars into the great beyond. Sky above, ocean below. Just like you said I could! You have saved me, Noni-di.'

Be that as it may, Cellular is where the Noni vein in Shishu's notebook runs out. His poem with the kiss is the final one of its kind. In the preface, Shishu regretfully mentions that his next poetry journal, covering the rest of his time in Cellular, was lost. By the time the notebook picks up again in 1938, he was back at Alipore Central and his poems had all turned Red.

∽

The trigger for the second and final hunger strike was the hospital. Food had become edible after the first strike but medical care was still scarce. Inmates continued to die of illnesses—malaria, dysentery, tuberculosis—that adequate treatment would've managed. When repeated appeals failed to yield reform, they sent a petition to the Viceroy of India on 9 July 1937. Signed by 239 inmates, the petition described the abject conditions within Cellular and demanded immediate repatriation of all political prisoners to mainland jails. There was no response. The hunger strike began on 24 July. This time, Shishu joined the very first wave. Soon, 230 men were refusing food.

This strike had a character quite unlike the first. The Communist Consolidation members had by now won over several warders to their cause. They in turn had built contacts on the island outside the jail, and even amongst employees of the S. S. *Maharaja*, which plied the Andaman Sea once every ten days. Two-way communication was thus in place between the Consolidation inside Cellular and their comrades on the mainland, bypassing prison authorities.

The familiar arsenal of horror was soon unleashed on the strikers: floggings, standing handcuffs, and the dreaded force-feedings. But this time, the Consolidation's network enabled the news to reach the mainland press within days. Every major newspaper broke the story, to tremendous public outrage. These reactions, in turn, promptly reached Cellular via the same network and boosted strike morale. A fraction of the Consolidation had strategized to be non-strikers who kept up the mainland newsfeed. And every time a striker was force-fed, dozens of non-strikers raised deafening slogans that tore through the wings. Between hunger strikers and their agitating supporters, nearly 300 inmates were in participation. The strike had taken on the shape of an all-out prison revolt.

As the Viceroy remained unmoved, mass protests broke out throughout mainland India, especially in Bengal. On 2 August, Rabindranath Tagore wrote a scathing public appeal, expressing solidarity with the strike. Weeks passed. Prisoners in mainland jails began hunger strikes in support. Students hit the streets, workers held demonstrations. The impasse was finally broken through the intervention of Tagore and Gandhi. Neither were sympathetic towards the militant activity that had filled Cellular Jail. But this did nothing to dim their outrage at the horrors of the penal island.

They met with the Viceroy and convinced him to stand down. The strike was called off on 28 August. It had lasted thirty-six days. The strikers had won: Cellular would cease to be a prison.

The first batch of repatriated prisoners left Cellular Jail on 22 September 1937. Shishu had arrived with the very first batch, on 21 August 1932, and left with the very last, on 14 January 1938.

∽

The S. S. *Maharaja* once again, thought Shishu, but what a difference! Not lashes of rain but sweet winter light. Not a roller-coaster but a glide on calm seas. Not away from but towards. On the morning of 18 January, the men crowded the deck as the ship entered Diamond Harbour and was within sight of shore. They laughed and they cried, in disbelief and joy. They gulped great lungfuls of air. None of them had expected to make it back. Moored at Takta Ghat, they filed down the gangplank and took their first wobbly steps. Setting foot once more on the mainland, Shishu felt reborn. He had survived a special hell. Why me, he wondered, where so many had fallen? It felt like a lucky draw. Riding the police van back to Alipore Central, past glimpses of the city he thought he'd never see again, he resolved to breathe meaning into this chance rebirth.

chapter 3

SHISHU'S SECOND STINT AT ALIPORE Central Jail felt vastly different from the first. Back then he was lonely, and with Tarun Sangha dissolved, lost. This time he was a freshly ruddered ideologue with his tribe all around him: Ambika-da, Sushil-da, Doityo. After years at Cellular's solitary cell, he was back to ward living, his days abuzz with debate and keeping up with communist literature.

His poems from this phase stand out from the rest. In content they are unabashedly the work of a cub communist, brimming with canonical imagery. Their shrillness seems out of character. Shishu had surely noticed, because he packs this tranche into a separate section. As he sat curating these poems nearly fifty years later, his faith in revolution spent, did he browse them fondly like he would childhood photographs? Did the unrequited passion in them make him wince? Regardless, he was evidently convinced of their place in the notebook. Here's the final verse of a typical poem:

Long Live Revolution
(1939)

...
The bolts will be thrown open
With donations in blood
The chains will be shattered
As the proletariat take the world
No time now to look back
Onward, immortal soldiers,
'Long Live Revolution!'

Hammer, sickle, workers, peasants, crush, rise, chains, shatter, freedom, revolution—these are recurrent words in this section. The colour red is liberally deployed, such as: A new era dawns/ with a red dress on/ a red flag aloft/ a red lamp lit/ it knocks on the door. And plenty of blood, as in **Time For Change** (1939):

> The world hasn't a thing
> Your blood didn't stain
> As the leeches get rich
> On your honeyed veins.
> ...
>
> Forge a new road
> And follow it ahead
> Paint the whole world
> With your blood—red.

Another poem from 1939 skewers the lacy urban revolutionaries, who wilt like spring flowers at the first hint of state violence. And spells out their fate when the oppressed do rise: Along with oppressors/ the imposters too shall witness/ the thunder fist of the oppressed!

The mood, in general, is more ferocious than in his poems before and since. Moreover, unlike the rest of the notebook, for a few poems in this phase Shishu uses English. Here's one in full:

Those Who Labour
(1938)

> You will plough
> And then you'll sow
> They'll reap it all
> Surely you know.
>
> The bricks you lay
> The palace you build
> All those doors
> To you are sealed.
>
> So the world is—
> Must build it anew
> This one is

For a favoured few.

Arise ye wretched
Arise ye deprived
Shatter your shackles
Your belt so tight.

Vested will be
None with favour
All will enjoy
Those who labour.

The least self-conscious in this set is a poem where the proletariat speaks, in a voice knowing and at a simmer. For this Shishu deploys his native Borishailya dialect, percussive yet musical, to great effect. Was he channelling his memory of the Goila woodcutter? This is the notebook's only dialect poem. Here's an excerpt for a taste of how it sounds:

> kawler maalik kawl salaayna
> haal dhawrena zomidaarey
> maaler poyda kori moraa
> hyara to shawb dawhol kawrey!
>
> aytokal to roilam boiyaa
> dhawmmer kawl to lawre na rey
> thokbaazi shyash kawrte oibo
> thohi ki aar baarey baarey?

Much is surely lost in my translation:

Our Lot
(1940)

...
Mill owners never mill
Landlords they never plough
It's we who raise the goods
They grab it all, and how!

We've sat around forever
With vanes of justice stuck
The swindling now must end
You think we're all lame ducks?

Some of the poems hew close to the party literature Shishu was consuming. One, 'Fascists Will Be Crushed' (1940), is inspired by a speech given on 2 August 1935 at the World Congress in Moscow by Georgi Dimitrov, the Bulgarian communist leader, then head of the Third Communist International. Dimitrov, in a clear break from the Comintern's previous position, issued a fresh line advocating communist forces worldwide to join with non-communists in their campaign to defeat the rising menace of fascism. Atop his poem, Shishu copied an excerpt from this long speech:

> The imperialist circles are trying to shift the whole burden of the crisis onto the shoulders of the working people. That is why they need fascism.
>
> They are trying to solve the problem of markets by enslaving the weak nations, by intensifying colonial oppression and repartitioning the world anew by means of war. That is why they need fascism.
>
> They are striving to forestall the growth of the forces of revolution by smashing the revolutionary movement of the workers and peasants and by undertaking a military attack against the Soviet Union—the bulwark of the world proletariat. That is why they need fascism.

The underlining is his, and I found that these bits are italicized in the published speech. Shishu had likely copied this excerpt into his jail journal when originally writing the poem. The war had begun. Communist literature was clearly still reaching Alipore Central and the speech had moved him. The poem, an amped version of the excerpt, is venomous. Opening with 'imperialist vultures', it heaves with phrases like 'rapacious fascist wolves' and ends with a dire threat to those who 'dare touch even a needle's point' of the beloved

Soviet land, 'guiding light of the world's workers'.

Shishu's Soviet love shines forth in other poems from this phase. In 1939, he translated into Bangla two popular patriotic Soviet songs from their English versions. One song, 'Wide is my Motherland', opens with these lines that he jotted down atop his translation:

> Soviet land! So dear to every toiler
> Peace and progress build their hopes on thee
> There's no other land the whole world over
> Where a man walks the earth so proud and free!

This song made its debut in a 1936 film. The other, 'Kakhovka', a Soviet war ballad, also first appeared in a film, in 1935, with a rousing refrain: *We are a peaceful people/ but our armoured train/ stands ready on the siding.* Both are infectious marching tunes, given to raucous choral renditions. It is intriguing how quickly they had made their way into Alipore Central Jail. I can picture Shishu and his comrades singing them lustily in the ward, their voices reverberating off the high bare walls.

As the world enters a long and debilitating war, there is Shishu at twenty-five, a lifer in a British colonial jail, a communist and a Soviet loyalist, singing 'Kakhovka'. He doesn't know that the Soviet Union has signed a friendly pact with the 'fascist wolves'. Nor that when that pact breaks, his beloved land will ally with the 'imperialist vultures'. And upend the ground beneath him yet again.

∞

22 October 1939
Tarpasha
Dhaka District
British India

Noni broke into a half-run. She was late, but also felt propelled by a coil of thrill. The streets were hushed at dusk, freshly drained of cacophony. A sadness tinged the air. It was Bijoya Dashomi, Durga Pujo had just ended. She drew the end of her sari over her head against the autumn chill, and across her torso. I hope that hides the turmeric stain from cooking dinner, she thought. She'd had no time to change. The day had slipped away from her. Her hands were never dry, as the saying went. Luckily she already had a going-out sari on: her white Tangail with a broad red border. She'd worn it to the sindoor-khela ceremony in the afternoon, joining the neighbourhood's married women to see Durga off before her immersion. They had smeared each other with vermilion—face, neck, the odd bit in the eye—amidst much mirth. She had dusted most of the red off but it was still thick on her parting and spilled onto her forehead. She was rushing to the evening's cultural program, where she'd been invited to read her poems. Hira had taken their three boys—ages eight, five, and two—and gone ahead to the pandal in the school yard. Her three-month-old girl did fall asleep on schedule and the elderly neighbour would happily watch her for an hour or two. But her plan went awry when the baby awoke amidst her cooking dinner, inconsolable, needing the breast. And now she was late. To a public reading of her own poetry! The baby would need her again soon. Yet here was a stolen moment, to be savoured.

At the venue, Noni climbs the rickety dais clutching a sheaf of paper and takes her seat. Seeing her arrive, her eldest boy bolts ahead to the foot of the dais. When her turn comes, he peers up at her, head tipped back. Standing on the dais, so high, as high as the sky. She looks absurdly tall, like the Durga idol that was immersed in the Padma earlier today, her parting smeared with red, her face aglow, just as beautiful and awe-inspiring. The crowd falls into a hush. She clears her throat and reads. Then applause.

When Noni's eldest boy, my Baba, recalled this seventy-five years later, he couldn't remember anything of the poems. Only that her voice was resonant and sounded like a goddess's might. That she seemed to cradle the words before releasing them into the evening. He remembered the sound of applause, like hard rain. He had looked back at the crowd and seen them admire his mother. When she came down from the dais to be with the family he could hardly believe his luck. He had barged in on her a few days before as she worked on a poem, and felt stung when she'd swatted him away. But now he understood. On the walk back home, he had reached up for her hand and when she looked down and caught his eye, they had shared a smile.

∽

Noni had always tried to keep a bit of herself sequestered for poetry. But it was getting harder. She had four children, soon to be five, six, then seven. And a household to run. Not that life had been unkind. Her plate was very full but that fullness was not without pleasure. She liked her little home on the water, raised on stilts, with its corrugated tin roof. It was one in a row of similar homes along the Deegholi canal off the Padma. These were employee quarters of the Ralli Brothers Jute Company where Hira worked. She liked her community of neighbours. And much else besides. The afternoon light, for example, that scattered off the water and stole through the gaps in the floor planks, tessellating the walls. Or at night, the slip-slap of oars from a passing boat in the canal.

One such boat had recently brought by a Singer sewing machine, Hira's gift to her at the birth of their first daughter. I grew up seeing it. The machine was black and gold, well-oiled, and had a polished wooden hood. Its hidden chamber for spare bobbins was a nest for my childhood imaginings. Noni would become an expert at sewing clothes, for her children, then her grandchildren. Her Singer would travel enormous distances, across a fresh scar on the map, and remain her companion for over sixty years. But all that was later. Right now, the Singer was part of the blessings she counted. She thought of the stalks of foxtail millet her eldest boy often plucked on his walk home from school. Of him bursting in with a millet bunch, then the glow on his face as she pounded the papery husks off the fistful of grain and with milk made a creamy pudding, his favourite. She thought of the flowers in her small garden out front, where she held poetry-reading sessions. She had escaped the clutches of rural life at her in-law's home in Bikna and come into her own.

This new nuclear living had drawn Noni closer to Hira, a willowy man, withdrawn and unworldly. She had learned of his foiled revolutionary aspiration. An ace student who had quit college to plunge into Gandhi's non-cooperation movement. When Gandhi abruptly called it off, a bereft Hira had swung towards militant nationalism, like many Bengali youth at the time. Which is when his alarmed family had reigned him in with marriage. And now he was a hobbled horse, on the beaten track. Without a college degree he lived well below his station, as a part-time accounting clerk, working only six months in the year around the jute harvest. The rest of the time Noni often took the children to her parental home in Mahilara. But she missed him when away, his melancholy interior. Hira stooped over a charcoal etching—a few deft strokes, then smear. Or sitting on the back porch overlooking the water, his gaze intent on the faraway.

Hira had kept his friends from his revolutionary days. When they dropped by, he would nudge Noni to read her poems to them, then hang back to bask in the attention. This would usually be followed by dinner and chinwag deep into the night. At one such gathering in 1940, Noni heard that Subhas Bose had been evicted from the Congress Party. 'This was all Gandhi's doing,' Hira's friends seethed, 'he pulled the strings. Just as he had forced Subhas—the elected president, recall—to resign last year. All because his favoured candidate didn't win! And now this.'

'But on what basis?' Hira asked.

'The charge is indiscipline,' one said. 'With Britain dragging us into war, Subhas had pressed Congress to issue a six-month ultimatum for self-rule. Too radical for Gandhi.'

'They also got nervous of his leftist tilt,' added another. 'The faction he formed within Congress last year has allied itself with socialist and labour parties. Not to mention his open disdain for the Gandhian line that violence has no role. The high command called it a revolt!'

'And let's not forget our Bengal Congress heavies who backed Gandhi,' a third hissed. 'Especially Satin-da. Think about it. Satin-da, licking Gandhi's sandals, to give Subhas the boot! Congress is now finished in Bengal. Those namby-pambies are never going to kick Britain out. Subhas is the only way.'

'Imagine,' Hira mused, 'how Shishu feels now, wasting in jail as his leader changes colour. So many bright lives....'

Noni thought of Shishu. He had surely heard the news. She knew how hard he'd been hit when Satin-da had dissolved Tarun Sangha nine years before. Perhaps this fresh blow would mean little. But what did he feel exactly? Noni didn't know. Shishu was not writing her as often as he used to.

∽

Shishu was indeed in a maelstrom but it had nothing to do with Satin Sen. At the start of the war, he had felt quite settled as a communist—his Soviet love, anti-fascism, anti-imperialism all of a piece and burning bright. If imperialist Britain wanted to fight fascist Germany, it was their problem. Why should India, with Britain's boot on her neck, supply men and material? This was his party—CPI's—line in 1940. Subhas Bose was giving rousing speeches in Calcutta's Maidan grounds along similar lines, drawing tens of thousands. Shishu and his comrades, behind bars only a couple miles away, had longed to attend.

All of this ruptured when Hitler attacked the Soviet Union in June 1941. By the end of that year, with the Japanese attack on Pearl Harbor drawing America into the war, CPI's official line underwent a tectonic shift. This is the people's war, it now said, the world against fascists. And since Britain was fighting alongside the Soviets it was no longer an enemy but a friend. If the first bit could still be digested, the latter was pure poison for Shishu and his comrades. They were in jail for fighting imperialist Britain and now it was their friend? Shishu remembered Srimanta's words from years ago: 'Careful of communists! They have to follow Moscow's line. India's freedom is not their priority.' He felt like a speck of dust spinning out in space. Did anyone care? And all this time he had believed he was part of something big.

Shishu's grief train had only just begun. The CPI further congealed its stance in July 1942 by declaring support for Britain and the war. The colonial government responded by immediately legalizing it for the first time, and released all its leaders from jail. To nationalists of every stripe this smelled of quid pro quo. Communists were labelled colonial pimps. Things only got worse for them in August, when Gandhi declared his Quit India movement. As India erupted in a furious insurrection against British rule—railway tracks uprooted, telegraph poles downed, police stations ransacked—the CPI opposed it, to pervasive outrage. Even within jail, Shishu and his comrades suffered daily humiliation at the hands of other inmates, especially the fresh arrivals flooding in from the Quit India clashes.

Meanwhile, Subhas Bose had escaped to Germany and, in a move shocking many, sought Hitler's alliance to oust the British. When that failed, he sided with Japan as it prepared to attack India. In *People's War*, the CPI mouthpiece, Shishu read a vicious takedown of Bose, calling him a quisling and 'Tojo's dog', after Japan's prime minister Hideki Tojo. And then the photograph of Subhas shaking Hitler's hand, with Himmler looking on? Or the cartoon of him as an obese cat, being held up to a microphone by Goebbels? As a die-hard Subhas fan, like every Bengali he knew, Shishu was gutted. It was all too much to bear.

Ambika-da, Shishu's senior comrade from his Cellular days and now a ward-mate in Alipore Central, noticed his crushed state and pulled Shishu aside one day. 'Ei,' he gently nudged, 'what's going on with you?'

And it all poured out of Shishu in a slurry. Subhas lost. Britain supposedly a friend. Communists despised. Fascists about to bomb Calcutta. The release brought him a surge of relief, but as Ambika-da's pep talk progressed it ebbed out, leaving behind a parched coast. Shishu felt something singe within him and evaporate. Something tender and essential. It wasn't so much what Ambika-da said as what Shishu heard. That everything was relative, nothing was pure. That compromise was oxygen. That organized resistance, counterintuitively, really meant submission.

'Look at Subhas,' Ambika-da was saying, 'our soul-brother, Soviet sympathizer, leader of the Congress Left. Imagine the vortex within him that pushes him into the arms of fascists. Do I support his path? Never! Do I understand him? Absolutely. India's freedom is Subhas's priority. By any means necessary.'

'And yes,' he continued, 'this is a tough season to be an Indian communist. The party line has forced us into a hounded corner. But this is a time of churn. It will end. Remember that the promise of Soviet revolution is intact. And without destroying the fascists there is no hereafter. Revolution is our priority. If that takes a foul bedfellow, so be it. Any means necessary.'

His final words drove a stiletto of ice through Shishu. 'You're what, twenty-eight? I'm past fifty. Let me tell you something. To age is to embrace imperfection. You don't flee it. Where would you go? You settle, even in a chipped marriage. Because the alternative is loneliness.' Shishu got a glimpse of the void. He saw with chilling clarity what the fight was really about. Not for freedom or justice or rights. But against the void.

Looking back, he would mark this as the moment when serpents first got into his Eden, if he ever had one. When he began living life at half pressure.

∽

As the war came to him, Shishu learned that you absorb shocks better when deflated. Japan first bombed Calcutta on 20 December 1942. The air raid sirens had sounded that evening, as they had for days. But this time there was no all-clear. Shishu heard the rumble of the bombers overhead, coming in from the east. Then the sudden impact, the ear-splitting report. The jail walls shuddered. A guard posted on the roof came flying down, ashen. He'd seen the north sky burst into flames, towards the city centre, a mile away. The bombing lasted an hour. Japanese sorties pounded the city nearly every night for the following week, with a particularly heavy bout on Christmas eve. Bits of cinder, carried by the southerly breeze from the river, littered the jail grounds. A noxious pall hung in the air. Many inmates were stricken, but Shishu felt a perverse thrill. He thought it'd be hilarious if the jail was hit. Would it make a headline in *Pravda*? 'Fascists kill Comrades jailed by our Imperialist ally!' He knew 'pravda' meant truth. The whole truth? In the event, the truth didn't even make the Calcutta papers. The British administration heavily censored all news and photographs related to the bombings, including the panicked exodus from the city. Britain, recently routed by Japan in Singapore and Burma, could ill afford to lose India. Calcutta—its port and garrison city at the eastern front, teeming with Allied soldiers—could not be seen as damaged. The official yarn of 'there were very few casualties' and 'damage was of the most meagre sort' was shredded by a brave British editor, Ian Stephens, of a Calcutta daily. His editorials lashed out at the government's denials and outright lies. Britain's focus on managing the optics of Calcutta's damage, at grave cost to its citizenry, continued a year later when Japan's air raids grew even more audacious.

On 5 December 1943, Calcutta was struck in broad daylight by two successive waves of Japanese bombers, 250 strong. This grievous attack merited a minor mention in the papers the next day: 'A number of bombs' were dropped on the 'Calcutta area' but the damage had been 'slight'. In fact, Calcutta Port's dockyards had been ravaged, with structures levelled, parked vessels destroyed and an inferno in its coal berths sending up a towering plume of black smoke visible for miles. The central business district had been hit. As had several residential neighbourhoods including Alipore, leaving 12-foot impact craters. Shishu had felt the blast in his chest, a welter of flash-crackheat-dust. Like a monstrous lightning strike next door, but more impactful because it had come out of a clear blue sky. His wish, for the jail to be hit, had come within a hair of coming true, on a Sunday morning of sweet winter light.

Air defence of its second city in shambles, Britain mounted a speedy cover-up. The day's official death toll—335—excluded seamen trapped aboard the sacked vessels, dock laborers incinerated in their quarters, and many more. The true count would never be known.

On another day of catastrophe bound for the history books, the German Luftwaffe had bombed London killing 436. But Calcutta's blitz would be buried by colonial censors. Generations of Indians would never know that an Indian metropolis had been repeatedly bombed in World War II.

But Shishu was there. He had seen it, even from behind bars. He had heard and smelled and felt. He knew.

∽

These airstrikes on Calcutta had come amidst a historic famine. Starving masses from Bengal's ravaged districts had flooded into the city only to die, their skeletal bodies piling up on the streets. The famine was man-made. Britain had expected Japan to mount a coastal attack on Bengal. To deny them provisions or transport upon landing, Britain enforced widespread confiscation of grain and boats from rural Bengal, to the ruin of its population. The countryside was put to the torch—standing crops, bamboo groves, bridges. The coastal invasion never came. But this brutal 'denial' led to a raging famine, killing an estimated 3 million Bengalis over two years.

Shishu had read news of the city's assorted horrors—the grain rotting in the government warehouses, the thriving black marketeers, the wasting bodies prostituted for a meal, the plaintive wail of Bengal's rice farmers themselves begging the city for not even rice but the water it was cooked in—'phyan daao!' He'd read of the relief kitchens that had come up all over the city. They had set one up within Alipore Central, with inmates donating part of their rations. He and his comrades would face the usual jibes from the Congressis in the kitchen: 'Guess who caused this famine?' they would taunt, 'your pals, the Brits! And you're working for famine relief? Brother, you are confused!'

None of this bothered Shishu much any more. His hide had grown thick by now. Or so he thought, until the incident with the dog. They had been out in the jail yard for their exercise hour when they saw it saunter in, carrying something in its mouth. As it sat down in a corner to gnaw in peace, a guard nearby gave a shriek and raised his baton to chase it away. The dog fled, leaving its meal behind. That's when Shishu saw it. A child's forearm, bony and brown, with little flesh on offer.

Bullseye
(1943)

> The dead fill the homes, their
> Stench haunts the streets
> Foxes roam the yards
> Little limbs in maw
> Thieves are now saints
> And cheap flesh is the law.
> ...
> A mother drapes her girl
> On the guillotine of lust
> To the bullseye of ruin
> The blood-arrow thrusts.

The strident Red streak in Shishu's poems runs out in 1941. The notebook has no poems from 1942, a telling hiatus. When he resurfaced, Shishu's voice had shifted, as in the poem above. Here's another sample from this time: a tonal rap, its meter much snappier in his Bangla original:

Dead Parade
(1944)

> ...
> Corpses spill from
> The fat cat's treasury
> The loan shark's greed
> Has topped all charts.
> See the court gear up
> To grill them all fat cats
> Here come the dead
> In a silent march.

Hira had wanted to send his family away to the village. With the war on, even tiny provincial Tarpasha felt unsafe for women and girls. Its proximity to the major ferry terminal at Mawa meant clots of Allied soldiers roaming the streets, looking for fights and other fulfilment. But the family could not be sent. Britain's brutal 'denial' policy got in the way. They had drowned every boat, skiff, dinghy. Or stacked them up and set them alight. For water-bound Barisal district this meant death. Food was scarce in every village. A terrible time to host extra mouths, even for Noni's relatively well-off father in Mahilara. So the family stayed put in Tarpasha for the war.

Noni remembers a young widow, her three hungry children. Her rickety shack at the edge of town, with a tattered burlap curtain as the door. There was always a clutch of Tommies waiting to take their turn. The children had to be outside too. Waiting, but for other things. One time she saw a Tommy pull out candy bars. The candy changing hands, from a fleshy pink hand to reedy brown ones. The crinkle of wrapper. The burly soldier, the blue of his eyes so faded that he looks blind. Is he bored or being kind? The stick-figure children, their bright eyes wide with fear and thrill. Their mouths full of unfamiliar cloy, quick chew and swallow. Noni imagined these were her children. The thought made her retch.

∽

The perfect storm of horror that Britain's war had unleashed on Bengal one day ended. Its festering wounds would spawn further storms in a year. But for now, there were good tidings. At thirty-one, Shishu was free. He was released from jail in September 1945, within weeks of the Allied victory in the Pacific. Walking out, he felt a stab of nostalgia for the fourteen-year-old boy that had gone in, his yolk all bright and runny. Not hard-boiled like now.

Free life was disorienting. At his cousin's Kalighat home, Shishu had to contend with droves of fawning visitors. With their admiring eyes. With phrases like 'our pride and Bengal's', 'ultimate sacrifice', 'fearless soldier'. Shishu tuned them out and watched, like a gecko on the wall. The gecko had questions. Who was he now? Could he offer up his life as he had then? Answer: he didn't think so. He watched his visitors watch him. They gawked at a battle-hardened revolutionary, a seventeen-year jailbird. And a card-carrying communist—the party had just issued his card now that he was out. But within, what about within? Maybe just a shrunken shell, Shishu felt, a raisin compared to his fourteen-year-old self taut with belief.

The first letter he received post-release was from Noni-di. She wrote from Tarpasha congratulating him. Writing her back felt like a lifeline and Shishu pounced on it. If only Noni-di was around, she would read him within minutes and tell him who he was. He decided he had to get out of Calcutta, towards her. Durga Pujo was around the corner, his first as a free man since 1928. He hadn't seen his family in that long. The news of his father's passing had reached him in jail, like a sigh buried amidst the din of war. Would he feel the heft of it now, standing on the land, his father's and his? 'I'm going home to Barisal, Noni-di,' he wrote, 'for pujo.' Putting the idea down on paper felt good. 'Are you coming too?' She was weighed down at Tarpasha, Shishu knew. But this was the first pujo post-war, the festive time when families gathered annually to share both grief and relief. Extra grief this time, extra relief. 'Please come, Noni-di.' Surely she would? Shishu had so much to tell her.

chapter 4

AS HE AGED, SHISHU OFTEN picked through that first trip back to Barisal like one fondles an old scar. It was the *Florican* once more that had carried him back, propelled by its massive steam-powered paddles. But the real propulsion, he remembered, had been Noni-di. The thought of seeing her again. The swell of a quiet crystalline thrill, even though he hadn't heard back from her. This memory always left Shishu wrenched for his younger self. The letter he had written Noni begging her to come was their last before losing touch. But he didn't know it then. She had good reasons to not come, of course. Too close to delivery. Her seventh child. And travel precarious, with the war just over. He heard this news at Noni's parental home in Mahilara, a short distance from Goila, where he was visiting his mother, and was crushed.

That first year post-release felt like a blur in hindsight. One of those years you could easily unfurl into a decade. But if he had to pick highlights? The actual travel back to Barisal would certainly jostle in. It was utterly disorienting. On the train heading east from Sealdah to Khulna, as they crossed the Ichamoti into east Bengal and all that electric green reared up at him, he had found himself reliving how those colours had drained away when heading west seventeen years before. His heart had leapt and sunk at once. A peculiar mix of looking forward and back, the present too slippery to hold on to. Parts of it felt like a movie playing in reverse. The shattered mirror gathers up to become whole again. Except, you know that it can never be whole again.

And that legendary steamer curry Shishu had eaten in the *Florican*'s dining room while still docked at Khulna. The first mouthful and time had slowed down. He had craved this for so long! The heat and perfume of the curry, the silk of the meat. Ah bliss! But soon it felt like he had taken a bite through a layer cake of memories.

One layer from when he'd eaten this as a child on a trip with his father. Another from the last time he was on the *Florican* en route to being hanged, wishing this as his final meal. And a third of the present meal that he could not stay present to. It evaporated, like calligraphy with water on sun-baked rock.

As night fell, he had stood on the deck and seen jots of light approach, like a cloud of fireflies. Up close they became vending boats. Fish and rice, luchi-torkari, paan and smokes. But above all, sweets. And one of the boats had paat kheer. He couldn't believe his luck. He hadn't had any in maybe twenty years. He had gently unwrapped the banana-leaf packet and dug into the sweet, soft mess, the caramelized milky grains melting in his mouth. It was so exquisite that he had bought two batches of twenty packets to carry home. One for his family and one for Noni-di's. It turned out that she wasn't there to receive it, but her nieces and nephews had happily devoured the sweets.

Then there was Srimanta. They had exchanged letters right after his release. He was in Barisal town and had agreed to come to the ferry terminal to receive Shishu. He was going to spend pujo at his village, Chandshi, close to Goila, where Shishu was headed. They had naturally decided to travel together. Shishu had been looking forward to this. But as the *Florican* took the last bend on the Kirtankhola and Barisal town came into view, his stomach knotted up. He could see Bell's Park, the bungalows on foreshore road, the jhau trees beyond. They all looked just the same. But he knew how much he had changed, how far he had wandered since leaving these moist shores. Who was Srimanta now, he wondered. As the *Florican* docked, he scanned the pier for his childhood friend. A portly man with thinning hair seemed the most likely candidate. It was quite a shock. Shishu was sure Srimanta found him equally unrecognizable. They each hesitated before waving.

And so Shishu would go, cueing up the bioscope in his mind's eye. Scenes from that first year of freedom mobbing him like unruly aspirants at a pageant. Pick me! No, me! Me!

Early October, 1945
En route to Chandshi
Barisal district
British India

By the time Shishu and Srimanta caught a skiff it was evening. Chandshi would take at least four hours riding the Kirtankhola north, with shortcuts on rivulets and wispy canals that draped the low river country here in a filigree. The two men chatted with a surface ease while holding back. Their equation had shifted, Shishu knew. He was no longer the sidekick. Many regarded him as the hero of an epic sacrifice. He could see Srimanta wrestle with this, whereas his muscle memory sought Srimanta's comradeship, as before. At thirteen, he didn't care what he fought for as long as it was by his friend's side. As nightfall hushed the river, Shishu shared this with Srimanta. The ensuing laughter and reminiscence lightened the air. They soon turned off into a narrow canal. And Srimanta opened up.

Even with no moon the open river is never entirely dark. Reflected starlight hovers over it in a luminous mist. But within a Barisal canal, the darkness is of a cave. The vegetation closes in. Heavy canopies of rain trees, braided vines, shaggy date palms. The shore and water get tangled in one inky clot. Sometimes you hear the water growl, like a hungry gut, as the incoming tide rushes even the thinnest capillary of the deltaic network. No rhythmic splash of the oars here. The boatman levers forward by stabbing the muddy canal bottom with a long bamboo pole. To you the darkness is a silky solid, but he knows every upcoming bend. Shishu realized how much of this land he was, of this water. How much he had missed this darkness, the submission to it. He savoured the embrace of home and listened to his friend speak.

Srimanta filled Shishu in on his journey since Tarun Sangha was dissolved in 1931. He had followed Hiralal-da into joining the CPI but his heart was not in it. 'I never believed India's freedom was their priority,' Srimanta said, 'they were perennially beholden to Moscow.' Shishu remembered him saying this even as a teenager.

'And we saw that during the war.' Buffeted by taunts in jail, Shishu knew this only too well. 'Matters came to a head for me in 1942, when all of India convulsed with the Quit India movement and we, the communists, stood by the British, even as they starved and strangled Bengal! That's when I quit.' Shishu felt a familiar pang: his spirited friend had acted and he had not. 'It was a terrible time. I would've probably gone into a rudderless tailspin. It was pure luck that saved me. On a visit home to Chandshi, I met Jogendranath Mandal. His village, Moistarkandi, is right next to mine. Have you heard of him?' Shishu had a flashback from ten years before—1935, Cellular Jail, study session atop the central tower, Doityo speaking about Indian communism's blind spot on caste, the need for more Ambedkars, one rising in Bengal, a young lawyer in the Barisal High Court, a Namasudra Dalit from rural poverty. Jogen Mandal. Yes, he had heard the name. 'Well, Ambedkar founded his Scheduled Castes Federation party in 1942. I was in an ideological crisis, searching for a home. When Jogen-da formed SCF's Bengal chapter in 1943, I slid right in.'

Shishu felt he was thirteen again. Srimanta had dashed ahead, found something exciting and was going to tell him about it. There was comfort in this old pattern, like a worn couch. Srimanta, now fired up, spoke of his leader.

Much had happened while Shishu was in jail. In 1935, the British had granted a large measure of administrative autonomy to India and allowed elections, both at the centre and in the provinces. The first elections were held in 1937. In Bengal, Jogen Mandal had won from Barisal's north Bakargunj, defeating a powerful upper-caste incumbent, the only Scheduled Caste candidate in the entire country to have contested in a General category seat. That first provincial government was led by the Krishak-Praja Party, with Fazlul Huq as Bengal's prime minister. There had been much power wrangling since. The Muslim League now held the reins in Bengal, with the SCF as an ally. And Jogen-da was a sitting minister. The next elections, delayed by the war, had just been announced by Viceroy Wavell. Bengal would go to the polls in five months. But Jogen-da was already in campaign mode. And he was in Moistarkandi now for the holidays. Did Shishu want to meet him?

Shishu watched himself from the outside. He saw the familiar tug. But also an unfamiliar heft. Or was it inertia? He couldn't, didn't want to, move fast any more. But he did want to know more about SCF. What did they stand for?

'Quite simply,' Srimanta said, 'this is about low-caste representation. But also about class conflict, in the terms you and I have heard in communist study circles. Think of it this way: Brits and upper castes are capital, low castes and Muslims are labour. This is certainly true in Bengal. A united Dalit–Muslim front is therefore a natural class response. They are poor, marginalized, exploited by the same forces. The SCF advocates such unity. We have forged ties with the Muslim League since 1943. Our other focus is on land reforms and peasants' rights. The League, as you know, claims to speak for all Muslims while looking out mainly for the ashraf elite. The Muslim masses, the vast ajlaf majority, are with SCF.'

Shishu couldn't help look back twenty years, at a rare instance of him pushing back on Srimanta about Tarun Sangha's tactics of harassing Muslims during the Patuakhali satyagraha. And Srimanta's flip assertion of Muslim backwardness. How well his friend had recalibrated. Shishu felt a stab of admiration. Why were things so much stickier for him?

'Look,' Srimanta pressed on, 'Dalits and Muslims together make up about 80 per cent of Bengal. In Barisal district that figure is closer to 90 per cent. Bengal belongs to Muslim peasants, fisherfolk, boatmen; to Hindu weavers, carpenters, tanners, and the vast swathe of those we call untouchables—Jogen-da being one such. I am a Brahmin's son, so are you. We belong in that thin crust they're now calling kebab,' he let out a chuckle, 'you know, the top three castes: Kayastha, Baidya, Brahmin. K–B–B. We make up less than 5 per cent and perennially rule the rest, claiming we know what's best for them. Look at the Bengal Congress, consider their top leadership. Kebabs every one, like our very own Satin-da. Forget the top, do they even have a mid-rung leader who is Muslim or low-caste? In all of Bengal? No, right? OK, some may consider Congress a crypto-Hindu party. So let's turn to Bengal's communist leadership. What do you see? Kebabs up and down. This cannot go on. Something will need to give.'

Jh-jhawpaashhsss! They had emerged back on the open river and a section of the bank had calved near them. The loud splash shattered the stillness of the night and rocked their boat. 'See, even the river agrees,' quipped Srimanta. Then he finished up: 'Jogen-da is a Namasudra Dalit, an MLA, and a minister, whose family still makes a living building boats. If you come you'll see. He has the lived experience. I believe in his cause. And as a kebab, my only role is to support him as a foot soldier.'

Their boatman, Idris Miah, was a wiry man with a scruffy beard and a tattered lungi. Shishu saw his muscular back gleam in the starlight, his work hard enough for sweat even on this cool October night. In the long tradition of subcontinental drivers, Idris would speak only if spoken to. 'What do you think of all this, Idris-bhai,' Shishu asked. Idris immediately intoned, 'Zzoyo zzoyo Zugen Mondol!' Long live Jogen Mandal. 'I am also from Moistarkandi, kawrta. He is my leader and of all us boatmen.'

Shishu abruptly felt overcome by a thick fatigue. Was there a universe in which he and Srimanta ferried passengers, freeing up time for Idris and his friends to read, to debate, to decide, to change their own lives? The math didn't work out. Was Jogen Mandal an exception? Could he really be of the mud and the ministry at once? Seemed like such a vast wingspan. Shishu dearly wanted to be warmed by Srimanta's fire. Srimanta, who always made sense, even when he was wrong. 'Idris-bhai decides it,' he said aloud, 'I must meet your Jogen-da, Srimanta.'

ട

Mid-October 1945
Moistarkandi
Barisal district
British India

As they arrived, Jogen Mandal was working on a boat in his yard. Shishu saw a chocolate massif of a man sawing wood, barefoot, bathed in sawdust. He wore a thin undershirt, too small for his barrel chest. A short sarong of unbleached cotton hung to his knees. The rhythm of the work made his arms bulge and his shoulder-length curls bounce. Noticing visitors, he looked up and flashed them a blinding smile.

Shishu hadn't seen the other avatars of Jogen Mandal but had heard Srimanta describe them—Jogen in a three-piece suit and a chain watch, addressing the Barisal Bar Association; Jogen in a long kurta and wide-bordered dhuti, with a shawl draped on one shoulder, addressing the Bengal Assembly. But when in Moistarkandi, it was always the undershirt and short sarong.

'Ei je, Srimanta,' Jogen boomed. They called him the 'Barisal gun' after the cannon-like reports of the bore tide rolling up the Meghna. Up close, Shishu saw he had the quiet gloss of a Barisal canal shaded by rain trees. Was he getting hypnotized? The man certainly had a magnetic presence.

'Jogen-da, my childhood friend Shishu,' Srimanta introduced him. 'Of the 1929 Barisal action, remember? He's just out after serving nearly seventeen years, five of those in Cellular.'

'Arrey! What an honour! Wait, wait, let me wash my hands. Ei, who's around? Get us some moori-lonka!'

As Jogen Mandal wrapped him in a bear hug, Shishu felt the man's heft. He led them to sit cross-legged on the mud porch running along the scrappy two-roomed hutment. When this man sits, Shishu noticed, he sits like a tree. He occupies space. And when he laughs out loud he sways like a banyan in a storm, his nimbus of curls the wind-whipped canopy. But there is a moonlit quiet in his eyes.

Shishu had discovered while walking to Moistarkandi that it really was an extension of Chandshi, its low-caste enclave, so to speak, on a marshy stretch outside the village. The homes here were visibly poor, low-slung and made of scavenged material. And the Namasudra cluster, where Jogen's family lived, was at the farthest end. No one here owned any land. All did manual work, even the women.

Someone brought out a bell-metal plate piled with puffed rice, mustard oil, and green chillies in bowls. 'That's our only plate,' Jogen chortled, 'you two share it. Ei, pour my moori in here,' he pointed to a pocket he'd made with a fold of his sarong. Mixing his moori with a bit of oil, he scooped up a mouthful and crunched a bite off a green chilli. 'Aah,' he said through chews, 'nothing like moori after hard work. I've been helping my uncle on that boat all morning.' After a few more mouthfuls he switched gears. 'You know, your timing is good, Srimanta. There's a meeting this afternoon. At Mahilara. You come too, Shishu. It's nearby, I'll row over myself. You're stopped at Goila? Then let's meet at Gournadi. Or stay for lunch. But it'll either be more moori or if you're lucky some fermented rice,' he guffawed. 'In our homes we only make one hot meal, when everyone gets back in the evening.'

The meeting was over a demand of tenant farmers who worked Mahilara's surrounding beels that became rice paddies half the year. They had been losing crops year after year to flooding. The slope of these beels was such that a short canal—about a mile and a half— would easily drain the excess water into the main canal on which the ferry plied to Mahilara, and save the crops. The opposition had come from Mahilara's upper-caste landlords, who had filed a spurious lawsuit. Their complaint: drainage via the proposed canal would raise the water level in the main canal and place Mahilara's streets in ankle-deep water during the rains. An experienced lawyer, Jogen knew the case wouldn't stick. But his moral force lay elsewhere. 'Think about this: mass starvation versus a few wet feet,' he said. Shishu thought he saw a flicker of hot coals in those calm eyes. 'Hundreds of bilya peasants versus twenty landlord families. The peasants here happen to be all Muslims and their landlords Hindu. When they protest, the landlords unleash hired thugs. And who are these? Poor Kahars and

Bagdis, all Dalits like me, armed to the teeth on behalf of their upper-caste employers. And then everybody—Hindu Mahasabha, Muslim League, even Congress—calls it a Hindu–Muslim riot!' Jogen's eyes twinkled now. 'If the aam gets sliced different ways, you know it must be about elections. Not about the aam.' Shishu noticed the clever wordplay: aam could mean mango or the masses.

He wondered if one of those twenty complainant landlord families was Noni-di's. It seemed highly likely. He was suddenly relieved that she hadn't come.

Mid-October 1945
Mahilara
Barisal district
British India

'Have you ever heard of farming without farmers?' Jogen's voice boomed. 'You haven't. So, whatever the farmer needs to farm he should have the right to.' Listening to the speech, Shishu was struck by Jogen's style—rustic yet substantive, speckled with jokes. He scanned the crowd, at least 200 strong. Most were bilya peasants, in loincloths, their wiry bodies bare, their heads wrapped in thin gamcha towels, occasionally cracking up with raucous laughter. But there were a few others. Ah, there was the answer to his question from earlier in the day: Noni-di's father stood at the edge of the crowd. A bit stooped now with age, but still a tall patrician figure, as pale as a European, his brow knitted in irritation. Retired from his court work, Shishu was sure, dependent on his feudal income and therefore clearly unhappy with this agitation. That's my great-grandfather he is looking at.

Drawing from his years of litigating land disputes, Jogen was breaking down Barisal's byzantine hierarchy of feudal ownership for his lay audience. Each level collected taxes from the one below—jomidar, talukdar, neem-talukdar, gerosto-ryot. Four rungs of ownership to the same parcel of land that they never touched. This pyramid sat atop sharecroppers who actually worked the land

and whose payments went up the food chain. And payments were naturally due even when crops failed. All the risk and responsibility of the crop rested at the bottom rung: with the landless peasants.

Shishu stood surrounded by these peasants, he saw their eyes aflame with indignation. 'Therefore,' Jogen was wrapping up, 'the peasant will do what he needs to do. This is his hold, his stand.' He then distilled the agitation into action: the peasants would carve the canal themselves. 'Get here tomorrow at the crack of dawn,' he bellowed, 'bring your shovels, bring baskets, bring arms and heads! You move earth away on your heads all the time. If there is even a hundred of you, how long can this job take? I will join you.' The crowd, electrified, roared—'Zzoyo zzoyo Zugen Mondol!'

When Shishu arrived at the dig at daybreak, he found Jogen already there. He watched a sitting minister strip to a loincloth and get down to shovelling earth with practised ease. Hundreds of peasants worked alongside him, energized manifold by his presence. Shishu and Srimanta soon waded in. Shishu, hardened by manual labour in jail, was able to keep up. But Srimanta wilted quickly, much to his embarrassment. By the end of the day the canal was done. Jogen had worked all day, stopping for smokes and cold, fermented rice when the peasants did. And no one seemed particularly exercised about any of this. The peasants simply saw him as one of their own. As they stood around afterwards, mind and body calm with fatigue, mood light from dabbling in risk, and also from the deep play of collective action, Shishu saw that the flame in their eyes had been doused. After decades of being haunted by the Goila woodcutter, he put that ghost to rest in the hands of Jogen Mandal.

Other things had been put to rest that day at Mahilara, Shishu felt. It had been his maiden taste of hands-on class warfare. After a dozen years of chewing the cud of theory in jail, here at last was some practice. Jogen Mandal, Shishu was now convinced, not only had charisma but also preternatural span. At one point during the day, in the thick of the dig, Srimanta, sporting a wild grin, had caught Shishu's eye. Shishu knew what his friend was saying: see what we are building here in Barisal? A caste–class revolution! Come on, join us!

Srimanta seemed so freshly in love. His thrill was infectious. But Shishu could not get the wind up to jump ship. Something had become cauterized in him. He was entangled in a commitment, with none of the spark of belief but all the comfort of habit. A full-time CPI worker, with a ₹20 per month stipend and a Calcutta tram monthly pass. The party assigned duties and he performed them. That's who he was: a worker, now on pujo vacation. He remembered Ambika-da's words well: you cannot flee imperfection. The chill in them gripped him anew. He was happy for Srimanta, but that peripatetic path was not for him. Every fresh pasture had its own potholes. Mahilara had forced him to square with where he was: in a slack marriage, but a marriage all the same. If he saw a ravishing woman walk by, he would crane his neck. But he would not follow her home.

∽

What else would Shishu share about that year if asked? Maybe that in March 1946, Jogen Mandal's campaign in north Bakarganj was mortally wounded by Congress cadres. He was defending his home seat that he had won in 1937 in a historic upset. The upper-caste interests of Batajore–Mahilara–Gournadi–Chandshi, aligned with the Congress, were not about to allow a repeat. Shishu read anguished letters from Srimanta, who was witnessing a barrage of brutal tactics: smear campaign against the candidate, booth capture, ballot-box stuffing, voter intimidation or actual assault. And above all, bribes—cash, clothing, even cattle. This would become a playbook that every political party would need to adopt, or perish. The harbinger of a cottage industry in free India.

Yes, Jogen lost his home seat. But he won from Patuakhali, in the Scheduled Castes category. 'And you know who won at Patuakhali in the General category, of course,' wrote Srimanta, 'our Satin-da, the Congressman. Congress had fielded an SC candidate there as well. They tried all their usual tricks. But Jogen-da held. And that is SCF's solo win in Bengal. Congress played dirty and bludgeoned us. But you know what really hurts? That they will now claim to be the voice of the low-castes.' SCF was routed in the provincial assembly elections of 1946. Even Ambedkar lost. Of the 151 candidates SCF had fielded in various provinces, two won. And of the thirty seats in the Bengal Legislative Assembly reserved for Scheduled Castes, Congress bagged twenty-four, with straw-man candidates who carried no weight post-election. This body blow, exacerbated by Partition the following year, effectively stubbed out the movement for Dalit autonomy in Bengal.

Shishu had witnessed the Congress juggernaut first-hand, both the muscle and the money. CPI, above ground only since 1942 and in its debut electoral foray in 1946, had fielded nineteen candidates in Bengal. When on campaign duty at the Budge Budge jute mill outside Calcutta, Shishu had seen Congress cadres hand out cash and clothes. They moved in clots and viciously beat up CPI campaigners. His party's trade union office at Bowbazar had become a field hospital. But CPI managed to eke out wins in three seats. One of them Shishu had campaigned for in the tea estates of north Bengal. Srimanta had ribbed him over this, smarting from having fought in a losing seat: 'What's your secret winning formula?'

Srimanta's letters became upbeat once more in late June. The elections for the Constituent Assembly had been announced for 18 July 1946. The provincial legislatures would elect candidates. But the Bombay Presidency, Ambedkar's home province, had turned against him. Moreover, Congress was determined to keep Ambedkar out. Sardar Patel had publicly proclaimed that 'apart from the doors, even the windows of the Constituent Assembly are closed for Dr Ambedkar. Let us see how he gets in.' Jogen Mandal, having barely scraped back into the Bengal Legislative Assembly and now the law minister, threw his entire weight behind meeting this challenge. With just three weeks in hand, he filed nomination papers for Ambedkar from the Jessore–Khulna constituency and went on a whirlwind tour to elicit support. He campaigned in Rangpur, Tangail, Khulna, Faridpur, with his young followers raising awareness about Ambedkar. In the halls of the Bengal Assembly, he coaxed four Congress MLAs into going against their party diktat. When Congress got wind of this, it forcibly held one of them in seclusion, who was rescued in the nick of time. An independent MLA pledged his support only the night before. When the dust had settled, the final tally showed Ambedkar with seven votes, one more than Sarat Chandra Bose, the Congress heavy. Of the candidates from Bengal, Ambedkar had scored the highest. He was in. And Sardar Patel had got his answer.

A jubilant Srimanta wrote Shishu: 'We did it! And with the most votes, imagine! Six of the seven are low-caste Bangals and one is a tribal.' His letter listed them—Jogendranath Mandal, Namasudra, SCF, Barisal; Mukunda Behari Mullick, Namasudra, Independent, Khulna; Dwarikanath Baruri, Namasudra, Congress, Faridpur; Gayanath Biswas, Namasudra, Congress, Tangail; Nagendra Narayan Ray, Rajbangshi, Independent, Rangpur; Kshetranath Singha, Rajbangshi, Congress, Rangpur; Bir Birsa, Adivasi, Congress, Murshidabad. 'It is Jogen-da and low-caste Bangals who have sent Ambedkar to the Constituent Assembly, skirting every roadblock the Congress put up. SCF may be dead, but this fact will live. For this alone, free India will remember Jogen-da, don't you think?'

They would not, Shishu found out later. Without Jogen Mandal's gritty campaign in the teeth of existential erasure, Ambedkar could not have architected India's Constitution. And without Ambedkar, it would have likely not been such an extraordinary document. In particular, constitutional provisions for India's low-caste masses were unimaginable in the zeitgeist. But Jogen Mandal, the oyster of that pearl, would get washed away by the tide of time.

∽

> *The old world is dying, and the new world struggles to be born: now is the time of monsters.*
>
> —Antonio Gramsci

That was such a ferocious year, Shishu felt looking back at 1946. Thick with events, each a major inflection. As if history too had been bottled up in jail and was bolting out in a torrent. The Naval Uprising in February. The provincial elections in March. The Constituent Assembly in July. The Great Calcutta Killings in August.

The Noakhali massacre in October. The Tebhaga peasant revolt starting in November. It was relentless. And not without reason. The war over and Britain deep in debt to the Indian exchequer, the time of the Raj was up. That spell of urgency infused all parties. It animated the air.

But Shishu did not see it this way at the time. The full slap of history lands only in hindsight. In the moment, he was atop a tsunami yet to crest, oblivious of its monstrous height. The carnage would be visible only after the wave had receded. Some things were visible, though, moments that stayed with him. Through his party work that year, he had seen a bit of Bengal. This was his first sense of the field, of what they were up against, those like him who had pledged to fight for a free India. Things he didn't know when he had plunged in at fourteen. When sifting through those memories, a few always bubbled up.

Late February 1946
Alipurduar
Jalpaiguri district
British India

'It is all written right here,' the wizened elder said, brushing his forehead with a gnarled forefinger, 'based on our previous births. What can the landlord do? It is he who has kept us alive. Besides, no matter what,' he raised an open palm as if to quiet a protest, 'our Rani-ma needs to be given a vote.'

The party had sent Shishu to north Bengal to campaign for their candidate, Ratanlal Brahmin, from the Darjeeling seat. He was to spend a week visiting tea plantations along the Himalayan foothills, embed with the labourers, convince them of the party line, and secure their vote. He had come to a tiny hamlet of Rajbangshi Dalits, tea labourers all, in the grip of grinding poverty. Dark wiry men, their midriffs caved in, with only tattered loincloths against the late-winter chill. The women wore little more. Shishu sat with them one evening in a flimsy shack of corrugated tin. He spoke about who might be responsible for their plight, about workers' rights. They gave him a patient listen. And then their elder spoke—about fate, about previous births, about his vote for Rani-ma. Shishu felt gut-punched. A great gust had stripped his task to its absurd core. Rani-ma was the queen of these parts. The matriarch of the Jalpaiguri royal family, who the Congress had fielded as their candidate, and who lived in a distant palace. She had never set foot here but dominated the muscle memory of these ravaged bodies. And Shishu was to compete with that, with abstract ideas of labour and capital?

But he could at least communicate here, because the Rajbangshis spoke a dialect of Bangla, albeit unfamiliar. At his next stop, the labourers were Totos: tribal inhabitants of hill Bengal with whom Shishu shared no language at all. He had arrived early evening and would need to spend the night with them. After a few failed attempts to engage, he fell into watching them. As one watches wildlife, he realized.

The poverty here was even more acute than at the Rajbangshi hamlet. Shishu had seen nothing like this in fecund south Bengal. He was in a hut packed with a dozen men, one goat, and a few chickens. At its centre was a glowering fire, on it a spouted brass pitcher, in which tea was on a continuous boil. Whoever wanted some would pour himself a bowlful. No milk or sugar, of course. Tea leaves the tea labourers got for free. While sipping, Shishu noticed the brew was the colour of stale blood. And in a flash, he recalled his Red poems, heaving with *workers' blood*. Giddy and indulgent, that's how they seemed now. But he would keep them, he decided, as a record of how little he had seen when writing those words.

All night long, the labourers toasted themselves and sipped tea. Some dozed on their haunches. The fire crackled and cast a copper glow on their bare bodies. They looked otherworldly. Had they eaten any dinner? None that Shishu had seen. He tried to ask and was greeted with vacant eyes. At one point the goat sidled up to the chickens and caused a flutter. Do these men not sleep? Or was it he who was keeping them up? He wondered what they thought he was doing here. A column of bloated bedbugs crawled up a rattan wall. A couple of men idly popped them with their thumbnails, leaving streaks of blood. Shishu joined them. It was the only way he could take part.

17 August 1946
Fern Road
Calcutta
British India

The stain remained on the wall. Although it was the thick of monsoons, the rain did not reach it. Irregular, about the size of a human head, it faded from red to brown, and later a vague grey. This was the exterior wall of the rooming house that Shishu shared with other party whole-timers. On it, a mob of medical students had brained a man, a man they knew. They had first thrashed him with a femur bone, a teaching aid from their anatomy class. Their victim's stain survived for years, it seemed to Shishu. He saw it daily, on his way in and out. He saw it on visits, after he had moved away. Or maybe you always see a stain if you know where to look.

This was the second day of the riots. The peak of the violence. The killing spree was no longer sporadic. It had spun out through Calcutta in a feverish spiral of tit for tat. A diverse metropolis had with shocking speed curdled into Hindu and Muslim enclaves, barricaded and bunkered—a portent for the entire country in exactly a year. Armed vigilantes roamed the streets. Shishu heard of Hindus being killed in Metiabruz, Khidirpur, Park Circus. But his neighbourhood was in Ballygunge, a Hindu area. The victims here were Muslim.

He had planned to stay in today after what he'd run into last afternoon. The killings had already begun in Bowbazar where he was, and he was rushing home. On Rashbehari Avenue, he saw a Muslim man being pulled off a tram, which trundled on as if nothing unusual had occurred. Within minutes, a mob closed in on the man, armed with bamboo rods. Shishu heard the first scream and didn't wait for the rest.

But today he was home. He heard frantic banging on the front door. And a guttural groan, breathless and raspy with fear. He rushed to the door and swung it open to find old Ismail, his rheumy eyes flared in panic. A trickle of blood had tinged his white beard. 'Bnachao!' he gasped, through dried spittle. His pursuers were not far behind, one brandished a cured human femur, like a club. Shishu blanked out for a bit. What was he seeing? This was Ismail, who vended eggs on their street. Shishu and his comrades were regulars, as were these medical students who lived next door. In fact, Shishu had had one of those eggs this morning. And just last week, when Ismail's sciatica had acted up, these doctors-to-be had helped him with pills. In the seconds it took Shishu to gather his wits enough to pull Ismail in, someone yanked him away from the door and slammed it shut. Shishu spun around and found it was his landlord. Then he heard the frightful crack. Of a skull smashed against a brick wall.

19 December 1946
Borgaccha village
Rangpur district
British India

'This time we only broom-beat them like the trash they are,' the woman said, her eyes flashing in the dimly lit room, 'and blinded them with chilli powder. But next time, I swear we'll shred them with fish blades!'

A couple dozen people huddled around a lantern in a hut of rattan and thatch. A bitterly cold night outside and a heated meeting within. The speaker was Joymoni, a Rajbangshi Dalit peasant who had shown Shishu around earlier that day. She had the gravitas of one cured by hardship, laced with a fiery streak. And she was not the only one. Shishu had never seen so many peasant women at a party meeting before. Three days ago, a posse of police and private militia had killed two of them and injured several. Then, they had dragged Joymoni away in a rape attempt, but the women had beaten them back. They were talking about that now—Joymoni, Phuli, Rashmoni, and others.

The party had sent Shishu to Rangpur to support Comrade Moni Singha. Shishu was familiar with the legend of Moni-da and was a bit in awe: the declassed feudal prince, a Mymensingh royal who stands with his subjects, Hajong tribal sharecroppers. Fresh off of leading a revolt against feudal families including his own over equitable crop shares, Moni-da was now in Rangpur, where a similar movement called Tebhaga had spread like wildfire. But to his surprise, Shishu found it was not Moni-da who was in charge here, but the peasant women.

Tebhaga—literally 'thirds'—was the peasants' demand. The business of divvying up a landlord's crop was handled by jotedars, a class of shifty middlemen. Traditionally, the sharecroppers brought in the harvest to the jotedar's compound, threshed it there, and got paid half the grain. Since they bore all material costs and risks for the crop, this arrangement was far from fair. Moreover, jotedars frequently defrauded them when measuring out their half. Disaffection over this had been brewing for years and exploded during the amon (autumn) harvest of 1946. The peasants demanded to thresh the grain in their own compounds, keep two-thirds, and give a third to the jotedar. As they began bringing the harvest into their homes in late November, the crackdown was immediate. Jotedar militias, with police support, unleashed a firestorm of violence. They set peasant homes and grain silos alight, brutalized them with batons, guns, and rape. This only hardened the peasants' resolve. The resistance, led by women, fought back with brooms, kitchen blades, and dust leavened with chilli powder. What they lacked in arsenal they made up for in numbers. By mid-December, the Tebhaga movement had flared up across nineteen districts in both east and west Bengal. Rangpur was a hotspot.

Joymoni had taken Shishu around Borgaccha earlier today. The clash here had happened three days ago in the paddies outside the village, next to a beel aptly called Raktodaho—Blood-hollow. Goons with batons had tried to stop the harvest. The peasant women pushed them back. The forces retreated, then returned with guns. The women tried to flee. One was felled in the fields. Another was chased into the village and shot beside a pond. Shishu was shown the spot, the moist earth still stained. The women had turned it into a shrine: covered with a basket, flowers in the morning, lit lamps at night. The incident had primed them into wicks themselves, it seemed to Shishu. It was they who had called the meeting to organize a protest.

Shishu looked around the room now. A solo lantern on the floor cast an eerie up-glow on some of the faces. Most were peasants, Muslims, and low-caste Hindus. The same coalition as in Barisal last year, he noticed with relief. The sectarian bloodbaths in Calcutta and Noakhali still fresh, yet the solidarity here was intact. The women were up front, their men behind. A couple of village elders sat in the back, their hookahs purring. There were a few party whole-timers like himself, men and women. A bearded man with a sage-like mien sat very still. And Moni-da—thickset, with a scruffy moustache and a piercing gaze, who mainly listened as the peasants spoke. Also, scrunched against a wall, a gaunt youth was immersed in sketching the scene. So the party had sent someone to make a visual record? Shishu missed his own sketchbook. He hadn't had time to touch it since leaving jail. In the end, the resolution was a long march to Satibari, 60 kilometres away. It would take three days. A protracted show of force against jotedar tyranny. They would start the next morning.

Much of what Shishu heard that night he only understood much later. For instance, when Joymoni spoke of the pressure of sexual servitude from jotedars that peasant women routinely faced. They had put up with the Allied soldiers through the famine years and now jotedars. 'We have had enough!' she declared. Then, turning to her husband she growled: 'And that goes for you too!' With that she had folded in domestic abuse, including marital rape, into the 'enough'. This incendiary act, bucking every norm, took Shishu's breath away. The men in the room flinched; Joymoni's husband glowered. Yes, Shishu thought later, the party's outreach had helped empower peasant women, especially during the famine. But empowerment cannot be scripted, it has its own tune. Their combustion during Tebhaga was spontaneous. Equal partners in farm labour but unequal in all else, pincered by hunger and sexual assault, the Tebhaga women had exploded in a natural geyser.

The next morning, over two hundred peasants and volunteers had gathered despite the short notice. Their march to Satibari soon began, with Joymoni at the head. The women lead the slogans: 'Adhi nai, tebhaga chai!' 'Jaan debo tobu dhaan debo na!' (Not half, we want two-thirds! We'll give our lives but not our rice!) As their long column passed a shorn field, Shishu noticed the young artist from last night crouched in it, doing a furious sketch, before rushing in to join them.

∽

When thinking of Rangpur, Shishu always remembered Joymoni's radiance during the Satibari march, her buoyant stride. He wondered what happened to her in a few years when the resistance became armed, their demand blooming from crop shares to dismantling the entire feudal machine. And the Communist Party yanked the rug from under its frontline women by asking them to 'go back to the kitchen'.

He also remembered the Satibari police lock-up, where several of them had landed at the end of the long march. In their cell was a Sufi mystic from Shah Jalal's dargah in Sylhet, who had nothing to do with the march or with Tebhaga. He happened to be visiting Satibari, got picked up in the melee, and seemed mildly amused by it all. As the night deepened, he plucked on his one-stringed drone and sang with an impish smile in his Sylheti dialect:

awba hokir mollazee
zhulnar maazhe undure katssey
tokhit rakhsoni

Ah, fakir mullah sir
a rat is nibbling through your bag
you're paying no heed

With the fullness of hindsight, Shishu could not imagine a more apt song for that falling apart, leaky time. Or a better portent of what was to come.

chapter 5

The writer, like a murderer, needs a motive.

—Janet Malcolm

YOU ALREADY KNOW WHAT WAS to come. Partition. Humanity oozing out of the two cracks like lava, terrified and exhausted. Millions and millions. Clotting and cleaving now and then, but moving, always moving. The largest mass migration in human history. It ruptured old bonds and new coalitions alike. And it blew Shishu and Noni apart.

Lava can be of two types. One moves slow, with a hot, molten core, its wrinkled skin cooling into glassy ropes of rock. Another moves fluffy and fast, shooting out bits of fire, congealing into rubble whose jagged edges can draw blood. Both build the land that comes after. Refugees are no different.

∽

Let me tell you something that may not come as a surprise: Shishu's ghost talks to me. I've had an ongoing chat with him, a freewheeling exchange, ever since I found the notebook. A crusty spirit he is, mouthy and combative, exasperated with all that he's seen across several decades of being dead—very different from the man Shishu was when alive. I have managed to fend him off thus far. But at this point, at Partition, he really wants in. So I am going to have to occasionally unmute our private chatter.

'Did you know this was coming?' I ask the ghost.

'The actual partition? Not even in February, no,' he shakes his head, reliving an old incredulity. 'The date was set for August but the deed was already finalized in June. So really four months from conception to delivery. Less than half the time for a human baby.

Is it any wonder, then, that the results were less than human? A miscarried foetus, that's what we got,' his lips curl in disgust, 'and we've been forcing it to live ever since!'

'You were there. Help me understand what happened.'

He narrows his eyes: 'The what? Or the why?'

'Oh, I don't know. Aren't they related? And what do I do with this inherited scab that never seems to fall off?'

'Yes, I feel bad for you. All you have are stories. Reams and reams. Seventy-five years of mewling.'

'Mewling? Isn't that a bit harsh?'

'Well, what else should I call it? Upper-caste mewling is what it is. I'm talking now of Bengal, mind you, not Punjab. Look at all the Partition classics in Bangla. As if 15 August 1947 was the Big Bang. Such helpless shock! Why? Our existence was about upholding a cracked system we had floated atop for ages. Why were we surprised when it exploded and overthrew us? And after it happened, was there any attempt to reflect, to acknowledge the cause? No!' A bony forefinger stabs air. 'Instead, since the early fifties we have built this cottage industry of pathos: innocents evicted from a land of burnished gold where everybody, Hindus Muslims Dalits, lived in a cosy tangle. Manufactured memories! But if you repeat something enough it becomes the truth. And if you repeat it for three generations it becomes canon.'

'So, it's all fake then. The uprooting, the loss, the panicked leaving under the cover of darkness. Then starting over in cramped slums, derided and despised as parasites. All fake?'

'I am not saying the rupture is fake. And the trauma in any rupture is real. But the memory of a rupture ought to contain its cause. The *why* lives inside the *what*. Let's say you were drilling for oil for years and caused an earthquake. Can you deny the drilling when remembering the earthquake? And our kind were the top soil, mobile. We had relatively soft landings after the explosion. Think of the boulders below: east Bengal's low-caste masses. Political football! Under Jogen-da's leadership they had rightly allied with Muslims against upper-caste tyranny. They had stayed put when their land became Pakistan. And what happened? Jinnah died, all promises were broken, and they became sitting targets. I was in Barisal during the massacres of 1950, remember. Most upper castes had left by then. I saw Muslim peasants butcher their Dalit brethren. These people had been one body under Jogen-da, one at Tebhaga. But now there was a madness abroad. Jogen-da rushed over from Karachi. A frantic firefighter, by then stripped of all tools, trying to battle a raging inferno. Then, ravaged, he fled to India in October 1950. Think about that: Jogendranath Mandal, Pakistan's then minister of law, fleeing! Think of his orphaned people, the Bangal Dalits. Trapped like frogs in water coming to a boil. Have they written a Partition classic? Or what about Joymoni, the Rajbangshi Dalit Tebhaga leader I've told you about. Where did she go? Probably begging on the streets of Calcutta in the fifties. Is her grandchild writing her story? Unlikely. Because they couldn't rebuild as easily as us. Their exodus west oozed for decades. Bengal's wound was not a clean amputation like Punjab's. Besides, the unlettered need generations to pick up the pen, even without an apocalypse. But their story is central to this. And we must remember that, even as we fill the airwaves with our own.'

'Let's say they were at fault, my ancestors and yours. They launched the dominoes, caused this monumental fracture and all the ensuing illness. But why should the crack run through me? I don't even have the benefit of real memories like you. Good or bad. I am a landless, unrooted child of a refugee. And yet, on a recent visit to the land, it called out to me, like a banshee. What am I supposed to do with that?'

'Oh, you visited Barisal, did you?' he lights up. 'You went to Bikna but not Mahilara? Ah, too bad. I'd ask you about that towering silk cotton tree at the edge of Mahilara. It was under it that Jogen-da had given his striking speech before our canal dig. Such a noble tree, huge buttress roots,' his mind drifts before he catches himself. 'Anyway, listen, there is no magic bullet. We upper-caste Bangals were in a systemic debt. Centuries of rank exploitation, violence, and humiliation of a vast majority. The price: eviction, lost property, root rupture. And maybe a couple generations of phantom root-ache.

Seems fair to me. Yes, yes, our eviction didn't fix everything. But it allowed an entire people to bloom: Bengali Muslims. And yes, many others haven't paid their debts yet—North India's feudal cohorts, for instance. But we have, to some extent. For the low-caste Bangals, though, the accounts remain terribly unsettled. They were owed the same debt as the Muslims, their co-oppressed, but paid even more than us, their oppressors. They were robbed by both sides.' He pauses, a bit winded, then his gaze softens. 'Trust me, the pangs will fade. Look around. How many in your generation even identify as Bangal? We are nearly done. A lost people. If anything remains it'll be those imagined memories. Unless the low-caste Bangals speak. And they have now begun, albeit in a slow trickle. Read Adhir Biswas. Harishankar Jaladas. Manoranjan Byapari.'

'I will, I promise. You're right, of course. It's a glaring absence. But I can't help think that you keep circling back to their story to avoid talking about yourself. About what this did to you.'

'Ah, that,' he cracks a wry smile. 'India became free. Well, some sort of free. For us Bangals that freedom meant homelessness. I became an unfree freedom fighter,' a contorted chuckle leaves him, 'a fugitive cowering in the shadows.'

'Why? Where were you?'

'Underground. In Chandshi, Barisal. The party was in disarray, you understand. Congress took charge of free India. They banned CPI in March 1948 and jailed the leadership. I went east, a stateless communist in East Pakistan. We worked to revive Tebhaga, which had been hobbled by Partition, and had some success. This naturally alarmed the Muslim League, freshly swollen with confidence in new Pakistan. They were determined to break the Dalit–Muslim peasant coalition that Tebhaga had forged. "Tebhaga keno, choubhaga paabi", they assured Muslim peasants—why two-thirds, you'll get it all! Those commies duping you are Indian agents, they said. We have achieved Pakistan, all Hindus will leave soon and their land will be yours! Their campaign was highly effective. And they began arresting us, as spies and anti-nationals. By mid-1949 we were on the run. Meanwhile, CPI had expressly barred its members in East Pakistan from coming to

India. Why? Because the party had embraced a blanket denial of Hindu–Muslim violence. It was all class dialectics, you see. Hindu members haemorrhaging west would contradict that line!' He lets out a cackle. 'I wasn't laughing then, of course. Trapped, I went into hiding. Srimanta was happy to help, so I headed to Chandshi. The ban on CPI was lifted in early 1950 but the party couldn't really function until late that year. I stayed hunkered down until mid-1951, when I was called west for the upcoming Bengal elections. And I was back in India, essentially for good.'

'Wait, wait. Slow down. Rewind to 1950. Mid-February. You are in Barisal. What do you see?'

'Hellscape.' He pauses, eyes shut, then sucks in a chestful of air before going on. 'Riverbanks strewn with bloated corpses. Dogs and vultures feeding. Muladi, Lakutiya, Madhobpasha, Koibartakhali. Men slaughtered, young women taken as booty. Thousands of mostly low-caste Hindus killed in a matter of days, in Barisal district alone. The violence had a celebratory edge. This was no riot, this was a one-sided massacre.' He looks away, then down at his hands. 'And there was absolutely nothing anyone could do. Not even Jogen-da, as law minister. His escape to India snuffed out Srimanta. My sparkling friend was never the same,' his voice cracks. 'Something broke in me too. The colossal betrayal of the most vulnerable was too much to bear. This Barisal could never be mine. I was a rolling stone, a party worker, but this wound gouged even me.'

'I'm so sorry.' I had forced him somewhere he didn't want to be. 'Your poems from this period suggest that you had coped by looking outside, at global events.'

'This is true. We were in a tight corner at home. And we had made some bad mistakes. But it was a banner season for communism abroad. Mao had just founded the People's Republic of China. Ho had risen in Vietnam. All of eastern Europe had turned Red, as had parts of Africa. And this amidst the withdrawal of colonial powers. It felt like a new world order.' The memory perks him up. 'No wonder America got spooked! This is when the Cold War begins. And at home, let's not forget Telangana—India's first full-fledged, militant agrarian revolution. Peasants wrested control of an enormous tract from feudal landlords and built self-administered communes. They held it not for one or two days, but for five years! In fact, our post-Partition Tebhaga phase was inspired by Telangana's armed liberation model. They were crushed, of course, and twelve peasant youths were put on death row. Having been there myself I felt great solidarity.'

'I know. I've read your anguished eulogy to them. All eight pages of it,' I rib him. We've grown quite free like that.

'Yes, well, it was a little long,' he chortles and sheepishly adds, 'I had a lot of free time on my hands in hiding.'

'So, did you have any news of Noni at this time?'

'None at all. Her parental family in Mahilara was gone, thank god. But they'd left even before I came to Chandshi. So I had no news of her. The massacres had spread to other districts: Khulna, Faridpur, Jessore, Dhaka. Had she already left Tarpasha? I didn't know and feared the worst. And you know,' he says ruefully, 'when I finally saw her after all those decades, neither of us could really bring up words. I never found out the story of her crossing.'

∽

A woman, thirty-seven, sits under a shady tamarind tree. She is slender and attractive, even in a plain, red-bordered, white cotton sari, even on a day like today. Her wire-rimmed glasses add to her melancholy gravitas. She sits amidst an amorphous pile of luggage, her children strewn in a famished heap. She scans her surroundings. Her boys are sixteen, fourteen, and ten; the oldest two have gone in search of food. Her girls are eight, six, four, and two. She is three months pregnant, but she doesn't show. There are other things she doesn't show. Her rising panic, for instance. All that is familiar is behind her. A lot of what she loves is with her. And the future is a black hole.

That's Noni at East Pakistan's Goalando ferry terminal on 8 March 1948. The sixteen-year-old is my Baba. The family waits for a train to cross over into freshly severed India.

Where is her husband? He couldn't come because that would

mean losing his job. A few neighbouring families were leaving, and Hira found this a good opportunity to send Noni and the children to safety. He would stay at Tarpasha and send money for their upkeep. Just until the madness subsided. Then he'd bring them back. This couldn't possibly last. Remember 1905? They had tried to slice Bengal in halves once before and failed. The same would happen this time. But things felt brittle in the interim. And with all the girls in his family, it was best to send them away. That's what everyone around Hira had said. Only temporarily. Something about that insistence rang hollow to Noni. And deepened her dread.

It was only afternoon but much had already happened. The family left Tarpasha early that morning in a skiff. Out the Deegholi canal and then via a network of rivulets, it had taken them three hours to arrive at the Padma River. As soon as their skiff crunched into a sandbar to dock they had scrambled ashore, their steps sinking into soft river sand already blistering hot. They scrambled because on the other side of the sandbar a massive paddleboat steamer had arrived and was filling up fast. The jetty was a jerry-rigged affair: a swaying contraption of ropes, planks, and bamboo, with the Padma churning below. The boys darted ahead with the luggage and staked out a spot on the back deck. Noni had just settled down with the girls when the steamer set off, brimming with its load of the unmoored. The family was afloat on the mammoth Padma, its far shore barely visible.

The steamer reached Goalando at 3 p.m. The train to Sealdah wouldn't arrive for a few hours. The disgorged crowd scurried, desperate for a rice meal. There had been none on the long sail. Goalando was a bustling terminus, connecting the rail and ferry systems. A row of food shacks sold all manner of hot meals. Hundreds thronged them, the lines grew interminably long. Noni had settled her family under the tamarind tree and sent her two oldest for food. The boys came back empty-handed. The lines had turned riotous. Hunger was laced with mounting anxiety: the upcoming train ride was overnight or longer, and there was to be no hot food on it either.

Help came from unexpected quarters. Across the street from the tamarind tree was a warren of hutments: Goalando's red light area. The women had noticed the stranded family. With the threat of salty language, they cut a path through the crowd and helped the boys secure two vats—rice in one, fish stew in the other. Not just any fish: Padma's ilish, closest to the Bengali heart. The ravenous family inhaled the food. Their new friends served and fussed over them. They played with the girls. They lavishly praised Noni, for her beauty and her strength. They wished her well and shed a tear for her, on the eve of her leaving home forever.

Soon the train arrived and there was fresh bedlam. The crowd surged, thronging the doors. Noni's boys dove through the unbarred windows and secured a seat, before pulling in the luggage and the girls, also through the windows. Noni clambered up the steps of the railcar, carrying her two-year-old. This was challenging with no platform and the first step several feet off the ground. The car was bursting at the seams. Noni and the girls were settled atop their luggage with great difficulty. The boys hung on to the upper racks. They were the lucky ones. As the train began moving, many bags were left behind, many men barely hung on to the door handles.

Night fell. The train had no electricity. The heat was intense. Outside was a mild March night, but inside a jam-packed crowd sweltered in the dark, in its own heat and angst. People lit the occasional match to check on their group. Hira had unwittingly chosen to move the family during a window of relative calm: after the tense post-Partition months but before the massacres of 1950 and the ensuing tidal wave west. Noni's train experienced none of the violent horrors of similar journeys months before at the Lahore–Amritsar border. But they knew those stories. And it was dark. The train stopped at every station. Wailing children kept the petrified adults distracted. Some, overcome by fatigue, even dozed off.

In the morning they arrived at Darshana, the border crossing. The train was detained here all day for extensive, and rude, inspection by troops of the newly formed East Pakistan Ansars. Food and water were scarce. Women suffered the interminable wait until darkness to relieve themselves. The train was released in the late evening and reached Gede around 9 p.m. to another round of checking, this time by Indian authorities. It finally left for Sealdah around midnight and reached the following morning.

10 March 1948. After two days and two nights the family arrived in Calcutta. From Sealdah station they shared a 12-foot lorry with three other families, piling atop their luggage. As the truck juddered and began to move, Noni's four-year old girl let out a wail: her mountain was wobbly! Noni pacified her with a handful of puffed rice. The truck careened through the streets of north Calcutta and Noni got her first glimpse of the city that would be her home for the next fifty-two years.

They soon arrived at the place Hira's contact had found for the family. It was a house in the northern outskirts occupied by refugees, one family to a room. Theirs was 10'x10', on the ground floor, with the door partially blocked by the stairwell, under which the cooking would have to be done. And the only window opened onto a foetid drain. In one corner of the inner courtyard, they saw a pile of gunny sacks, seeping blood. Human or animal, they didn't know and didn't try to find out.

Noni set about cleaning up. Her family had crossed over, unhurt and intact. This would be their defining event, here on out. But she had no time to register that. Too much to do. Her kids were hungry. The kitchen needed setting up. She would soon nest this dank spandrel. And it would be home for a dozen years.

§

But here's the thing. Truth—the whole truth—resembles the home of an inveterate packrat. Filled to the rafters with a confused jumble of cartons, the kitchen overflowing with mouldy dishes, the stench ripe. It is not a place one visits by choice. What we do when presenting it, say in a museum, is clear up the clutter, so the visitor will linger awhile rather than flee. What gets thrown out in that cleaning is naturally a function of who is doing it.

Act 3
Embers

In 2002, the privately funded British Empire and Commonwealth Museum, which aimed to present the imperial age from multiple perspectives, opened in Bristol after more than a decade of planning. In a slant rhyme to the end of empire, it closed its doors six years later and went into liquidation in 2013 amid sordid reports about the unauthorized sale of loaned objects. The chairman of the museum's board of trustees said: 'I think the time has not yet arrived for the proper story of Empire and Commonwealth to be told.'

—Maya Jasanoff

*I sat alone in school
while our tongue sat outside
whining, like a dog*

—Jitendra Vasava

PRELUDE: THE TUSSLE

'WHAT IS ALL THIS?' SHISHU'S ghost looks sceptical.

'You could call it a tiling of time,' I offer gingerly, 'with objects.' Did that sound too precious? I blurt out what I hope is a hook: 'It is Noni's life during the decades you had lost touch. I thought you'd be interested.'

'Ah!' he yelps in mock enthusiasm, 'this is one of those effete museums, where you harvest little family mementos, scraps of second-hand memories, add yeast, let rise, then bake,' his arms sweep a bloated shape, 'into some sort of Grand Memorial!'

'Wait, you're going to judge without viewing it?'

'Look, I hate to tell you this but what you're attempting here goes against our cultural grain.'

'How?'

'We have never kept archives, unlike the Greeks, the Romans, the Chinese. We have never time-stamped our work. Nor in most cases signed them. Ancient India had no notion of history. Does that absence say anything?'

'What does *that* have to do with *this*?'

'Let me bring the two closer. Is there a serious museum on the Partition, an event that impacted over a billion lives? In any of the three countries that emerged from it?'

'One opened at Amritsar in 2017, but it's really about Punjab. So, no.'

'What about the Bengal Famine? The defining event for all Bengalis. Over 3 million dead. With historic spasms downstream, notably the Great Calcutta Killings, which made Partition inevitable. Is there a museum on it, in either Bengal?'

'No,' I feel like a thick student.

'And why is that? Because those are built by energetic lest-we-forget people. Here in the fecund tropics, we don't let memory get in the way of life. We know, if left alone, nature always overruns even the finest edifice.'

'You can't be serious! Are you really saying that our amnesia is a thoughtful practice and not the path of least effort? Besides, why would memory get in the way? It is how we figure out who we are. Who others are. And what we share. It seems essential to life.'

'Forgetting is just as essential,' he says with an enigmatic smile. 'Memory is an unreliable filtrate. A trickster that shifts shape. Like fat in good meat our best memories are marbled with forgetting. It is the melting away that makes the morsel luscious.'

'Fine, I can accept that. Forgetting is undervalued, you're right. It can help heal.'

'Ah, let's be careful,' his eyes have a lingering glint, 'forgetting needs closer scrutiny. It comes in various shades. For instance, in the days leading up to 15 August 1947, a pall of smoke had blanketed Delhi. Why? Because the British were burning documents en masse, to avoid the wrong hands. The rest they had already shipped to London, bound for deep bunkers. And India was just the start. Egypt 1956, Malaya 1957, Trinidad and Tobago 1961, Kenya 1963, British Guiana 1965. In colony after colony, they frantically erased their tracks on the way out. Incinerators when available, dumped in the ocean when the coast was near. A wholesale erasure of definitional stories. Like lobotomy. So, you see, memory for us is a crippled venture.'

'OK, here's what I've heard so far: we are culturally amnesiac and colonially lobotomized. And our best defence against burnt or inaccessible archives are wisps of hand-me-down stories. It is uphill, I agree. So then, what? We give up?'

'No, we skirt the hill. Let me give an example. There are no museums on the Bengal Famine, yes? But two legendary auteurs have made films on it. Have you seen them?'

'I have, but how is that relevant?'

'I'll tell you. Satyajit Ray's *Ashani Sanket* is a straight-up memorial. A picturesque famine in technicolour. The starving lead with her plucked eyebrows intact. Quite possibly Ray's weakest film. Mrinal

Sen's *Akaler Sandhane*, on the other hand, takes a completely different tack. It is a film about the impossibility of making a film on the Famine.'

'A museum about its own impossibility—that's a compelling idea! But I wasn't trying to memorialize the big guns. Famine. Partition. I simply wanted to share Noni's life, from those missing decades. You know, the survival.'

'Ah, but that is precisely the impulse behind every museum. Lest we forget. The certainty baked into that makes me nervous. I wanted to alert you to the dangers of memorials. To the impossibility of X-raying the central, heritable, fracture of our people. A fracture that you carry and—admit it—why you waded into this whole farrago in the first place.'

'Come on,' I imagine taking his hoary hand, 'can't you help me out? Maybe we can do this together.'

'I'm not sure about this,' he grouses, 'but let's take a look.'

Thus was Shishu's spirit dragooned into collaboration. A spirit hostile towards remembrance, perhaps to hide the hurt at being unremembered.

1

PAPERWORK

'*Kaagaz Nahi Dikhayenge*'
Paper
1948

A printed form in Bangla text, 8" x11", on pink tissue-thin paper. It has mild tearing along one vertical and three horizontal folds. The header reads: 'West Bengal Government Refugee Registration Certificate'. The footer instructs the official to make triplicates with carbon paper: 'one copy to be sent to the Relief Commissioner's Office, one handed to the registered individual, and one kept for our records'. The smudged inking of the entries suggests this is a carbon copy. In addition to official fields for bookkeeping, there are six for the registrant to fill: *name, name of the head of family, current address, gender, caste,* and *where you came from.* The last field is further broken into: *district, subdivision, police station, village, post office.* It is signed at the bottom by the official and the registrant, and dated: 27 April 1948.

∞

'NONI-DI'S REFUGEE CERTIFICATE,' GHOST SHISHU exhaled, 'this is like running into an old friend! Notice the excellent preservation. A bit of tatter, yes, but remember, this is before plastic. And ours is a land wet and excitable. Floods, storms, riots. This bit of paper you protected better than your liver. And here's the address: 132, Bagmari Road. I'd been in that area numerous times throughout the fifties. Little did I know!'

'Some of the fields are curious,' I said, 'like "where you came from". What did they do with that information?'

'Nothing officially, as far as I know. But the refugees coalesced organically by district, even by village in some cases. We were entirely on our own, you see, in an unfamiliar land. India had no plans for our resettlement, unlike the refugees from West Pakistan. They didn't build us a Chandigarh. We built our own squats. Starting 1949, squatter colonies mushroomed across Calcutta's outskirts and all along its suburban railway tracks. Our volunteers would route new arrivals at Sealdah station to the suitable colony. From Jessore? Go to Bijoygarh. From Khulna? Go to Senhati. From Barisal? Go to Habra. And so on. We defaced Calcutta forever,' he croaked with glee, 'the empire's second city would never again be squatter-free!'

'What about the caste data?'

'That is an Indian tic,' he chuckled. 'Is any tentacle of our state free of it? It became operational later, when low-caste arrivals were banished outside West Bengal. But this is still 1948. Note the infrastructure for refugee relief this document suggests, however minimal. The early arrivals, like Noni-di, had little trouble getting certified. Your family was in the first wave. The first million. Mainly upper-caste, middle-class, employable. You eked out your own footholds. The certificate meant state-subsidized grain, merit stipends for students, access to the employment exchange. But this didn't last. The later cohorts faced a vastly different reality.'

'What was your experience?'

'The relief system buckled under the massive surge after the 1950 massacres. Over two million that year alone. And progressively less mobile: the lower-middle classes, the low-caste rural poor. Sealdah station became a manifest hell, teeming with skeletal humans in rags, the living barely discernible from the dead. Disease broke out. By the time I crossed over in 1951, there was a raging underground racket for forged documents. Touts stalked new arrivals. I couldn't pay and ran around from pillar to post,' the memory brought on a wry smile. 'Eventually the party helped me out, but it took several years.'

'That is absurd!' I cried in disbelief. 'You had put your life on the line to free India and free India refused to recognize you as a refugee?'

'Look, I was no exception,' he said with a gritty calm. 'That was the Partition's Big Bang effect. A wilful amnesia about the before. As if time itself had been reset. The new country was busy putting out fires, focused solely on the future. If you had fled East Pakistan you were a Bangal refugee, period. A body without place. An encroaching insect. Legions of Bangal freedom fighters like me had to start over. Many perished in dire poverty much before the 1970s, when the Indian government tracked down some of us to hand out little copper plaques, in recognition of our sacrifice. That,' he hissed, 'was the true absurdity!' He paused, shaken by his own outburst, before going on: 'Anyway, tell me what this caption says. Kaagaz...I don't read Hindi, I refused to learn it.'

'It says: Won't Show Our Papers. This was a slogan during the nationwide protests of 2019–20.'

'Ah yes, against the government's planned citizen's register. Asking for all sorts of documents now, aren't they, including ancestral data, to mark you a citizen!'

'Millions don't have these, as you can imagine. This has kindled widespread anxiety, especially amongst Bangals. In Assam, a border state like Bengal where they've tried this, refugee certificates were rejected as proof of ancestral citizenship. Nearly 2 million did not make the cut, most of them Bangal, born in India. Many were sent to detention camps, countless dragged through draining court appeals....'

'Of course,' he cut in acidly, 'the Partition tank rolls on! Keep together as an inherited trait, like caste. Good thing I never married. My descendants would've had a terrible time proving they were Indian.'

'Did you never get documents made? Your voter card or passport?'

'See, us Bangal refugees were a formidable voting bloc,' he tittered, 'every political party wanted a piece of us. So the voter card was easy. But the passport I never bothered with,' the bitter mirth ebbed as his face hardened, 'I had no place I wanted to go.'

2
VANITY

Stolen
Small mirror with shelf
Pre-1950

A 15"x20" mirror of bevelled glass with an ornamental arabesque peak. Its wood frame is carved in a rope weave and polished. A shelf at its base, also of polished wood, houses a slim drawer with one pull-out brass ring. The overall finish is of high quality.

MY RAVISHING AUNT BA IS at this mirror, putting on eyeliner. This is one of my earliest memories, possibly from 1969. She is in her mid-twenties, getting ready for work. Her bangles tinkle as she expertly traces each eyelid to a wingtip swish. Her crisp cotton sari rustles. I am four and transfixed. She looks impossibly statuesque. Post-bath and pre-make-up, she has prayed at the triptych of gods on the shelf and lit some incense. Padmini brand: a small, yellow-orange box with a metal-rimmed hole to jam a bolus of sticky incense into. Its lit tip glows now, a tendril of smoke clouding the mirror. A cloying perfume thickens the air. Aunt Ba puts finishing touches to her hair. Then she turns, sees me agape, and breaks into a dazzling smile.

Nearly fifty years from that morning, I learned that this mirror was a stolen object. That Noni's second son, my tall and strapping Uncle Blue, had done the deed. Blue got into bodybuilding after the family had crossed over and by 1950, at sixteen, had blossomed into a neighbourhood tough. And, in bad company, as my mother put it, when telling me the story. Sometime in the middle of that year, he and some of his muscled pals tried to forcibly take over the ground floor of a home in Bagmari. It belonged to one Bashir Ali, who also owned the property where my family lived. In the event, it was a foiled attempt. The boys kicked up a row, and when city workers showed up they fled, but not before looting the home on their way out. That's when Blue had filched this mirror. The other boys had taken more valuable things, Ma assured me.

∽

'So, this was cause for shame, then?' Shishu's ghost pinned me with eagle eyes, scowling. 'Tainted your memory, did it?'

'It certainly shook me,' I admitted. 'I've seen this mirror even in the early eighties. My family had used it for over thirty years. And it wasn't just the theft, but also how the story was told.'

'How do you mean?'

'Ma first saw this mirror in 1962 when she married into the family. So it's hearsay for her too. When I asked her why Uncle Blue had gone to forcibly occupy someone's home, she said Muslims were being evicted then, so those homes were being taken over. I pressed, why were they being evicted? She backpedalled: no no, they were leaving on their own and Hindus were buying up their properties. But these boys weren't buyers, I protested, they had broken in! At this she threw up her hands: I'm just telling it like I heard it. I tried again, a different time, and the story shifted somewhat. She said Blue and his gang had gone to occupy the ground floor but Bashir Ali refused to rent it out. That occupy–rent construct I found painful. A feint, but so transparent! Like a toddler covering her eyes and believing she's invisible.'

'See, this is what you children of refugees don't get: depravity and its denial are why you exist,' he said, cold and bilious, 'that is how one survives horror. You are doing the equivalent of cringing at the birth canal.' He saw me flinch and his tone shifted: 'It's our fault, really. We erase it. We raise you to be free. Then you go digging decades later and find a shard that cuts you. But you have no context. You can't see the feverish chaos of Calcutta in 1950. Nor the currents swirling around Blue. You don't know that dislocated boy who stole a mirror worthy of his beautiful sisters. Yet his urge is what you are made of.'

Shishu's Ghost Provides Context

You have to understand that Partition was not one wound but two, with entirely different outcomes. The gash in the west caused an immediate and horrific haemorrhage. Over 6 million Sikhs and Hindus fled east from West Pakistan and a similar number of Muslims fled west from India. A massive population exchange within a few months. Then the bleeding stopped and the stitching could begin. Abandoned properties and other assets were used in a systematic rehabilitation effort and to provide reparations. India built enormous camps in Punjab and Haryana to temporarily house the West Pakistan refugees, complete with sanitation crews and field hospitals. Within a few years most were resettled in planned townships, including one designed by Le Corbusier. And that was that. Partition refugees had been taken care of. Or so Delhi claimed. But what of the gash in the east? That story is very different.

Just as much of India moved on, the eastern gash began its first spurt of serious bleeding. Prior to 1950, the flow here was driven less by violence than dread. The massacres of 1950 changed that. And these millions, brutalized and dispossessed like the west-gash refugees two years before, now arrived in an India with its sympathy capital overspent. No crisp camps for them, no planned cities. Delhi insisted they had to go back, even though it was obvious that they could not. Trains disgorged them daily at Sealdah by the thousands. They swarmed Calcutta's streets and its outskirts. As things spun out of control, West Bengal's Congress chief minister pleaded repeatedly with Nehru for help, to no avail. Then, retaliatory violence broke out against West Bengal's Muslims and they began fleeing to East Pakistan. That got Nehru's attention, damaging as this was to his secular project. In April 1950, he signed a pact with Pakistan's prime minister, Liaquat Ali Khan, in which both nations promised to protect their religious minorities. The pact was unevenly enforced: it stanched the eastbound flow of Bengali Muslims, but not the westbound flow of mainly low-caste Bengali Hindus. And it provided no succour to the exhausted masses already here, with nowhere to turn.

So what did they do? They coalesced and fought back. With help from my party. Which, recall, was on the backfoot at this time, barely above ground. Bangal refugees and CPI, both down and out, both shafted by the Congress administration, formed a symbiotic binary, each leveraging the other to catapult onto firm ground within a few years. This astonishing feat was led by my very own Ambika-da: now a Bangal refugee himself, atop his identities as a freedom-fighting legend and a firebrand communist leader.

Armed with little more than bamboo and thatch, the human flotsam set up nests in Calcutta's outskirts. Much of the land they squatted on was government owned but some was privately held. When the police or hired goons showed up, the refugees banded together to deflect them, often with women as the protective outer layer. If the police won today, if their shacks were razed, they simply came back tomorrow and rebuilt them. How can you match the resilience of the desperate homeless? They had lost everything, including fear. The state, besieged already, they would wear out. By May 1950, Calcutta's southern edge was carpeted with mammoth squatter colonies, with names like Bijoygarh (Fort Triumph) and Azadgarh (Fort Liberty). In another year, rows upon rows of bamboo-rattan shanties sprouted all along the city's eastern train tracks, from Jadavpur in the south to Kanchrapara in the north. These hapless Bangals tattooed a word into Calcutta's psyche forever: jabordakhol—taken by force.

The jabordakhol air was promiscuous. With law enforcement in shambles, it emboldened all, including the already settled refugees and stray criminal elements. There were vacant properties in the city abandoned by Muslims to grab. Or why not capture it even if it isn't vacant, the owner is Muslim after all. Those people are slaughtering and looting us across the border, don't you read the news? Wait, but you aren't even a refugee! So what, I am Hindu, aren't I? Thus the mad logic went in the spiralling chaos. This is when your Uncle Blue had attempted a jabordakhol and stolen the mirror. This is the air he was breathing. Around him, entire mansions were being grabbed, and countless acres of land. Actually, here are some numbers: by the end of 1950, Bangal refugees had built 149 colonies across West Bengal, squatting on 2.4 million acres, sheltering about 150,000 people. The Congress government tried to evict them by enacting a law, essentially unenforceable given the hobbled state machinery. But it was the perfect fuel: the Bangal-CPI nexus was forged in the heat of resisting this law.

In mid-1950, Ambika-da began the painstaking work of organizing in the colonies, going door to door. He ideated and co-founded the United Central Refugee Council: a pan-political body on Bangal refugee welfare. The UCRC's leadership was largely Bangal, with Ambika-da as general secretary. Its central committee, while CPI-dominated, had members from all the major Left parties and even the right-wing Hindu Mahasabha. And importantly, reflecting its grassroots focus, it had members from forty-three of the colonies. UCRC's inaugural rally was held on 13 August 1950 at the Calcutta Maidan and 50,000 refugees showed up. Their homeless blues had been repurposed into political Red! I'll bet Blue had attended this rally. Brawny Bangal youth like him were prime UCRC recruits.

UCRC pressed the government to stop squatter colony evictions and settle the refugees afloat on the streets. Their tactic was to take Calcutta hostage with periodic chaos—meetings, processions, protests. They would snarl traffic while being beaten back by police batons and tear gas, in full view of the rush-hour crowd. Calcutta was forced to confront its new precariat—the Bangal refugees. The unwashed thousands surged through the city's main arterials, gaunt men and women, with embers for eyes. Their energy was of a spring uncoiled. Their voices rent the air. 'Amra kara?' a lead called—who are we? 'Bastuhara!' the crowd roared—the homeless! You see us as insects, now behold the locust storm!

The give and take was hard-boiled: the refugees were used as political muscle and in return received support building a semblance of civility and ease in their squats. UCRC worked closely with the colony committees, which had emerged organically. Initially made up of founders, they later became elected bodies that administered each colony, even meting out rudimentary justice. They set up schools, libraries, playgrounds, built sewer lines and dug wells. By 1952, there were even a few hospitals and colleges. What these colonies achieved was emergent self-governance, at scale, in the teeth of extinction. This has happened elsewhere. For example, the multi-national refugee camp in Calais, called the Jungle, circa 2015. Or the Rohingya refugee camp in Kutupalong, circa 2017. But here's the important difference: the 1950s Bangal colonies received no state aid and none from abroad either, with all the rich countries still recovering from World War II. You know what Calcutta called Bangals at the time? Pond scum. Indestructible when dry, inexorable when wet, and if left alone takes over any stationary waterbody. They meant it as a slur, of course, but I always took it as a compliment.

While tending to Bangal refugee welfare, UCRC also cultivated them as a leftist voting bloc. By the end of 1951, most had voter cards. The 1952 Bengal Assembly elections were around the corner, the first in free India. CPI was in the fray. Ambika-da was running. In fact, it was he who pulled me out of hiding in Barisal and brought me over to campaign for him in the colonies. The CPI leadership within UCRC worked to leverage the enormous Bangal vote to bring a leftist government to power. They managed this vote bank with a disciplined cadre hierarchy, a tactic that would become a template in West Bengal politics. Via colony-level outreach, they imbued the refugees with a sense of mission, an awareness of their collective force. They built a formidable refugee-powered campaign machine that could be deployed at will. Election campaigns became a burning crusade. A shrill, feverish business. This naked aggression of the precariat would be a Calcutta fixture from now on, honed as a political tool. The cast of characters shifted with time: fresh migrants, slums instead of colonies, new political parties. But the quid-pro-quo formula endured.

Buoyed by the Bangals, CPI won a massive haul of 69 seats in the 1952 elections—up from 3 in 1946—to become the largest Opposition party in the state assembly. In another fifteen years, they would upend the Congress Party to form a leftist government in West Bengal. By then, their base was further inflated by additional squatter colonies, hundreds of which had been already legitimized, with hundreds more to come. And the eviction law became a figment of memory.

So, as you can see, the Bangals radically altered Calcutta's landscape, both physical and political. But I should point out here that Bangals were not a monolith. There were at least three kinds. One, the first-wave Bangals, like your family, who, with a room and a job in the city, got down to assimilation. Risk-averse, they stayed largely out of sight, with little incentive for political engagement. Two, the colony Bangals, who settled on land illegally grabbed. The colonies were the world of the lower-middle classes: some education, a sense of self, their collective precarity a propulsion to band together. This made them a bank of political capital and therefore the most visible and engaged group, as we've seen.

The third category was also largely invisible: the illiterate rural poor, unemployable and without the gumption to grab land. They were at the mercy of the state, crammed into abandoned World War II army barracks and warehouses, like so much cargo. These were the PL camps—Permanent Liability, that's how the state saw them. An oddly resigned view, I find. These camps were rank hellholes, with no sanitation or healthcare. In the largest, Cooper's Camp, eighty latrines served 100,000. Inmates survived on a meagre dole that they stood to lose if they sought livelihood outside. Stripped of every trapping of humanity—health, work, purpose, even privacy—they lived in a primal dimness, like maggots in rotting flesh. Countless died.

There was movement between these groups, of course. For example, some first-wave Bangals moved into colonies seeking more room, maybe a little veggie patch. Some PL Bangals escaped into survival, in the decade India took to decide that they were, in fact, human and needed rehabilitation. Many were then transported to rudimentary settlements in far-flung lands, unfamiliar and inhospitable—Dandakaranya, Kalahandi, Andamans. The rest remained in the camps, even seventy years later, generationally damaged. Their state-issued PL tag a self-fulfilling prophecy.

Look at me, I've been going on and on! Let me wrap up where

I began: the two gashes. The one in the west bled heavily for a few months after August 1947 then stopped. In the east, the heavy bleeding began in 1950, but that gash oozed for the next sixty years, punctuated by spurts after every spasm of subcontinental violence, with major ones in 1964, 1971, and 1993. How many Bangals have crossed into India since 1947? Fifteen million is a low estimate. More than twice that of the western gash, but smeared across decades. The wound in the east never got stitched. See, our Partition never ended.

There you have it. The Bangal backdrop. Quite an earful, eh? And all of this dredged up by one look in that mirror! Well, I am an old windbag. And you pushed my biggest button. But now my throat is dry and I need a drink.

3

BRINK

December 1951
132, Bagmari Road
Calcutta

NONI IS SLEEPLESS ON A chilly night. She is worried sick. Her oldest son, my Baba, hasn't come home. He's been doing this quite often. What is going on with him? He always was the model boy, quiet and conscientious, academically gifted, attached to her. But he's been drifting away lately. Noni senses two separate threads in her anxiety and pries them apart. She's concerned about him, yes. But her panic arises from what his drifting means for her family. Her second son she has little control over. She hears he has become a neighbourhood tough. Her third son is only thirteen. And then the five girls, the youngest just three. This was already a gruelling load, with Hira in Tarpasha. He needed to remain across the border; with no college degree he had no prospects here. Then came the bombshell a few months ago: he had caught a mysterious illness. Waves of crushing pain in his jaws and cheeks that came and went with no apparent reason. When a bout hit he was pinned helpless, unable to work. But he had to; his pay cheques were keeping the family alive. Ever since hearing this news, Noni has had to think about the role Baba must now play, the urgency in him taking on the mantle of the provider, being her partner in raising the family. He is what stands between their survival and ruin. And here he was, spending nights somewhere out in the big bad city. He'd been evasive so far when asked. But she'll wait no more. She needs to know where he goes and why.

The baby whinged in her sleep. Turning to pat her down, Noni glanced around the room and thought: did I ever imagine living like this? A slim cot and a desk pressed against a scabrous wall, usually reserved for Baba. Her two other sons slept in a neighbourhood dorm. For herself and the girls, she made a bed taking up the entire floor. This required care because an open drain flowed through the room, with an ill-fitting plank for a lid. What was the drain for? Someone had said this room is where Bashir Ali's family did their Eid slaughter. Could be. This home was quite the mansion, two storeys wrapped around an inner courtyard. It had housed one family before, imagine, and now held eight: four upstairs and four down. The six upstairs rooms were spacious, with high ceilings, stained glass, crystal doorknobs. The eight rooms below were less generous, but all had plenty of light and air. Except hers, tucked behind the stairwell. No, she didn't blame Hira for this. His timing had been excellent and the neighbours he'd sent them with were well-connected business folk who were doing him a favour. They'd already taken over this house and it was natural she'd be given the room no one wanted. But whether or not this was the abattoir, Noni mused, we sleep on a drain. Good thing my father didn't live to see this. Or that I cook under the stairs. And not even there if it rains, when I drag the stove inside and smoke up the room. Or that the money always runs out before the month ends and I have to borrow from the lady upstairs.

    She heard a plaintive whistle from the tracks to the west. It bloomed, then faded, as the night train from Sealdah hurtled north. Towards the border? Noni wasn't sure why the sound made tears spring up. Brushing them off brusquely she focused on the positive. Hira still had a job. The children were healthy on the rice–lentils–vegetables she cooked. She tried to manage a bit of fish, at least once a day, so essential for their brain. No one could say they weren't well-dressed. Her trusty Singer machine had been a lifesaver. The ration shop sold cheap fabric by the bolt. She made little dresses for the girls, shirts for the boys, all the same print. The leftovers she gathered into a curtain, for her one window, which had to remain shut against the stench from the cowshed right outside. But this meant fresh milk nearby, didn't it? As if on cue, an animal rustled and lowed in the dark. Was it nearly dawn? Her thoughts arced back to the start: Baba. Baba was the biggest positive. He had a bright future. He was going to pull them out of this. He had to. Noni would make sure.

∽

Baba, now twenty, was a senior at Scottish Church College, reading physics on a merit scholarship. These were hard-earned feathers in the refugee boy's cap. But a new obsession had derailed his academic focus. Not wine, nor women, as Noni might have feared, but song. Hindustani classical music, to be exact. His interest in this was not new. He had grown up steeped in it with his uncles in Mahilara. His baro-mama—Shishu's first political mentor Shankar-da—was a gifted singer who took Baba to musical events. His mejomama, a sublime flautist, would clamber onto the bandstand at weddings with specific requests for the shehnai players. But all that was rural Barisal. This was Calcutta, the very mecca of Hindustani classical music. Baba had got his maiden glimpse of this rarefied world a few months ago. A college friend, Ajit, who trained on the sitar under Vilayat Khan, had invited Baba to a soiree at his guru's home in Park Circus. It was a monsoon evening. Dashing in with Ajit, sopping wet, Baba stepped on a live wire of music. And nothing was ever the same.

Only much later did he grasp the full extent of that evening's gift. Performing that day was not only Vilayat Khan, the future sitar maestro, then an electric young genius, but also Amir Khan, the vocalist magician, then India's leading exponent of the khayal form. And Baba had sat within a few feet of these gods, breathing the same air. If Vilayat was the dazzling fireworks of a lightning storm, Amir was the full moon reflected on water, its hypnotic gravitas folding one in. One aroused, the other stilled. Both drove him to tears, to an ethereal place he didn't know existed. How could he climb down from this high? He needed his hits and sought them with the energy of a new addict. With Ajit as his partner in crime, he chased mehfils—intimate performances in wealthy Calcutta homes, open to those in the know. Especially those in Chatubabu–Latubabu's mansion on Beadon Street. The past few months had been a blur, a tour of the heavens. He'd heard Allauddin Khan's sarod, Bismillah Khan's shehnai, Akhil Bandhu Ghosh's thumri, Siddheshwari Devi's kajri, Begum Akhtar's ghazal with Keramatullah Khan accompanying her on the tabla, Nikhil Banerjee's sitar, whose liquid play he preferred to Ravi Shankar's force. And on and on. Each had only further stoked his hunger. And heightened his sense of doom. The news of Hira's illness had laced his bender with a perverse intensity. He knew what was coming. He knew this had to end. But how would he live without it?

Then came winter and things got ratcheted up a notch. This was the season when musical giants from all over India gathered in Calcutta for performances every night, all night long. The city was flooded with music. The same city that was racked with political unrest, its sidewalks heaving with destitute Bangals, their women's bodies being exchanged for food. Baba, a cleaved boy in a cleaved city, swept up in a musical vortex, took deep drags of the magic each night and weaved home in the morning to his hovel, too bleary for college.

Even half a century later, he had graphic recall of the concert he'd come home from on the morning of Noni's intervention. Nikhil Banerjee on a tear, with Samta Prasad on the tabla, finishing in a volcanic jhala. A performance that seemed impossible to top. Then, at two in the morning, Amir Khan takes the stage. Eyes closed, caressing his nape as was his habit, he began with a low alaap of Bhatiyar. Almost a hum. And within minutes, the audience, afire after Nikhil, were transfixed in Khan-sahab's web, oblivious to what had come before. He sang for nearly three hours, gliding from Bhatiyar to Ahir Bhairon, and finally to Lalit as the horizon limned with red. Ah, Amir Khan singing Lalit at dawn! That. That is heaven on earth, Baba had murmured, and I was there.

∽

Noni was on her haunches firing up her coal stove under the stairs when she saw Baba walk in. The inner courtyard was already filled with the morning thrum. The daily squabbles over the one toilet shared by nearly forty residents. Women slapping laundry near the open-top water tank, men bathing. No, she couldn't talk to him here. Nor in their room, where she'd just set the girls up with their school work. What about the roof? That wouldn't work either, people were hanging up laundry there. Where, then? The stove had caught on, she noticed, with a head of smoke that needed to settle. She stood up and blocked Baba's path as he made to enter their room. Something in her eyes made him follow her. They crossed the courtyard, walked out the front door, on the main road, past the mosque, towards Bagmari Muslim Burial Ground. Neither spoke a word. Noni had decided the graveyard would give her the privacy she needed. So, as they go in through the arched gate, we will wait for them outside, in the winter light slanting and sweet.

They emerged in short order. Noni only had a few minutes before the hot coals in her stove needed attention. Both their faces were tear-streaked. But the boy's looked like a crumpled paper lantern. As if a weight-bearing strut had shattered within. Noni had reined in her firstborn.

Baba soon gave up physics and got on the path of lucrative employment, training at a newly founded institute for marine engineers, a long bus ride away. Noni would wake before dawn to make him breakfast and a packed lunch on her coal stove. When his institute moved to a sprawling residential campus in the southern exurbs, she rode the bus hours each way to bring him sugar-palm fritters and other dainties. Baba graduated in 1954 and landed a job immediately. The dress shirt he wore to his interview was stitched by Noni. He would be gone a lot on sea voyages, his generous pay the family's life raft. His passion for music was never reignited.

§

Shishu's ghost fell silent for a bit, then sheepishly said: 'I'm sorry if I implied earlier that all first-wave Bangals got quick toeholds in the city. I knew many fell through the cracks. But I didn't know your family had come this close. Hira-da apart and ill,' he shook his head, 'poor Noni-di!'

'And what about Baba?' I bristled.

'I feel for both of them. He was clearly central to her mission.

Both sustained damage, I'm sure. For Baba, his crushed ardour must've had an effect. You know what they say: hurt people hurt people.'

'Oh yes, that he did. Most of all, himself. His love for Noni was a rich, unconditional sort. Hers could not have been. He didn't understand this until the end of his life. By then, she was long gone and he had mauled many.'

'That is such a streak through Bangal homes,' he nodded in recognition, 'all those hurt engines with hurt drivers. But did you kids see any of this growing up?'

'To us, Baba was distant and dour, with a hair-trigger temper. We leapt to life when he left for work and became funerary upon his return. He must've already been burnt out, having raised his large brood of siblings. But I realized that much later. At the time, he felt like an ogre. And we could tell that Noni was a second power centre. She was affectionate, in her way, towards us, her grandkids, and towards her other children. But to Baba she was stone cold.'

'I see. Survival battle over, but the weapons had failed to retract. Yet another Bangal pattern,' he sighed. 'It is so hard for me to picture Noni-di cold,' he seemed pained. 'That's the price she paid. But she did get the job done. And I must highlight her immense talent for life. Those sugar-palm fritters? That is classic Noni-di!'

'Yes, she deployed her formidable talents to yoke Baba,' I quipped.

'And where would you be if she hadn't?' he snapped back. 'Forget you, where would Baba be? Floundering in the pitiless alleys of classical music, where even talent and training don't guarantee a living. And he a refugee boy with his father on the cusp of unemployment. She hurt him, yes, but also saved him a lot of hurt.' He saw the protest form in my eyes and changed track. 'You know, seeing Baba on the city streets reminded me of my own walks at the time. I may have run into him, unbeknownst. The elections were near, I was campaigning with Ambika-da all over the city and noticed posters for a film playing in the theatres: *Chinnamul* –The Uprooted. On Bangal refugees, the mainly low-caste rural surge that began in 1950. Potters, blacksmiths, goldsmiths, weavers. And the film was made in the thick of their arrival. No, not a documentary, a fiction feature. Have you seen it?'

Ghost Shishu's *Chinnamul* Detour

Of course, you haven't. Few have. But this is India's first film on the Partition. And the first Bengali film to make an international splash, at least in the Soviet Union. Nemai Ghosh's *Chinnamul* is neorealism before Satyajit Ray. Five years before *Pather Panchali*, in fact. Ghosh reached for a new language in this, his debut film. His actors blended with real refugees in the dystopia that was Sealdah station circa 1950. He wove in documentary footage of packed trains pulling in, of the tidal wave crashing onto the platforms. Of bodies barely alive, their meagre belongings, their flared eyes. His concealed camera tracked his actor–refugees waiting at a teeming platform, cheek by jowl with refugee families, the skeletal mother, her listless baby sitting in its own faeces. It followed them playing skilled Bangal tradesmen trying their luck in the city: the goldsmith hawking cheap combs on a busy street, alongside real Bangal hawkers; the blacksmith, job hunting in car repair shops and getting real rebuffs. Ghosh scotched the line between fact and fiction, using stark reality to tell a universal story of love and loss unfolding in an indifferent city. In real time.

And what did the city think of this film? The reaction was initially limp. Then, the famous Russian director V. I. Pudovkin came to Calcutta on a cultural delegation, saw the film and was awestruck. He carried it home and the Soviet state released the film simultaneously at 181 theatres in Moscow, Leningrad, Kiev, and elsewhere. Pudovkin also wrote a rousing review in *Pravda* on 6 December 1951. This foreign attention naturally meant Calcutta's critics were now full of praise. More importantly, the city did a double take on the dregs from the east clogging its streets, which it had grown used to sidestepping. It began to notice them as human, after seeing their plight on celluloid. We like to consume alive art, you know. Especially via blessings from abroad.

Ghosh made this film against tremendous odds. And broke

technical ground. But why did he do it at all? Because he was an ally. Not a Bangal, remember, but a fervent ally. Having spent formative years in Dhaka, he couldn't bear the wholesale degradation of a people unfolding on Calcutta's streets. He wrote the screenplay, did the camera. He rallied and found Bangal producers. He was a member of the Indian People's Theatre Association where he had close Bangal friends—Bijon Bhattacharya, Shobha Sen, Ritwik Ghatak—all of whom he roped in for this project. In fact, this is where Ritwik makes his debut, both as actor and assistant director. Ah, Ritwik! Our doomed prophet who would go on to make the classics on Bangal life: *Meghe Dhaka Tara, Subarnarekha, Jukti Takko Gappo*. Ritwik, who carried broken Bengal within him like a festering organ. It drove him to the madhouse and electric shocks. No, no, I won't get started on him! But you know, even Ritwik couldn't bring himself up to show what had happened to Bangals in the PL camps.

∽

December 1951
Ghushuri PL Camp
Across the river from Calcutta

Shishu was breathless. And not just from running. He felt like he was having an out-of-body experience. Did he just see what he saw? And was that really Ambika-da next to him, dissolved in a mess of tears and vomit? Ambika-da—intrepid hero of the Chittagong Armoury Raid, of Cellular Jail hunger strikes, of UCRC street clashes! Seeing him like this made it really hard for Shishu to fight the metallic taste of an oncoming retch in his own mouth. It was the smell that had brought it on, more than the sight. They were outside now, but the smell was still snared in his nostrils. And the sight? Could he ever unsee it?

It was not that they had no idea. Ambika-da had been tipped off about the disaster unfolding in the PL camps. The Congress administration had kept a tight lid on them, denying outsider access, particularly to the press. Ambika-da had made noise on this issue, campaigning mainly in the Bangal colonies. But with the elections drawing close, the decision now was that UCRC would sting a few PL camps to expose the government's rank failure. Accordingly, Ambika-da had led a small team, with a doctor and a photographer, who duped the guards and broke into Ghushuri. Shishu was in it.

The camp, on the industrial waterfront across the city, was a repurposed jute warehouse. Partition had gutted Bengal's jute industry, with the fields mainly in the east and the factories in the west. The row of Nissen huts—windowless half-cylinders of corrugated iron, 50'x25'—meant to hold jute, now held humans, some of whom had been jute peasants in their previous life. Now their days were spent in forced inactivity, on a ragged state-issued diet, behind barbed wire. Each hut housed up to twenty families who marked out their territories with bits of rubble. The days were hard, but the nights were much worse. Because the shutters to these huts had to be drawn, turning them into furnaces much of the year. If left open for air, prowling jackals poached sleeping babies. So, every night, the hefty doors mounted on rails were rolled shut. Inside, the inmates sweltered, each steeped in the night sounds and night smells of all the others. When the shutters were thrown open, the morning light often revealed death. Mainly of the elderly and the very young. They died from suffocation, from eating rotten dole, or drinking sewage-laced water from shallow wells hastily dug, from infections untreated. How many? What were their names? The state didn't know and didn't want to. Deaths mounted across West Bengal's PL camps—Cooper's, Dhubulia, Kashipur, and many more. Overstretched and unable to keep up even with mass cremations, the state tried to cover up the horror.

These things Shishu and his teammates knew. And yet, they were unprepared for what they found as they entered one of the Nissen huts. It was mid-morning; inmates were cooking lunch with their dry rations. Smoke from their makeshift stoves filled the hut, as did a riotous cacophony. Children ran around. Adults bickered. Old men dozed. No one paid the visitors any heed. As their senses adjusted, they were hit by an overpowering stench, and saw its source. A dozen bloated corpses piled against the back wall of the hut, like so much firewood. Right next to the churn of life. Wait, wasn't that Niranjan Barui over there, Shishu thought, the strapping peasant who was Jogen-da's lieutenant in the Mahilara canal dig six years ago? But he couldn't bring himself to ask. Niranjan, emaciated, was staring vacantly at a pan of rice coming to a boil. What had become of these people, Shishu wondered, his people! What did it take to cook and eat and sleep here, next to that putrid pile, knowing you could be on it tomorrow? They had made a gruelling escape from a massacre to this! How had it come to this?

Ambika-da began to retch and rushed out. The others hung back long enough for the photographer to take a few shots. Meanwhile a dishevelled young mother snagged Shishu, clutching her dead baby. The trucks for corpses only came once a week now, she began in a mutter. Then her voice swelled. And where were they taking them? She had heard they were throwing the babies into the jungles, for the wildlife. She had more flesh! Why doesn't the truck take her too? *Whyyyyyyyyy?*

Shishu ran as fast as he could but couldn't shake off her wail.

4
SOUVENIR

Survivor-1
Gold bead
1955

A 7 mm solid gold bead on a twine. The sturdy black twine, looped through two ears on the bead fixing it in place, has evenly spaced knots on it.

THIS IS THE LAST OF a string of twelve beads. The rest slid into the gap between Hira's income and Noni's refugee household expenses. The bead string was a gift from her father to Baba as a newborn, in 1931, to gird the baby's waist. The twine is original. The knots mark the missing beads.

Survivor-2
Currency note
1957

A one-rupee-note, issued in 1951 by the Government of Pakistan. On the back is a print of the Naulakha Pavilion, viewed through a scalloped arch of the Sheesh Mahal, both within Lahore Fort. All text on the note is in Urdu, except the denomination. The numeral '1' appears on the upper right corner in English, on the lower left in Urdu, and on the other two corners in Bangla.

Banking across the fresh border was a fraught business. Hira sent money to Noni through age-old hawala channels. Her pick-up point was the neighbourhood egg wholesaler. But the commission was steep: of the 250 rupees he sent her monthly she'd only get 200 in hand. Delivery, though, was largely reliable. Any delay meant a visit to the pawnshop or short-term debt. This specific rupee note rode with Hira, in his wallet, when he finally crossed over into India.

∽

'Look at that, the sublime Naulakha Pavilion,' ghost Shishu cooed in delight, 'a bit of Bengal in the martial heart of Lahore! Notice its deep, curving eaves, typical of the do-chala roofs of rural Bengal. To keep out the heavy Bengali rains,' he chuckled, 'in Lahore!'

'Why was this in Lahore?' I was intrigued. 'And why the name Naulakha?'

'Naulakha because it had cost a whopping nine lakhs to build! This was back in 1633, mind you, the year after work began on the Taj Mahal. Shah Jahan built Naulakha as a dainty summer retreat inside Lahore Fort. A Bengali hut, not of lowly mud and thatch, but of pristine white marble inlaid with exquisite pietra dura. But why did the emperor want a Bengali hut? Maybe to channel its moist rural idyll. The romantic rich build huts, you know, then as now. This one inspired others. Rudyard Kipling's sprawling retreat in Vermont, for instance, which he even named Naulakha. As a hat tip to the Bengali idyll, I'm sure, and not the cost.'

'But why was this on the currency?' I tried to bring him back on track.

'Ah, yes! Why indeed? The Pakistani ruling establishment, almost entirely Punjabi, was signalling to the country's Bengali east wing, one they habitually looked down upon. Naulakha was a rare symbol of a Punjab–Bengal syncretism. Notice the two Bangla numerals versus the one in Urdu? That's a similar signal; the east wing being more populous. We all know how that story ends. How the east wing splits away and why. But here, on the old currency, are traces of the west wing's feeble outreach. Now,' he peered at the caption cards, 'why do these two have the dates they do?'

'Um, that,' I hemmed, 'that's when I imagine they became souvenirs.'

'Eh?' he looked confused.

'1955 is when Baba got his job, Noni no longer needed to sell her gold. And 1957 is when Hira moved to India, so his Pakistani currency was no longer of use.'

'I see,' he frowned, 'so you think that shift is instant? I don't think it's clear at all when such objects become souvenirs. It's a mysterious process, impossible to time-stamp. Maybe it only happens when you've fully shed your refugee skin and can wear it as an accessory, like a leopard print, at the right occasion. And that can take generations.' To take the edge off of his scold, he draped a bony arm around me and switched subjects. 'So Noni-di crossed over in 1948 and Hira-da in 1957. Did they live apart for nine years?'

'Not quite. He couldn't travel but she would visit him, usually with the youngest in tow. Hira's illness was getting worse. Noni would sometimes be gone for months. And Baba ran the Bagmari household, even cooking, with help from the older girls. They had two more children during that period: a boy in 1953 and a girl in 1956.'

'So Noni-di now has ten children! All in that cramped room?'

'Yes. Until 1957. When a ground-floor room opened up because a family was leaving. And we occupied it. Now there was space for Hira, and Baba arranged to bring him over. Hira quit his job, travelled gingerly, and arrived in a brittle state. Baba immediately got him medical care with big-city experts. The diagnosis was trigeminal neuralgia. He even had neurosurgery, but nothing helped. Hira lived another fifteen years, with crushing pain, largely bedridden.'

5

PROSED POETRY

November 1958
132, Bagmari Road
Calcutta

NONI WAS COOKING BHUNI KHICHURI, Baba's favourite. He was home on leave. Waiting for the rice to dry out, she rested her back against the scabrous stairwell. She had begun to feel like resting lately. Like maybe the worst was over. The family was together. And thanks to Baba, no longer on a shoestring. Her hands were fuller than ever, but the older girls were a great help with housework. Hira was ill, yes, but he was here. Besides, in that second room she now had a window that actually opened. Into the inner courtyard, but still. On certain full-moon nights, with the angle just right, it let in liquid silver that pooled into a dent on the cement floor. She waited for this and felt poetry creep back into her heart. Like a long-lost friend.

Baba had arranged music lessons for the girls: vocals for one, sitar for another, tabla for a third. Tabla, a male purview, he had assigned to the family tomboy. He wanted his sisters to have the training that no one got him. This is how he got his musical fix, Noni could tell. And it tormented her. Yes, she felt enormous pride for Baba. Everyone in the neighbourhood reminded her that she should. They called her hajarir Ma—mother of the thousand-er—hinting at his salary. She wished she could freely ride that thermal swell. But she was tangled in stays of anguish and guilt that she could show nobody.

She had focused instead on what was doable. Sunday lunch that her children loved: goat meat in a thin gravy, bright red but not too spicy, with a simple white pulao of rice and ghee. For their birthdays, a quiet payesh of milk and rice, not too sweet and not too thick. The food even attracted her children's friends. Soon her kitchen prowess was a neighbourhood fact. They began to call her Draupadi, for making magical meals from virtually nothing. Then there were the cultural events she goaded her children into—all those music lessons needed expression. The venue was their building's covered porch facing the street. The occasion could be the Bengali New Year or Tagore's birthday or Bijoya Dashomi at the end of Durga Pujo. She helped put up curtains to create a dais for her children and their friends to perform. They sang and danced and play-acted. Sometimes she joined them, reading poetry, lately her own. Her family, her talented and beautiful children, had become the neighbourhood paragon.

And there were Baba's home leaves. He came loaded with gifts. Some were strange objects from faraway places. A snack from Japan that the sisters secretly agreed tasted terrible but would never admit to Baba. A package of Korean edibles so pretty yet unfamiliar that it would remain unopened for fifty years. But also the family's first radio, a handsome Grundig set, all polished wood and brass, its rich timbre a source of delight and further cachet with neighbours. And one time, from Takoradi in Ghana, an African talking parrot: wildly talented and deceptively dull grey except for a vivid red tail. Baba's arrival brought a festive jolt not just to the family but the entire street. For his younger siblings, though, it came laced with dread. Because he quizzed them on their lessons, on whether they had followed the instructions in his letters. And with him home Noni went into a cooking frenzy, every meal made special.

But this time, she seemed slower and somehow muted, Baba noticed. Was she all right? A week before he was scheduled to sail out again, Noni pulled Baba aside: 'Can you take me to the hospital?' she asked, as if in passing.

'Why, what's wrong, Ma?' Baba was filled with foreboding. No one had ever seen Noni unwell despite her brutal workload. But now she was getting on in years. 'Are you feeling ill?'

'No, I feel fine,' she said, averting his gaze, 'you all are about to have a sibling.'

Baba was stunned. Another pregnancy? So that's why she had seemed slow. Her shape never changed much. Besides, he'd been gone and wasn't paying close attention to it. The news left him whiplashed, a hard swing from worry to indignation. Too furious to speak, he saved his words for later.

༄

'It is time you gave up meat and fish.'

That is what Baba told Noni when bringing her back from the hospital with her eleventh child. It was the closest he could come to what he really wanted to say. Birth control didn't seem an option, perhaps due to taboo, or lack of access, or both. His words, though, were rather effective. Insidious, like a paper cut, there is much to unpack in them. One, that fish and meat aroused lust. Two, that Hira, being bed-bound, could not be the initiator. Whether or not these suggestions were well-founded, the reproach hit home. Noni gave up meat, but not fish. And this was her final pregnancy. A long innings for a woman who, as a fresh bride, had endured taunts of infertility.

༄

Shishu's ghost fell into a moody silence for a while, like he was wrestling with himself. He finally said: 'You couldn't possibly have heard this story growing up.'

'You're right,' I nodded, 'Baba only spoke of it in his final months. It slipped out, I think, his defences stripped by illness. He repeatedly relived the sting of that exchange from nearly sixty years before. What was she thinking, he would murmur, gazing mid-distance.'

'Aha re,' the ghost grimaced, 'he had walked with that pebble stuck in his sole for all that time!' Then he drew his lanky frame up and squared his shoulders. 'You could take Baba's side on this. He'd been handed the entire weight of his every-growing family. His rebuke was fair and it must've hurt him terribly to do it. But you have to understand: she was a full-blooded woman, my Noni-di. A Barisal woman brimming with tyaz. That's what we call it in our

Bangal dialect. Vitality, marrow, sap—none of these do it justice. Her tyaz,' his voice swelled, 'was the key ingredient that kept your family alive. And it also did other things. I for one wouldn't cherry-pick its effects,' he finished, flush with emotion.

'What was going on in your life at this time?' I asked, after he seemed calmer. 'I had found my footing just the year before,' he said, glad for the reprieve, 'I was single, you see, but with family still across the border. And a useless vagabond when it came to such matters. It was my brother who arranged to move them: his wife and children, and our mother and sister. By the time they came it was hard to find room in the colonies close to the city. They settled in Haat-thuba, a village 50 kilometres north-east of Calcutta, near the Bongaon border, where those fleeing Barisal had gathered. Bongaon, Thakurnagar, Haat-thuba, Habra—this belt is still thick with Barisal's low-caste refugee colonies, the domain of uprooted Namasudras and Matuas. Jogen-da lived in Bongaon, too, amidst his people. Anyway, now that my family had come over, I needed a job to help my brother. Being a party whole-timer simply wouldn't do. But I hadn't even finished school, remember, much less college. Jail had been my only school. Employment was tough, therefore, even with the party's help. After years of struggle, I got lucky in 1957. A vocational school had come up in Haat-thuba and it was residential. I became its hostel warden. Room-and-board was free, and the small salary I'd give to my brother. At forty-three, this was my first real job and I did it for a dozen years.'

∽

November 1958
Haat-thuba Vocational School
Hostel Warden's Room

It was night and Shishu was at his desk. The hurricane lantern cast a curdled glow on his notebook. The soot on its glass was more smeared than cleaned. Seeing this drew Bina-di's shrill voice into Shishu's head and made him chuckle. Bina-di: the crusty old lady in charge of keeping the hostel's lanterns in working order. Her mundane banter, her daily gripes, her excuses about scissors too dull to trim wicks. He had even written a poem satirizing her a couple of months ago. The thought of that poem, though, made him sad. Thirty years ago, he had used his wit on vicious parodies of life in British colonial jails. Now he used it to tease a defenceless elderly underling. How far his poetic vision had atrophied! But he mustn't be too hard on himself, he thought. He had only been able to reach for his poetry journal recently, after years of not having had the time. Building back a life post-Partition had cost him a decade. He didn't like his current poems but they kept him alive. He was going to use poetry to survive. Just as he had done in Cellular Jail.

Thinking of Cellular made him look around. Was this room that different from his cell there? It was similarly narrow, with a window at one end and a door at the other. The desk was one difference. And the door not being locked from the outside, of course. But the outside is nothing without the resources to enjoy it. Freedom had taught him this. But, no, he chided himself again, he was being unduly negative. He liked the job and his colleagues. He liked being surrounded by the young boarders. He enjoyed writing little inspirational lines for them at the end of each session. They will build this country, they need all the help they can get. And he? He would plug away at poetry, find his way back in. Long poems tired him now. He found that he could only bare himself in spare haiku-like bits. Like the one he had just written tonight:

Search
23 November 1958

Keeping my
Tiny self hidden
I have wanted
The wide world.

This one he quite liked. But good or not, he would keep at it. The hunt for words had kept him afloat before, it would again.

6
THE KNOB

Noni's Eleven
Black & white photograph
March 1963

Group photograph with a woman, fifty-two, seated at the centre surrounded by her seven daughters and four sons, ages thirty-two through four. Her husband, fifty-nine, sits next to her.

THE FAMILY GLOWS. THE CHILDREN are strikingly handsome. They attend, or have been to, good schools and colleges. Some play musical instruments, one sings, another is an athlete. Baba, dapper in white, is a newlywed. At the centre of the frame is Noni, Hira's gaunt and withdrawn figure beside her serving to further underscore her radiance. Owning her spot, she meets your gaze with a strength that is quiet and formidable. A half-smile plays on her lips, as if to say: I think we made it.

There is no pictorial record of the family's crossing into India, of Noni waiting at Goalando ferry terminal with her exhausted children. But a plethora of similar families were photographed. The world had gawked at the millions on the move. Disaster is always news, recovery rarely so. The picture here was taken exactly fifteen years later. The family, by then, was thriving. Noni and Baba, like many of their kind, had marshalled it through the storm into the harbour of middle class. The price they had paid for this passage remained off the books.

∽

This—my family's first and only group photo—appears in a Czech ethnographic memoir published in 1963 at Prague. The author,

Milada Ganguli, a Czech woman married to a Bengali, had lived in Calcutta for over twenty years by then. The book is an insider-outsider view of Bengali life, in text and photographs by her. Milada, a polymath and an ace photographer, also happened to be Noni's friend. But how did that come about?

By 1960, Baba had stopped sailing and found a well-paying shore job with a British company. He had moved the family from Bagmari to a rental in Calcutta's northern exurbs: the ground floor of a modest house, still cramped but a significant upgrade. Three rooms, plenty of light and air through large windows with classic wooden shutters. Across an inner courtyard their own kitchen, and a toilet shared with only one other family. Beyond the front gate, ponds, and open space; the river only a short walk away. This was Baranagar, a former playground of the colonial rich, dotted with stately vacation homes within generous grounds. In one of these homes, Abanindranath Tagore—India's pre-eminent artistic genius—had spent his final decade, living with the family of his grandson, Mohonlal Ganguli. Milada, married to Mohonlal, was raising two children in this home, a short walk from Noni's. Their daughters were classmates in school and inseparable teenagers. It is through them that Noni and Milada had met.

The photograph is captioned in the book thus: 'Mrs. Madhabi Sen with her husband and children'. Milada did not use Noni's real name, presumably to protect her friend's privacy.

What was the dynamic of this friendship? Noni had little free time. The family remembers Milada coming by at least once a week. She was fluent in Bangla and the two women chatted away in the kitchen as Noni worked. Milada had a keen appetite for all things Bengali and Noni was a natural fount, particularly in the realm of cuisine. Milada watched Noni deploy a panoply of techniques and her camera clicked away. Prepping vegetables, for example. Even the innocuous bottlegourd could elicit art: only triangles in certain dishes, only two-inch fingers in others. There were tricks to avoid stained fingers when handling sap-producing vegetables, like young jackfruit or plantain. And to rid the pesky fibres when slicing the core of a banana stem. Then there was all manner of shaak greens—notey, dhneki, bathua, hinchey—each needing different treatment. That they were crammed with nutrients was traditional Bangal knowledge that Noni had. These greens, lowly weeds usually ignored by West Bengalis, had now begun flooding the markets as Bangal refugees, desperate for a living, harvested them from the surrounding lands and sold them on the city streets.

That was just vegetables. Prepping fish—and more so, shellfish—had its own theatre that Milada eagerly documented. Not to mention the actual cooking, in which Noni's talent was legion, even with the most pedestrian ingredients. For instance, when she fried finely julienned potatoes to a crisp, they remained white; her fried pointed-gourds remained green. Any blackening would be shameful. Also, marked by her hardship days, Noni discarded nothing. She created magic with every part of the banana and the taro plants, with jackfruit pits, spinach ends, and vegetable peels. The effects were there for all to see: her children were in the pink of health. Milada took great interest in them, in their activities. She admired Noni's raising of such a magnificent brood.

What is clear is that Milada was drawn to Noni. And that Noni's girls visited Milada's home quite often. But no one remembers Noni ever doing so. Did the class barrier get in the way? Was Noni able to open up on her own terms? Did she share her poetry life with Milada, or did she recoil because of her Tagore connection? How close were they, really? We'll never know.

The family did not get a copy of Milada's book. Naturally so, as they didn't read Czech. But they didn't see their published photograph either, until it was shown to me by Milada's daughter exactly fifty years later, in 2013. She spoke fondly of my family and remembered being dazzled by them in her youth—a child raised under the wing of Abanindranath Tagore, in a mansion, surrounded by the city's artistic elite, with summers in Czechoslovakia.

'That caption: with her husband and children,' Shishu's ghost zeroed in. 'Notice how she puts it, the primacy she gives Noni-di. She had identified the system's sun!'

'I think you're reading too much into it,' I pushed back. 'This is a European, an educator with a master's degree from London. And a member of the Tagore clan. Her feminist angle is natural. Besides, Noni was her friend.'

'But why?' he gave a knowing chortle, 'why was one so exalted attracted to a refugee barely on firm ground? Because Noni-di had something special to offer. Yes?'

'Clearly Milada was special, too, in being open. But you're right,' I conceded, 'this wasn't the first time Noni got noticed by the cultural elite. Back in her Bagmari days, when things were downright dire, a famous writer who lived nearby had become friends with her. And in the late sixties, when the family moved to Behala in the south, a famous singer in the neighbourhood sought her out as a friend. All this clearly says something about Noni, which, I will admit, I didn't notice until seeing this photo. Her gaze in it was key, which Milada had captured. It made me wonder who Noni had been, behind the peripheral presence that had sweetened my childhood.'

Shishu's ghost, without a word, nodded vigorously and broke into a radiant grin.

7

CURDLED

January 1965
Haat-thuba
West Bengal

THE CPI HAD CLEAVED IN two a couple months before and its wake continued to buffet Shishu. An actual split? The party was no longer his home but it was still family. He couldn't believe it was now broken, with old-timers leaving in droves. Some joined the new faction, others stepped away entirely, stung by the in-fighting. It left him bereft. Things looked blurry, like in a dust storm. Ambika-da had been gone a couple years now but Shishu grieved that loss afresh. He yearned for a trusted senior to talk to. You've pushed past fifty, he chided himself, but you still need help navigating tight corners. It's like Noni-di had said all those years ago: you'll always be a shishu!

He knew that a showdown had been brewing. Nehru's pro-Soviet stance since the early fifties had tipped a section within the party towards Congress, raising the hackles of the rest. Then came Stalin's death, followed by the fusillade of horror stories that Khrushchev uncorked. The party line still came from Moscow, but Calcutta's die-hard Stalinists privately viewed Khrushchev as a liar, a revisionist upstart who had mauled their socialist utopia. Shishu felt dazed, unsure what to believe. Evidence of Stalin's atrocities mounted. Had everything so far been propaganda and this the truth? Or was it the other way round? By the late fifties, whether repelled by Stalin or by Khrushchev, a rebel faction within the CPI had veered towards China. India's 1962 war with China further inflamed this fissure because the party had not opposed it. The pro-China faction simmered for two years before finally splintering away in November 1964. It called itself CPI(M), the M—for Marxist—pointedly suggesting that the mothership had lost its way. But where did all that leave Shishu?

He decided to reach out to Maity-da, an old comrade and jailmate from his Alipore days. Like him, Maity-da barely made a living. He worked for pennies as a proofreader at *Udayan*, a Soviet journal translated and printed in Calcutta. It had been nearly a year since Shishu last visited him, around the time of the 1964 riots. Maity-da lived in a slum in Gobra, in Calcutta's Park Circus neighbourhood. Shishu walked past cowsheds and shanties, and across a set of unprotected train tracks. This slum, nestled in a graveyard, had been drained of Muslims in an earlier riot. But Park Circus being predominantly Muslim meant they still occupied pockets not far off. On his last visit, Maity-da had pointed out to him a neighbour, a pot-bellied man strolling his baby girl in a bright red pram. 'See him,' Maity-da had breathed, as if struggling to contain acid reflux, 'when Muslim homes and shops nearby were being attacked and looted last week, that man calmly crossed the tracks, walked into such a home and stole that pram.' He paused, his leathery face mottled in anguish. 'Yes, I know that across the border Muslims are slaughtering thousands, and millions are fleeing west yet again. And that this man hurt nobody. But, you know, in some ways this feels worse. This normalized easy hatred, for anybody to tap into. Even that timid man. This is not going back into the scabbard. And this freedom to hate,' he finished almost in a whisper, 'this freedom is what you and I went to jail for, Shishu.'

Nearing Maity-da's home, Shishu mulled over that episode from last year. He was eager to talk to Maity-da, eager for his vulnerable wisdom in these scattershot times. What did he think of the party's split? Which way was he going to go?

The flimsy rattan door was ajar. It creaked as Shishu pushed in. Maity-da was ill in bed, painfully thin. He seemed glad to see Shishu but could barely speak. His neighbours were helping with food, not that anyone in the slum had very much extra. His illness was undiagnosed, there was no money for doctors or medicines. Maity-da was single but had relatives somewhere outside the city.

Where? Shishu felt strapped to an anvil of helplessness. He didn't have much to spare himself. There was nothing he could do except creep away, heartsick. Before leaving he took a good look at Maity-da: the glazed eyes, the sunken cheeks, the half-open mouth caked with dried spittle. Here was proof that you could die of serving the greater common good.

On the evening train back to Haat-thuba, Shishu was overcome by vertigo, a sense of everything falling apart. He had to grit his teeth to steady himself. At his desk that night he thrashed around for a way out, wrestling with words for hours. Eventually with fatigue came calm. And a dogged manifesto:

Rose Garden
23 January 1965

Let my land
Be arid Sahara
I'll keep sowing
A patch of Persian rose.

☙

23 January 1965
Saturday night
The Grand Hotel, Chowringhee
Calcutta

Miss Shefali, the city's top cabaret act, had taken the floor. The spotlight followed her, shadows playing on her fleshy curves as she wriggled to the music, covering ground. A flick of a jewelled arm, a thrust of a shapely leg, a waist minced around a bare navel. She swayed like a hooded snake to the swell of the saxophone. The fringe on her bikini top quivered, her sequinned skirt sparkled, her bare feet were a blur as the drums worked a crescendo. She twirled and laughed, head thrown back, her hip-length hair a satin curtain in the wind. From the murky gloom beyond the pool of light, a hundred gazes were helpless moths to her flame. One of them was Baba's, with Ma's next to him, equally agog.

Shefali danced and Baba watched. Neither had any inkling of how similar they were. Bangal refugees both, survivors and gritty arrivistes in the city. Each an engine hitched to a dependent cohort. Each straining to shed their past and hiding it well meanwhile: loss dressed as urgent can-do. Their kind had infiltrated the city. In business, politics, science, performing arts, restaurants, carpentry, textiles, street vending—every conceivable shelf the metropolis had on offer. In the lower rungs they sniffed each other out to band together. But up the ladder, losing this glue was imperative.

After the show was over, the dance floor was opened to the attending guests. Baba grabbed Ma as the lights dimmed and the band struck up a slow tune. A spinning globe of purple descended from overhead bathing everything in an ethereal light. That magical scene was the highlight for Ma, from a night that had overwhelmed all her senses with firsts. She was at a British company bash at the city's prime party address, with its vast ballroom of mirrors and crystal chandeliers, the soaring vaulted ceiling, the liveried waiters, the unfamiliar foods, the parquet dance floor, the music, the cabaret show. On and on. And now this!

Baba had no face. His white collar and shirtfront floated free in the inkiness into which his dark suit had disappeared. He had no arms. His disembodied cuffs glowed like bleached bones but were attached to no hands. Looking down at herself Ma saw that her black silk sari had melted away, only the gold lamè motifs winked like marooned jewels. This was disorienting for a minute, then enormously fun. The purple light! It had drained all but the pale tones from the room. And emboldened a young brown couple shy about public intimacy. They giggled and clung to each other. Neither knew how to dance but it mattered not at all.

His employer encouraged wives at such parties but Baba had other reasons to bring Ma out. They'd had a bruising fight a couple months before. So much so that she'd left for her parents' with their newborn daughter. Now that she had returned Baba wanted to make it up to her. He knew things had been hard for Ma. He had moved the family yet again, an incremental improvement—this rental was upstairs, with balconies—but still not spacious enough to fit everyone. He and Ma slept with their baby in the living room. Besides, Noni was difficult, Baba knew. Even for Ma, who was perennially willing to compromise. So he wanted to take her out for a night on the town. They dressed to the nines: she in her best silk, he in his nattiest suit. As the taxi sped away from their drab lane in the city's northern fringe and towards Calcutta's fanciest nightclub, Baba felt buoyant.

This changed at a traffic light, twenty minutes in. They had stopped next to the Esplanade Mansions—a vision of cupolas, balustrades, louvered windows—home to the city's most exclusive residences. Baba had time to scan its towering facade, uplit and stately. He had time to reach in and fondle a hard crystal of resentment. His company had offered him a flat here, but only for his nuclear family. So he'd had to turn them down. If he lived here the Grand Hotel would be a short walk. Would he ever live the life he strove for? Or was he forever tethered? The light turned green and his mood lifted. He looked over at his gorgeous wife, gazing out the cab window at the night city. He savoured the rustle of her sari, the clink of her bangles. He felt he had broken free, at least for tonight.

∽

Baba by now is erasing entire chapters of himself. That is how he is coping with his double life, the clashing worlds brought on by a refugee's speedy rise up the corporate ladder. But he doesn't know this. He hasn't had the time to be mindful, to register the losses. For instance, in November 1964, his company had sent him to marshal a vessel back from Assam to Calcutta—a five-day sail on the waters of East Pakistan, through its entire length. En route he had stopped for supplies at Jhalokathi, his first time back at his ancestral land since Partition. Ma happened to be at her parents' then, so Baba wrote to her about this voyage, luckily, creating a record. His letter is a vibrant read, chock-full of granular details of what he sees. But in their interstices are chilling absences. No memories jogged, no yearning, no curiosity. As if he felt nothing at all and didn't even notice that he didn't. As if he was visiting a brand-new land, not the home he had fled. Not the land where fresh massacres only months before had caused yet another exodus.

He did pick up two hefty Kirtankhola ilish at Jhalokathi, however. Stashed in his galley freezer, the fish made it to Calcutta for the family to enjoy with great fanfare. Noni pulled out all the stops: some pieces she fried, others she steamed with mustard paste, still others she stewed with pumpkin Barisal style, and the rest she made into her famed ilish pulao. She even invited her sister to join in the feast, who, overcome with emotion, refused to wash her hands after eating, wanting her fleeting contact with Barisal to linger. In his letter, Baba dismisses his aunt's effusion as mindless excess. 'It is interesting,' he observes with the detachment of an anthropologist, 'how sentimental some people can get over their homeland.'

Only sixteen years in, he seems entirely assimilated. Or at least that is the pose, one in which he will raise his children—bereft of his Bangal dialect, with not a whiff of Barisal. We will never hear the Borishailya tongue at home, not even between him and Noni. We won't hear the songs. There will be no nostalgia for a lost homeland. No longing for the people, the rivers, the trees left behind.

Baba must have meant well, but he didn't know. You can unlearn your own language to escape the rudeness of memory. But events still pile up, with or without an identity to congeal around. Once dislocation takes root, once there is that first shadow of doubt, it cannot be willed away. And it seeps across generations, like blood.

∽

In the wee hours, the young couple leaves the glittering party and heads back to their dreary home, drenched in the night's magic. Their baby is sleeping with Noni tonight, so their bed in the living room is a little less cramped. We'll leave them as they sink into each other. This may have been the night they made me.

∽

'I see what you're doing,' the ghost looked pensive, 'you're trying to read your rings, as in a tree. That's hard to do without cutting it down, you know. Even drilling for a sample core can hurt.' He fell into a moody silence, before going on.

Ghost Shishu on 1965

It was a bruising time for me. The party's split was dominant, yes, but broadly there was something much bigger afoot. See, this is when the curdled nature of Bangal life starts to become clear. The earlier waves are in various stages of settlement. And a fresh tide has just slammed in, after the latest round of mayhem in East Pakistan.

I'm glad to see your Baba doing well. Many employable early arrivals like him had by now reached the upper echelons. The rootless have little ballast, you know, they can rise fast! And this was true across classes. In fact, I would argue that manual-labouring Bangals settled faster in many cases than their pen-pushing counterparts. They were more nimble, less hindered by middle-class hesitations. Many started out hawking fruit on sidewalks, or sanding furniture in grimy workshops, and soon had a little shopfront and shack in one of the colonies, which by now were in the hundreds. Not all, of course, some took the lumpen route and became political ammunition. But either way, being settled also meant seeing oneself apart from the next wave of the unwashed. This is an old story. Immigrants everywhere do this, as they look up and away in the new country. If you've risen to comfort you might feel compassion. But seeing yourself in that heap of bones on the station platform? That's hard. Because erasing that memory was crucial to your survival. In '64–'65, those heaps were rising once more at Sealdah and on the city streets. And this time, among those sidestepping them were other Bangals, who had shed their refugee skin by now and were on firm ground.

The new arrivals were overwhelmingly low-caste Hindu. The killings this time had the explicit tenor of a state-supported genocide. It seemed as if the goal was to kill enough so that the rest would be terrorized into abandoning property. Khulna, for example, East

Pakistan's only Hindu-majority district, turned Muslim-majority overnight, drained of its Namasudra Dalits—the same community that had bled heavily in Barisal in 1950. They surged west across the border and sought refuge in the Bongaon belt, cramming into Namasudra colonies there. As the existing ones were overrun, new colonies sprung up. I was right there, in Haat-thuba, with a ringside view. And I watched history repeat itself. This wave, stranded like the one in 1950, with their backs to the wall, got organized and built ground where there was none. And as before, political parties, including mine, swooped in to capitalize on this nascent vote bank. The pattern would repeat with each pulse of arrivals. Bangal refugees and West Bengal's political parties would remain locked in a symbiotic dance.

But the 1965 wave had arrived at a particularly chaotic moment. The Bengal Congress had finally weakened enough for the Left to make a bid for power—buoyed by Bangal muscle, recall. The political flux was compounded by a looming food shortage, which the fresh load of refugees had only worsened. Food riots would soon break out. And the city, including its settled Bangals, would view the new batch as pests.

What followed was half a decade of crippling instability, with no party able to hold on to power. The perfect crucible for revolution, yes? Ah, how I wish!

8

BLOOD FEVER

27 February 1971
Calcutta

THE DOUBLE-DECKER BUS LURCHED, BREAKING Shishu's reverie. He was at a window seat on the upper deck gazing out at the city, seeing yet not seeing. This split vision was the effect of the film he had just watched at the Cine Society on Central Avenue. *Las Hurdes* by Luis Buñuel. It had left him elated and gutted in equal measure, like two incoming waves at an angle crosshatching out. Such abject poverty in the heart of Europe? He had no idea. The land arid and pitiless, like parts of Bankura and Purulia. The people listless and dazed, as during the Bengal Famine, except their misery here was endemic. But so familiar. That's where his elation arose from, the resonance. At the post-screening discussion someone pointed out that this was a hard but staged look at Spain's Extremadura, an anodyne traveller's gaze. That this was Buñuel brutally mimicking contemporary Spanish documentaries on sub-Saharan poverty, while putting a spotlight on Spain's own. All that was fine. But what haunted Shishu was the gaunt donkey, collapsed under its load, being stung to death by hornets. He wasn't sure if that death was a bad thing.

Out the bus window, Calcutta looked to Shishu like that donkey: buckled and under siege. Bengal had been under President's Rule for the past year. The city saw pitched battles daily between various factions. Nearly 200 political murders in the last two months. Military convoys patrolling the streets. Workers on strike. Factories and shops shuttered. The swelling ranks of the jobless poached for muscle. Like that swarm of deadly hornets, it seemed to Shishu. Just then, the bus swerved onto Red Road, and he saw it: a statue of George V mounted on his steed, being pulled away on a flat-bed truck. But the king was backward, facing the oncoming traffic. Was this mere chance? Shishu felt a belly laugh bubble up. It was far too apt! This was standard punishment for villainy in rural Bengal: shave head, pour buttermilk, and mount backward on a donkey leaving the village. The king still had his crown, but anointed with decades of pigeon droppings. Placing him backward was a cheeky masterstroke. Buñuel would've approved! Others had noticed too and soon the bus roared with guffaws. Shishu's mood shifted. He remembered his first look at Calcutta over forty years ago, the empire's second city, through the barred window of a prison van, hurtling towards death row. How far-fetched it had seemed then that one day this city would be stripped of the British. And look at this absurd sight now!

There was absurdity, too, Shishu thought, in the reason for dismantling these fossils over twenty years after the fact. To protect them from Naxals, who had begun hacking off their heads and body parts. Not just of colonial statuary—those of Vidyasagar, Rabindranath, Rammohan, all condemned as bourgeois icons, had received similar attention. And not just statues either, they were cutting down living icons too. Or anyone they deemed an enemy of the people. For instance, Hemanta Basu's gruesome murder just last week. Just thinking about it got Shishu's blood up. Was it far-fetched to think that this acute chaos, this too would pass?

Ghost Shishu Interrupts

Wait, wait! That was such a rat-a-tat-tat year. So much happening at once. Let me set it up better before we get to Hemanta-da's murder.

My life had become a bit easier by now. I had found a government job two years before at the State Bank of India, as a teller at the Barasat branch. Mindless work, heavy in spurts, but with blocks of dead time at my desk that I could fill reading or writing. The pay was predictable, with a pension assured. I had the weekends off and usually went into the city. For instance, 27 February 1971 was a Saturday and I was in town with several errands. I'd been to the optician's at Lalbajar to pick up my prescription glasses. I hit the party office at Alimuddin Street. Yes, I had joined the CPI(M) by then. There I read the English journals I couldn't afford. The *Economic and Political Weekly*, for instance, was a favourite. I especially loved an acerbic column it carried, called Calcutta Diary. I then had a bite to eat at the Central Avenue Coffee House and went to the Cine Society, which was marking Buñuel turning seventy-one. Membership was practically free with my party card. I've seen so many magnificent films there, from all over the world!

Why am I telling you this? Because this is the peak of Naxal violence and counter killings. CPI(M) has splintered further in 1969. The new faction, fondly called Naxals and formally the CPI(ML)—L for Lenin, but their defining slogan is 'China's Chairman is our Chairman'—is amidst staging a militant insurgency. The Bengal government is in tatters. The former CPI has curdled into an alphabet soup of factions, all mutually hostile. Amidst a carpet sprout of Left parties, CPI(M) has shot up. Assembly elections are due in a week. The streets are alive with violent clashes, whether between political factions or gangsters is sometimes hard to tell. All of this is in West Bengal. What about in the east? 27 February is only days before Mujibur Rahman's historic speech at Dhaka, asserting his people's will to wrench off Pakistan's east wing. And weeks from the virulent genocide that Pakistan will unleash in response, causing yet another mass exodus westward. Starting mid-year, on this side of the border, India will ratchet up its brutal crackdown of Naxals. Both Bengals will be awash in blood.

That entire cauldron of horror is just about to tip over. Yet, even as it disgorged throughout that year—millions of Bangals dragged their broken bodies west on Jessore Road; tent cities filled up; a shambolic state government elected in April collapsed in June to President's Rule yet again; the streets saw at least three types of corpses: Naxals, their victims, and Bangal refugees; then war loomed—through all of this, I worked at the bank and spent Saturdays in the city. All of that was happening at once in the Calcutta of '71. Films and theatre, songs and laughter, political upheaval and a refugee surge, amidst a historic carnage. Life went on. Just like in the Calcutta of '43 and of '50. The carnage looked historic only in hindsight. You know, this dyslexia, this inability to read history unfolding outside our window, I feel it is both a feature and a bug. It is how we survive and why we repeat mistakes.

∽

'Here's what I am curious about,' Shishu's ghost said, 'you were a child in 1971, what did you see?'

'I only have the happy memories of a six-year-old,' I confessed, 'Baba had just moved the family to a rental in New Alipore, one of Calcutta's toniest neighbourhoods. The same home where you visited Noni twenty years later. There were still nine of us in three rooms, but it always felt spacious. With vast balconies, lots of light and air, across from a city park. My school was a short walk, my friends lived nearby. I remember this was the year I got my first book. Not a picture book, but one with text. I felt very grown-up. And you know how children pick up the slightest ripple of anxiety or excitement in the adults around them? I recall none.'

'Not even in December, during the war?'

'Not even then. The war lasted only two weeks and I do remember the blackouts. Because it was fun! Windowpanes had to be taped over with black paper that we kids cut up. Turning out the lights felt like a game. I recall no discussions at the dinner table, nothing especially animated anyway. And my family never hid emotions well. Had they felt threatened or moved by the killings elsewhere in the city, or across the border, it would show. I don't believe 1971 had touched us at all. But I do have this one image from the war. The equivalent of a UFO sighting. It evoked no fear, only wonder.'

'Oh?'

'It was a December night and the curfew was on. The city battened down, all lights out, everybody indoors. But Noni had stepped out on the balcony and I had followed her. The silent blackness felt unfamiliar, as if chilled to a thick tar. I remember my snot-green cardigan and the cold weaselling in. Then I heard a deafening screech and looked up. Pointed shapes with streaks of light were tearing up the night sky, as if sawing through granite. I remember the flush of seeing something new, something big and powerful, outside the realm of imagination. I had no idea those were air force jets. Noni did. She had seen bombers scream over Tarpasha thirty years before and knew what they could do. But she said nothing about that. All she did was murmur, as if to herself: "Those are heading east, towards our desh. Bangla Desh".'

'Ah, Noni-di,' the ghost shook his head, 'always so succinct! Yes, two words. That's what we've always called undivided Bengal: Bangla Desh. The land of Bengalis. And now, in 1971, those two words will coalesce into Bangladesh—a new country. The land of some Bengalis but not others. Born in a hellish carnage, its bloody afterbirth ejected west in a violent convulsion. Low-caste Hindus, yet again. By now you see the Bangal rhythm, yes? Get massacred, flee west, huddle in camps, become political fodder, assimilate while being treated like unfamiliar pests, even by settled Bangals. Each wave successively more destitute. Because the poorer you are, the harder it is to pry you off the land.' He looked away, as if wishing he hadn't said so much.

'I've read your poem from 30 March 1971, five days after the genocide began across East Pakistan. You called it "Joy Bangla!"—the war cry of the Mukti Bahini fighters. You praise and exhort them, but you also say: *did they love my golden land even more than me?* Anguished words!'

'Look, I was happy for them, all right?' He sounded evasive. 'And I was tired. I was pushing sixty,' he clammed up. 'But how did we even get here when talking about Hemanta Basu's murder? There, that's 1971 for you! Pull one thread and the whole cloth bunches up. Such a crosshatched time,' he let out a sigh, 'a time of lunacy. For a taste of which, let's get back to Hemanta-da. An old political warhorse. A freedom fighter and a close associate of Subhas Bose, a lifelong leftist. Never married.'

'So then, a lot like you?'

'Much bigger. I never entered electoral politics and he was the chairman of a major Left party, had been a minister in two coalition-Left governments by then, and was running in this election from a North Calcutta seat. But above all that, he was a kind man, who lived alone in a hole-in-the-wall, devoted to public service. I can still see his reedy frame, his soda-bottle glasses. His drooping moustache and mild, avuncular manner. On 20 February, he was attacked in broad daylight near his home and butchered. At seventy-six.'

∽

27 February 1971
Calcutta

In a sense it was the perfect murder. A political Rorschach test. No party claimed responsibility. Who you blamed only revealed who you were, but shed no light on the actual crime. The corridors of power were abuzz with finger-pointing and political points being scored. Outside, the general public seethed. Because an old man, frail and defenceless, had been brutally murdered. The wave of revulsion touched even the politically averse: the retiree, the stay-at-home mother, the workaday householder. Shishu saw them now from his bus window, marching in a silent procession down Harish Mukherjee Road. No party placards or paraphernalia. Ordinary people, many women and elderly. They were new to this, he could tell. But their handwritten signs, albeit inexperienced scrawls, smouldered with disgust. This dignified protest ruptured something in Shishu. He realized he was fuming. He needed to do something. But what? He got off at the next stop. He would walk with them. Waiting for the procession to catch up, he thought of a similar protest only six weeks before. After another gruesome murder in the city. Gopal Sen, the vice chancellor of Jadavpur University. Another upright and valued senior, an engineer and lifelong educator, who worked with his hands and believed in nation-building. Killed on campus on his final day before retirement. Why? Because he had disagreed that exams were a bourgeois practice that needed to be cancelled.

Shishu walked and felt bilious words roil up within him. Walking in shared silence with strangers helped. The raging fire quieted down to fervent coals. He hadn't felt this livid in a long time. Is this the revolution he and his comrades had dreamed of all those years in jail? Is this how Petrograd had felt from the inside in October 1917? Had his entire life been a gigantic lie? Back home at Haat-thuba that night, he didn't reach for his poetry journal. He couldn't. He let the heat simmer through Sunday. The poem came to him the day after, while at work.

Memorial
1 March 1971
State Bank of India
Barasat, West Bengal

What should I call
This idiot wind
That grinds out
Grotesque soul rubble?
No words size up.

But this I know:
Lives poured for others
Live on, pooled amidst them.
And cowards, who in mindless rage
Brandish the blood of heroes,
Land in history's
Putrid trash.

∽

'Who was putrid trash,' I probed, 'the Naxals?'

'I had felt like an unvented pressure cooker when writing that. But yes, the perpetrators of those senseless murders were despicable,' the ghost nodded, his mouth set in a grim line. 'And who were they? In Gopal Sen's case, I'd say it was pretty clear it was the Naxals. For Hemanta-da, the answer got buried in the fog of elections. Congress and CPI milked the public outrage to the hilt, successfully pinning the blame on CPI(M), then on track for absolute majority, which hurt us at the polls and we fell short. But Hemanta-da had been killed in Shyampukur, a North Calcutta neighbourhood that was a Naxal redoubt, out-of-bounds to CPI(M) for months. So, did the Naxals kill him? Or was it hired goons? And who benefited? The case went cold post-election. No one was ever charged. We never learned who killed the benign old man, or why. But it set a powerful precedent. From here on out, murders became a fixture in Bengal's electoral landscape.'

'And this was the Naxal's fault?'

'In large measure, yes. They managed to paint the time with a particular blood lust. Their fervid embrace of khatom—their annihilation motto—randomly tagging people as class enemies and savagely taking them out. That was beyond the pale. By the time their leaders realized this, it was too late. They had given the state plenty of reasons to pulverize them.'

'Isn't this a case of the old applying double standards to the new? Didn't you too want to annihilate? You killed a cop, didn't you?'

'And you think that is the same thing?' he looked stung and then held me in a steely gaze, 'I had been in Tebhaga, too, don't forget, where we fought for agrarian reform and against jotedar tyranny. The same fight that the Naxals built on twenty-five years later.' He paused and took a deep breath, 'Let me tell you a story. At this time, I lived with my brother's family in Haat-thuba. My nephew Shanto was then nine. I had given him a little notebook at the beginning of the year because he had shown interest in poetry and I wanted him to have a place to play with words. Our colony had Naxals, some active, others less so. Colony life is tight-knit and these Naxal youth would often stop by for a chat with me, sometimes leaving behind a copy of *Deshabrati*, their mouthpiece journal. One day mid-year, when Shanto was out playing, I saw his notebook lying around and flipped through it, curious to see what he had written so far. There were no poems, not even stray words, but row upon row of what looked like scores. I initially couldn't tell what I was looking at. Then

I noticed each row had a place and a date. Gopiballabhpur, April 1971. Debra, May 1971. That's when I knew: Shanto was keeping track of the Naxal khatom score, of class enemies eliminated. Where, when, how many. Where did he find these numbers? *Deshabrati* published them in each issue with much fanfare and urged for more. And why was Shanto keeping track? He must've listened in when these passionate young men and women talked, and likely looked up to them. Children mimic adults they admire. Scorekeeping must be grown-up work if *Deshabrati* was doing it. Maybe there was someone Shanto wanted to impress.'

'This does sound bad,' I had to agree, 'a nine-year-old obsessed with kill scores.'

'The point is, by then the Naxals themselves couldn't see past kill scores. Look,' he sighed, 'I'm not giving you a Naxal tutorial, you'll find reams in libraries. I understood what moved them, I had been there myself. I can still see their bright faces. Ah, as if they had invented fire! As if this was the first time students had joined peasants in revolution. What about the Narodniks in czarist Russia? How did that end? That was in the 1870s, the first volume of *Das Kapital* just out, the idea of class struggle still quite new. If that's too far in time and place, how about closer, in the 1940s and 50s, in Tebhaga, Telangana, Hajong? Yes, others had made fire before them, but they didn't want to read into those burns. They built a fresh inferno. And it turned a generation's best into moth smoke.'

9
REHAB ISLE

Building Material-1
Kitchen utensil, brass
1927

> A shallow kawrai—Indian wok—of solid brass, hand-beaten and 18 inches at the widest. A name in Bangla script is embossed on the outside rim.

THIS HAD BEEN PART OF Noni's wedding trousseau; the embossed name is hers. Growing up, I saw this kawrai come out on special occasions, like birthdays, when Noni made her legendary payesh in it. As she cooked down the sweetened milk and rice, the bubbles sang against the metal and filled the house with a caramel perfume. She would leave it in a shadowy corner to cool, where the payesh grew a creamy skin too tempting to not take a swipe of. We kids flocked to her as she poured it into a serving bowl later. For the payesh, yes, but also to lick the kawrai clean, scraping every last browned bit off its sleek golden belly with our fingers.

Building Material-2
Toy, copper and brass
1935

> A pichkiri—squirt gun—made of a smooth copper tube, a foot long and 2 inches in diameter, fitted with a brass piston ending in a wooden handle. Two screw-on brass heads provide choice of flow: a single jet or a shower. A name in Bangla script is embossed on the tube.

The name is Baba's, the pichkiri was a gift to him from Noni's father when he was four. Noni would bring it out for us kids every Holi, the copper scrubbed with old tamarind until shiny and pink. It didn't work very well, the piston had grown slack. We preferred our cheap plastic guns for their fiercer squirt. But Noni was eager for us to play with this pichkiri. We would load it and hound each other for close-range shots. She never joined us in our raucous water fights. But I remember her beaming as she looked on, a special light playing in her eyes. And I remember not understanding it. Why was she so thrilled when she wasn't even playing?

∽

8 March 1974
New Alipore
Calcutta

It was Holi. Noni stood at the threshold of an open terrace, watching her grandkids play with their friends. A dozen children pummelled each other with coloured water. They were past smearing faces with coloured abeer powder, making their eyes sting and mouths gritty. Past the surgical strikes with metallic paint that left them looking like unfinished surrealist canvases. Now, with the sun high and warm, the spring breeze sweet, it was time to get wet. Time for the squirt guns. They chased each other, squealing in delight, the attacker no less thrilled than the attacked. An older child lost patience with the squirting; the ammunition delivery felt far too piecemeal. Picking up the bucket of coloured water—the loading station for the guns—he dumped it on a surprised comrade. After an initial howl of protest, they all dissolved in helpless giggles. The bucket dunk had upped the ante. Nothing less would do now. No time to mix in colours, water alone was enough. The war wore on and wouldn't stop until lunchtime, when they would swarm indoors, ravenous.

Noni took in the scene, filled with a surge of mixed emotions. This day was always bittersweet for her. A time to look back and take stock. She had lost Hira two years before. A loss that had also brought relief, she recognized. He had suffered too much for too long. And is witnessing that not suffering? How many ages ago had she last seen his elegant artistic self? She strained to remember. That is who she wanted to keep. Not his wasting body and atrophied mind, doused in the stench of disinfectants. Had she been a good wife, Noni wondered, a good mother? Eight of her eleven children were now married. Even Blue, who she had been especially worried about. A loving and hard-headed woman had found Blue and settled him. Noni's three youngest children were still teenagers. But they were in Baba's and Ma's care, leaving her free to enjoy her brood of grandchildren, already a dozen strong and growing. Look at them play with Baba's pichkiri! Her heart swelled thinking of that defining March morning, exactly twenty-six years ago today. As her boat pushed off the Tarpasha dock, she had made herself a silent promise. That she would rebuild. Not just the sustenance, but also the joy. Tucked into one of her amorphous bundles in the boat's hold, along with her wedding kawrai, was this copper pichkiri. Baba would have children one day, she had thought, and they would play with it. Noni broke into a radiant smile at the memory. The pichkiri had travelled on the boat, the steamer, the train, the truck. Then over the decades from one rental home to the next. And look at it now, in use!

 Noni felt light. The albatross around her neck had finally taken flight. Maybe her accounts had more pluses than minuses. And plenty of reasons to be happy. But that feeling of lightness was dislocating. It brought news of a chilling void. She had grown old, with so many paths untrodden. Was fulfilling her potential one of them? Had she done all she could with the hand she was dealt? This bright March morning filled with children's laughter—was this it, the finish line tape of her marathon?

∽

26 January 1974
Cellular Jail, Port Blair
Andaman Islands

It all seemed a bit absurd. Shishu felt like an inept actor in a play. Here he was, back at Cellular Jail. Sitting in the central courtyard, amidst a ceremony. It was Republic Day, the flag had been raised earlier and the national anthem sung full-throated. Now, on a dais decked with flowers and tricolour frills, a pot-bellied politician was holding forth. On sacrifices made for freedom. His sacrifices, Shishu mused, among that of others. Oh, so many others. Ambika-da, Sushil-da, Niranjan-da, Doityo—so many comrades, all long gone. Shishu saw their faces, heard their irreverent laughter. Just as he saw that low-slung workshop, right there next to the dais, where he'd spent years in the oil mill chain gang. The past here felt so much thicker, the ceremony around him a mere skin against a torrent of stories, straining to rush in. The horrors, the triumphs, the camaraderie, the immersive awakening. Cellular had been a universe of all things acute, the place that had shaped him and one he had helped shut down—the hated Bastille in the Bay. And now, the state was going to build a national memorial here. Could they? Capture that collective roar, equal part groan and yawp?

Don't be ungracious, Shishu shushed himself. The state is trying to honour you, the former political inmates at Cellular. Decades late and many gone, ground out by penury, but still. They had rounded up a few dozen of the hundreds who had left these shores alive. No, rounded up is harsh—invited. And brought them over to Cellular for the ground-breaking of the memorial, on Republic Day, with all the attendant theatre. They had even chartered a ship for their honorees. Shishu had his own cabin! What a difference from his last voyage in 1932, locked in the hold of the S. S. *Maharaja*, sliding about in collective vomit. As the ship pulled into Aberdeen jetty yesterday, he had been out on the deck. So much had changed, but he recognized Mount Harriet, still a shaggy bear asleep. Looking up at the grim ramparts of Cellular Jail, he felt a twinge for his eighteen-year-old self, similarly craning his neck upon arrival. Something like envy. That kid didn't know what a romp he was in for. His life was a parcel still in the mail.

A titter of applause broke Shishu's reverie. The politician had finished speaking. It was time now for a lavish lunch. The rest of the day was a blur. First, a tour of the grounds. Shishu had heard that four of Cellular's seven wings had been demolished: two during the Japanese occupation during World War II and two more when building a hospital in the sixties. But it was still a shock, a good shock, to find his wing gone. Good riddance!

The honorees were then led to the dais to be feted with copper plaques and flowers. All were senior to Shishu and most, like him, Bangal refugees. Shishu scanned the faces, weathered and solemn, spectacled eyes vast and liquid, tinged with the memory of a fight now sacred. But had that fight been even more fierce than the one to survive in free India? What homes would they return to from this ceremony? To what slum or colony or hole-in-the-wall? To how much food? That old man, teetering on his cane to receive his plaque, why should he be gaunt and his clothes tattered? And why was it his eyes that shone with gratitude but not the politician's? Shishu felt his bile rise and decided to channel Doityo, who could find humour anywhere. I bet he's watching all of us right now, this pathetic crew, and roaring with laughter: 'Your youth and soul for a bit of copper!' When it was his turn, Shishu received his plaque in Doityo's name. Take that, Doityo!

The day wore on. Their pictures were taken for a planned gallery in the central tower. The tower's main pillar, they were told, would be laid with marble panels bearing the names of all freedom fighters who had served time in Cellular. Finally, at the ground-breaking, they took ceremonial turns at the shovel. Some gave speeches. Shishu decided not to. What could he say about Cellular, the only university he had ever attended?

By the end he felt jaded. He had heard the word 'freedom' one too many times today. With all that was plain by now about the freedom that had been won, standing at the site where the worst of its horrific price had been paid, he was overcome with fatigue.

Back at his ship's cabin that night, he reached for his poetry journal.

Cellular Redux
26 January 1974

Cellular Jail!
You broke many, but
We broke your spell
As a slaughterhouse
And turned you into
Our political alma mater

From the Bay
You had long faded
As the hated Bastille
Now resurrected, you
Raise a swell
In my stilled life.

What will you teach
The young?

༄

27 January 1974
Havelock Island
Andamans

'Can you tell who I am?' the woman smiled enigmatically, 'I never imagined I'd see you here, in the middle of the ocean!'

Middle-aged and pleasantly rotund, her mouth red with paan, she had blocked Shishu's path. Seeing that Shishu didn't have the foggiest idea, she broke into a toothy grin and warbled, 'You don't remember me, but I remember you! The tall man with kind eyes. Your hair is grey but otherwise you look just the same.' Others had gathered by now, intrigued by the visitors and smelling a yarn.

She called out to two strapping youths: 'Nitai and Gour, come here quick! Remember the story I've told you so many times about the Ghushuri camp?' The penny dropped for Shishu at the mention of Ghushuri. Could it be? 'I had scared you all away that day,' she chattered on, 'with my wailing and carrying on. The camp elders had scolded me later. But I wasn't all there, you know.' Shishu was now certain. Yes, it could be and it was. The scene resurfaced in him like a dead fish: the corpses like cordwood, a young waif berserk with grief, holding her dead baby that the truck had not yet come to collect. And here she was in front of him, over twenty years later, resplendent and whole. Magic? 'These are my sons,' she told Shishu, side-hugging the startled youths. 'Ei, you two,' she ordered them in a mock bark, 'this is like your grandfather. Touch his feet!' Then she grabbed Shishu by the hand and said: 'You have to come home for some tea! Your friends, too, all of you.'

3

Havelock Island was a revelation. Shishu had heard that hundreds of Bangal refugees—mainly Namasudra Dalits from Barisal and Khulna—had been settled here, a two-hour ferry ride from Port Blair. When he and a few of his Bangal comrades expressed interest in these villages, their handlers had arranged a visit. Exploring this small island on foot, touching the trees, smelling the air, Shishu felt a shiver of recognition. Here on a speck in the middle of the ocean, nearly a thousand miles from riverine rural Bengal, was a miniature replica, in all its fecund charm. He felt as if he was back in Barisal, only the rivers were missing.

Ambling down dirt tracks, the visitors ran into familiar fruit trees. Look at that, they cried, aam, jaam, kanthal, but even gaab and jamrul! And all the palms—narkel, shupuri, khejur. Nestled in the shade of familiar trees, were familiar homes with familiar flowers in their yards—jarul, tawgor, kawrobi. On a roadside they spotted a gawrjon tree, common in the Sundarbans. Did a Khulna refugee land here with a gawrjon seed in his belt, determined to recreate his homeland? Up ahead another familiar sight: a young mother sat amidst her children, shaving slivers from the spines of coconut fronds with a machete. 'What will you do with them?' they asked her in formal Bangla, knowing fully well. 'Brooms, what else?' she replied giggling, in an unabashed Bangal dialect that was music to Shishu's ears. It was what everyone spoke here. All around was a sheen of health—bright eyes, glossy skin, smooth mud porches. A woman walked by them unhurried, her long hair dripping post-bath, and flashed a radiant smile. Her whole being exuded an ease. Such was the air on this island.

Looking around, it was plain why the Namasudras had taken to Havelock like fish to water: the land appeared tailored for lower-riparian peasants. Much of its coast protected from the open ocean by other islands, Havelock had wooded hills in the centre, gently sloping to a wide swathe of flats, rich and drained by freshwater streams, ending in beaches of powdered sugar, lapped by turquoise waters teeming with fish. The state had allotted generous parcels to settlers, partly in the flats, good for paddies, and partly in the slopes, good for coconut and areca nut groves. The generosity was not pure: free India wished to populate the Andaman archipelago, much closer to foreign shores than its own, and bring it into the mainland's fold. But Andaman's reputation, as a dreaded penal colony across 'black waters', was tainted. The settlement scheme was open to all Indians, but it was the Namasudra refugees, fluent in working marshland and water, and too scarred to care about taboos, who had seized it with both hands. In Havelock, the fit could not have been more perfect. Five villages, housing nearly a thousand Bangals, hummed with life.

It was in one of these villages that Shishu had run into her, the phoenix from Ghushuri.

Ghost Shishu on Phoenix and Freedom

Over tea and puffed rice, Usharani told me her story. That was her name, Usharani Mondol. I didn't know this in Ghushuri but found out in Havelock, twenty-two years later.

Her family were Namasudra Dalits, landless labourers from Moistarkandi in Barisal—Jogen-da's village. When they fled the 1950 massacres, she was heavily pregnant. They washed up at the Ghushuri PL camp, where I saw her in December 1951. And in less than a year, she was here in Havelock. How? 'The pictures in the papers!' she exclaimed. I had forgotten all about it. The photographer in our UCRC team that Ambika-da had led into Ghushuri had documented the horror and those images had been splashed in the dailies. Usharani brought out a sleeve and carefully unwrapped it. In it was a newspaper cutting, yellowed and crumbling. A picture of a dishevelled woman in mid-yell, with a balled-up something in her arms. Those few dithered dots in a grainy image was the only photo of her firstborn, preserved like a precious heirloom. Her misplaced gratitude towards me made me cringe. Our mission that day had primarily been to embarrass the government pre-election. We hadn't followed up on the fate of the Ghushuri inmates.

Turns out, under the spotlight, the government had tried to clear out the camp quickly. 'Many of us got early allotments in the Andamans,' Usharani said, 'soon after they had picked out settlement sites here.' They were even shown promotional films on the islands, to fend off possible taboos. 'We saw a bioscope—trees, coconut palms, open fields. The land looked like Barisal! Why would we say no?' Remember, UCRC and all the Left parties were agitating against resettling Bangal refugees outside West Bengal. We did this throughout the fifties, the sixties, and deep into the seventies. And here I was, seeing how wrong we had been about the Andamans, in the flesh! Usharani arrived here in October 1952, aboard the S.S. *Maharaja*. Just as I had, twenty years before her. Like me she was packed in the hold, with other refugees. But unlike me, she was traveling to freedom. Freedom from history.

Her life thereafter had been a smooth sail. The state had given them ten bighas, along with farm implements and cash loans. They worked the land, producing both rice and coconut. Her husband also had a vegetable stall in the market and she earned a little by keeping chickens and ducks on the side. Their two-roomed home was comfortable and gleamed with care. She'd had two more children. Gour, twenty-one, was a desk clerk at the Havelock ferry terminal. Nitai, eighteen, still a student, loved the ocean. 'I feel something is missing,' he grinned, 'if I don't plunge in at least once a day!' And I thought, that is exactly how I had felt about the Kirtankhola growing up! These Bangals had been replanted so far away from Barisal's mammoth rivers, yet their water connection was intact—they were ocean Bangals now.

I was naturally thrilled for Usharani. 'Yes, life is good!' she beamed. 'You know the best thing here? Nobody steals, there's no reason to. We don't lock anything.' The sting of her dead child had dulled. And what of the old country, I wanted to know, did she miss Barisal? This brought up a bit of acid. 'What's there to miss?' she shot back, 'did we have anything there? We were everybody's punching bag! My children don't even know about Barisal. Our life is here,' she rapped the ground with her foot. As for the Indian mainland, she hadn't been back. Her sons spoke of it as a distant foggy shore. They had never been. And didn't seem very interested.

You have to understand, all these settlements in the Andamans were revenue villages. Not just in Havelock, but in Little Andamans, Mayabunder, Diglipur, and more. They were productive and paid taxes to the state. And nearly 85 per cent of these settlers were Namasudra refugees like Usharani—peasants, fishermen, boat builders, blacksmiths in their previous life. These hardy Bangals had diligently scrubbed off the P and the L seared on them in camp life. They were nobody's permanent liability. And they didn't see themselves as refugees either, but pioneers who had tamed this land. They had no use for history, no nostalgia. Time, for them, had begun right here, in their own hands.

They had challenges aplenty, with harsh monsoons and tenuous access to mainland supplies. But these islanders were living every Bangal peasant's dream. And mine! This is the revolution we had dreamed of. Enough land and water for all peasants willing and able, away from angry eyes and strong suckers of landlords and middlemen. And look at how it came about—by bureaucratic sleight!

Ha! Only for a few thousand, though, of the tens of millions who had wanted it.

The day before, at the ground-breaking ceremony at Cellular, I had repeatedly heard the word 'freedom'. At Havelock, I could feel that word as a lived doctrine, in all its ease and vigour. This is the freedom I thought I had fought for.

∽

'So, Cellular Jail had almost gone the Indian way,' I prodded Shishu's ghost, 'unremembered?'

'Yes, well, that would've been better, if you ask me. But with talk of a planned extension to the hospital in the late sixties and further demolition possible in the three remaining wings, a clamour went up. Activists lobbied. The government declared the proposed memorial in May 1969 and took another five years to break ground.'

'You really think that not remembering it at all would've been better? The most heinous penal island in the British empire?'

'Look, memorials make me nervous, all right? They are all about impossible flattening. Take a whole mountain, all its flora, fauna, light, fragrance, and make a pancake that someone can eat in an hour, maybe half. And if it happens to be part of the national canon, the pancake becomes a surface for territorial tattoos,' he hissed. 'The Cellular memorial is no different, hobbled by hagiography and misplaced highlights!'

'But you did accept the invite to the ground-breaking,' I teased.

'Yes, I had more social grace when alive than I do now as a ghost,' he retorted, 'I wouldn't accept if they asked me today. Besides, I freely roam the corridors of Cellular anyway. It is where I spend most of my time.' He then became pensive. 'It took another five years to build that memorial. The inauguration was on 11 February 1979. They had invited me but I didn't go.'

'Why not?'

'Because....' he faltered, then took a deep breath, 'because something was happening to me right then. Something big.'

10

RUPTURE

11 February 1979
Haat-thuba
West Bengal

SHISHU HADN'T SLEPT MUCH SINCE the police firing at Morichjhanpi. He obsessively scoured the Sunday papers for news this morning. The state had blockaded Morichjhanpi island in the Sundarbans, where thousands of Bangal refugees had gathered, denying them even food and medicine. The blockade began on Republic Day—a particularly cruel choice. And since the firing on 31 January the island was under a media curfew. This despite a high court ruling on 7 February to lift the blockade. No news had emerged from there in twelve days. But victims had begun to trickle out. Shishu had seen some of them, the 'why' in their vast liquid eyes. He felt like a man haunted.

At first they came in ones and twos. Then dozens. Over the past week their ranks had swelled. Like stunned bees from a smoked hive nearby. Shishu saw them slumped at the edges of the Haat-thuba market. Along the train tracks in the Bongaon–Barasat belt. Skin and bones, women too dazed to cover exposed breasts, children saucer-eyed in fear. Some with fresh wounds. A déjà vu of scenes from Sealdah 1950, 1964, 1971. Except this wave had not come from across the border. No, these Bangals had been brutalized within West Bengal. They came from Hasnabad, the gateway to the Sundarbans, where they had been rounded up. They were the fraction that had managed to flee the cattle trains dragging them back to Dandakaranya. Only a few were willing to talk. And they spoke less of the violence marking their bodies than the one on their souls. Why were those who had repeatedly claimed to be their saviour now killing them? Why invite and then evict? They hadn't asked for help, only permission to stay on a mud island in the jungle. Why then?

That sting infused Shishu's bloodstream. Their oozing wounds he could only see, but their betrayal he felt as his own. It filled him with an impotent rage. He had been helping a few affected families set up in Haat-thuba colony. But that felt like Band-Aid on a haemorrhage he couldn't yet fathom. This thing seemed so big. And there was so little news. He kept looking. Ah, here was something in the *Jugantar*. Jyoti Dutta, the intrepid senior journalist, had slipped through the state's vice grip. The first one on the ground! Shishu always looked forward to Dutta's reports, for truth hard-hitting and lyrical. But look at where his piece shows up! The lede was on the front page, yes, but pressed to the very bottom. Most of the report was relegated to page five. Before reading it, Shishu did a quick scan of the front page. The top headline: Iran's Islamic Revolution, about to overthrow the pro-West Shah regime. Just below that, Pakistan: Zia-ul-Haq's Hudood Ordinances had come into effect yesterday— eighty lashes for drinking, adulterers to be stoned to death, and other gruesome diktats. Yes, good to highlight repressive disasters far away, Shishu fumed, rather than illuminate the one unfolding at Calcutta's doorstep. Mid-page was coverage of a bonus for railway employees. And of belligerent residents heckling city workers for hitting a water main while installing a sewer pipe. Tucked below all of this, even below news of a street accident, was Dutta's report from Morichjhanpi.

Shishu read it, breathless. Dutta had broken the blockade and carried a boatload of food aid to the island. He detailed the state's tactics to stall him, despite him producing a copy of the court order. He had eventually sneaked across at nightfall, crossing the Korankhali River in a fishing dinghy by moonlight. That was the night of 9 February. The islanders immediately kindled fires to cook the rice he had brought in, their first in two weeks since the blockade began. Hunger was rife. All around the island Dutta saw stick-figure children by flickering firelight, waiting as their mothers cooked, listening to the soundtrack sweetest to Bengali ears: rice bubbling. Like the sound of a cavalry, ten thousand strong, trundling in to crush an eternal enemy. Shishu read on, his vision blurred by tears. Dutta had counted seventeen corpses, wrapped in rags, laid out on a moonlit mud shore. He listed their names and ages; thirteen of the seventeen were children, aged one to seven. Most had died of starvation during the blockade, he was told. But not all. Someone had unwrapped the smallest bundle for him. And Dutta had seen the moonlight catch the ragged edges of a bullet wound on baby fat.

The state had denied anyone had been killed at Morichjhanpi. And the UN had declared 1979 as the year of the child. Shishu couldn't read any more.

Shishu's Ghost on his Divorce

This was the darkest time in my life by far. Worse than death row. You know why? Because the state committing those atrocities was my party! Yes, CPI(M) had come to power in Bengal with a roaring mandate in mid-1977. And so many of us had been beside ourselves with joy. We finally had a people's party in charge! But Morichjhanpi was their first significant action as a ruling force. And it set the tone for the next thirty-four years they remained in power.

Let me tell you about the colossal betrayal that was Morichjhanpi. My party had demanded for decades that the Bangal refugees settled in Dandakaranya be brought back to Bengal. I had walked in raucous protest rallies back in 1958, when the Dandak project was first launched, even before refugee shipment began. Because these refugees, uniformly poor low-caste Bangals evicted from a moist delta, were being sent to a barren stretch straddling Chhattisgarh and Orissa. There is plenty of room for them here in Bengal, we had cried. I remember the UCRC had even surveyed possible sites and shared it with the government, including in the Sundarbans. But shipped to Dandak they were, by the trainloads, through the sixties and seventies, to a life precarious and bleak. Tilling unfit earth, abused as captive labour, dying like flies. And throughout that time, my party had volubly kept their plight in play. Only as political currency,

I saw the calculus later. Just as they had leveraged Bangal refugees to bloom in Bengal, my party had wooed the large Dandak Bangal vote to gain seats in the central Parliament, promising repatriation once they came to power. Then they did, in a landslide. And within months, thrilled Dandak Bangals streamed out in a mass exodus towards Bengal, with little idea of what they were walking into. They began arriving in March 1978, with the unerring homing instinct of olive ridley turtles, bound for a shore only ancestrally familiar. Ten thousand, twenty thousand, a hundred thousand. The state tried to put up roadblocks before they could reach the Sundarbans, pulled them off trains, thrashed them with batons. As they clotted up at Hasnabad, many were nabbed and forced back to Dandak. But many forged on, irrepressible, towards Morichjhanpi. And I understood how they knew to head there. Because their leaders had been close allies of my party for years. They had surely seen the UCRC land surveys, just as I had, which had specifically marked this island as a settlement site. A scrubby mudflat, uninhabited but habitation only a dinghy ride away, just inside the boundary of the Sundarbans reserve forest. They had waited decades for this. The silky mud here resembled the riverine tracts of Khulna and Barisal they had once fled, so unlike the pitiless red grit at Dandak. This is where they would squat. Like tens of millions of Bangals had all over West Bengal. That was their plan. And who could blame them? How would they know that the same people who had once done the thoughtful survey would now bludgeon them for trespassing on forest land?

That year, 1978, felt to me like a slow wreck. I couldn't believe what I was seeing. My party, buoyed to the throne by Bangal refugees, was now treating the ones at Morichjhanpi like so many termites. My party, who had fought to legalize hundreds of squatter colonies, now declared Morichjhanpi an illegal squat. I heard the chief minister spin conspiracy theories, that those aiding Morichjhanpi were out to undo his fledgling communist government! You know, I knew this man in my UCRC days—a fierce street fighter for Bangal refugees, Ambika-da's right hand. And his refugee relief minister was himself a colony Bangal, who had once squatted on government land! These powerful forces aligned against the Morichjhanpi settlers as they tried to get a foothold in the mud.

But something else, equally remarkable, happened that year. Bucking acute odds, those settlers built almost a gridded township with their bare hands. It housed over 30,000 at its peak. There were rattan-thatch homes raised on planks, uniformly laid out. A school, a library, a clinic, a playground. A market with a couple dozen stalls. A bidi factory, a bakery, a fishery, a forge, a boat workshop. Connected by streets of packed earth and girded by a raised embankment to keep out the salty tides. Their pluck and positivity stirred even Calcutta, a city jaded about Bangal refugees. Newspapers defied the state and filed reports from Morichjhanpi. I remember pictures of settlers working on homesteads: heads down, hands busy, focused. Of them fishing at dusk: the water flecked with their slim dinghies, the flared nets like dragonflies catching the late light. I remember a report Jyoti Dutta had filed in July 1978. He said, stepping on the island the first thing that hits you on the face, like a gust of fresh air, is their joy. They were half-starved but full of spirit. A wiry old man, who could afford to eat only once a day, exulted: 'We have erased our refugee tag! See these wide streets we've built? Even our grandchildren will walk on them.' I had seen an identical pioneer spirit in the Bangals at Havelock five years before. A different island with the same people—same history, same hands, same hearts. But Havelock had become a haven and Morichjhanpi was en route to hell.

As 1979 began, I thought, surely the state would let them stay? If you so much as put up a lean-to on a Calcutta sidewalk, that's enough inertia against evicting you. And these settlers had built an entire township! But no, the state ratcheted up the pressure with the blockade starting 26 January. Settler skiffs heading to the mainland on desperate runs for rations were rammed by police vessels and fired at on 31 January, killing many. The state ignored the high court's order to lift the blockade and many died of starvation. Over the next few months, the settlers faced virulent police repression, including rape of minor girls. Then, in mid-May, an armed police force about 3,500 strong, encircled the island in the dead of night and forcibly evicted the settlers over a three-day operation, killing many and injuring countless. The settlers, even the wounded, were packed into uncovered transport trucks in the furious May heat, then stuffed into train cars, and shipped back to Dandak. Many died en route, some even jumped off the moving trains. The Morichjhanpi township was set alight and razed to the ground. And the island restored to wilderness.

Notice that I keep saying 'killing many'. How many? No one knows. The cover-up was comprehensive. The state admitted to killing only two, both locals from habitation near Morichjhanpi. Perhaps they didn't count the settlers as human? Reliable eyewitnesses, like Jyoti Dutta, had found at least thirty-six dead at Morichjhanpi in early February. The settlers claimed hundreds had died of starvation over the blockaded months. And this even before the final purge in May, during which locals reported seeing corpses being flung en masse into the river. So we'll never know, because no investigation ever took place. And nobody was ever charged. But repression is not the story here. We are used to the state repressing the poor. And these were refugees, low-caste to boot. No, the main story here is deception, on a monumental scale.

All they wanted was a strip of mud to plant themselves in. Away from the rocky land they had been banished to, baked by a decade of drought, where nothing grew, where hard labour was extracted for free, where nobody listened. They fled that place because we had promised there was room for them here. When they arrived, trusting us, we brutalized them. Blocked their food supply. Poisoned their wells, which they had dug with no help from us. Burnt down their homes. Raped their women. Shot them and bloodied the wide waters of Korankhali. And shipped them back to Dandak. All in the name of protecting tigers. Ask around, the villagers in those parts will tell you that Morichjhanpi is when the tigers of Sundarbans became man-eaters. They had tasted the corpses tossed into the waters.

Morichjhanpi did something to me too. No, I didn't become a man-eater. But I did quit the party. I knew this would change nothing, but it was something I had to do.

Once I did, I began to see things, as if I'd been blinkered all this time. For instance, would the party have got away with the massacre had the settlers' names been Chatterji, Basu, Sengupta? No. Calcutta would've exploded in outrage. Their fellow caste members in the party would howl about human rights violations. But these settlers had names like Mondol, Goldar, Baroi. These were Namasudra Dalits. Jogen-da's people, but with no Jogen-da. They weren't even asserting their caste identity, mind you. They didn't know how. Look at the north, the south, the west of India—everywhere you'll find Dalits organized, with powerful leaders. But not in Bengal. Why? Because our Dalit movement was kneecapped with Jogen-da, back in 1950. Low-caste Bengalis have never had representation. They've been perennially preyed upon by whoever seeks power. Morichjhanpi is when I saw clearly that mine was a party of the upper castes. That all my life I had been an upper-caste communist. An oxymoron! We saw ourselves as caste-blind, we always knew what's best for the lower castes. But we never let them rise in the party. I remembered my friend Srimanta calling this out back in the forties. He would've got a huge kick over me quitting. Wish we could share a good laugh over it!

That's how I feel now, but at the time I didn't feel like laughing at all. I was distraught with grief and fury. I wanted to record this time in my poetry journal but couldn't bring up the words. And there was such a shroud of silence around. As if Calcutta's leftist intellectuals were cowed by this wanton show of communist force. There were a few exceptions, though. Shankho Ghosh, for example, the poet. He wrote a scathing poem around this time that gave me voice, perhaps to many of us. I had jotted it down in my journal.

Let me read you a bit where he calls out the party's shameful about-face on the Dandak refugees and its muscular muzzling of dissent:

> When you said, it was birthright
> When I say, it's a hoax
> Why did they have to rush here
> Unless at someone's coax?
> So what if life is hopeless,
> A long infertile cry
> If I speak up, your soldiers
> Will wring my throat awry!

But the real sting is at the end:

> You said: no, not in Dandak
> Plant them here, on mother soil
> When I do, I'm a showboat
> Leading rowdies to a boil.
> You have witnessed their dying breath
> And labelled it a whine
> From your lips—revolution
> Reaction, when from mine!

Reactionary! Revisionist! Those were the harshest insults, see. We communists lobbed them whenever cornered, like squids do ink.

All that said, leaving was painful. The party was my real family. I joined it as a stripling in Cellular Jail, back in 1935. Forty-four years! All those people I admired, all those words. Not that I had always felt aligned with the party line. My first patch of trouble was in 1942, when the party stood on the wrong side of history—with the British—while the country was ablaze in the Quit India movement. I had come close to quitting then, but Ambika-da had talked me out of it. There was more trouble in the decades that followed. Finding out about Stalin's atrocities, the CPI-CPI(M) split, the subsequent infighting, the Naxal bloodbath, then Mao's atrocities. All of these were blows I had weathered, and grown calluses. Look, I'd never been ambitious. I was content to be a cog. To be in a pack, with a leader I could look up to, working for a bigger cause. My relationship with the party had been like those marriages where you grind your teeth and hang on. Because you're scared of the unknown. That fear was no longer enough. Revulsion had taken over.

I didn't just quit the party, I quit politics altogether. I quit the familiar. I quit my bank job in Barasat and fled to a tiny village in Bankura. A speck of dry earth where a few diehards were trying to grow rice. I wanted to dive into physical labour. I couldn't bear to be alone with my thoughts. I felt entirely out of joint, like a left-handed man suddenly writing with his right. But also liberated in ways I didn't think possible. I was sixty-five and free. And filled with dread.

∽

'I was fourteen at this time, old enough to read newspapers. How come I knew nothing about Morichjhanpi, not even later?' I found this somewhat shocking.

'It wasn't just you,' Shishu's ghost intoned, 'few did. The censorship was intense while Morichjhanpi was unfolding. The state thwarted journalists at every step, threw them in jail, threatened newspapers with loss of ads. In parallel, they spun propaganda about Morichjhanpi: a noxious stew about an arms factory, foreign hands, a parallel government. This pincer movement—absence of facts and abundance of fiction—was unleashed on the public. That was during. What happened later was more fascinating. CPI(M) deployed tools straight out of Soviet and Chinese playbooks to erase Morichjhanpi. The silence and fear lingered for decades. You see, that chief minister stayed on the throne for nearly a quarter century. No one could speak about Morichjhanpi until his death in 2010. An anthology published in 2002, for instance, was swiftly pulled off the shelves. Shades of Stalin and Mao?'

That would explain it, but something else was bothering me. 'I'm thinking of my life at fourteen. I did maths homework and read novels. Wrote my first love letter. Whereas you? You were an anti-state radical, already on death row for political murder!'

'That was par for the course,' he waved as if scattering fumes, 'the conditions demanded it. That I succeeded in my attempt was unusual, my path was not. See, the fourteen-year-old is not a fixed thing. In history's lulls they are children, like you were. In its storms they are not. Look around, such a swell is coming up the world over. Speaking from experience though,' he exhaled, 'murder is rarely an effective method for real change.'

'Do you regret it?'

He scrutinized his fingers and fell into a pinched quiet. 'We do things in war that are unheard of in the animal kingdom,' he finally said, as if to himself, 'unnatural things that come with hefty price tags. They damage the young far more than the old.' Taking a deep breath, he looked squarely at me: 'To heal we need to remember. But we're good at myths, not memory. To remember, to truly remember it all, is painful.'

11
CODA

Memory
Black & white photograph
July 1932

> Family seated on a front porch stoop: an elderly couple flanked by two young women, one with a baby on her lap, and three children at their feet.

THE WOMAN WITH THE BABY is Noni, at her marital home in Bikna village, Barisal. The elderly couple are Hira's parents. Her sister-in-law with her three children complete the set. Noni here is twenty-one, moon-faced, and in the full bloom of youth. She looks pensive. And a bit blurry because Baba, the bonny yearling on her lap, had wriggled just as the shutter was pressed.

∽

Shishu's ghost was riveted by the photograph, his attention pinned on Noni: 'This must've been taken around the time I had sent her that long letter, in verse, just before shipping out to Cellular. This is the Noni-di I remember from when we parted five years before, in 1927. She looks just the same. This is the one who woke me, taught me to look and listen. When I last saw her, she was standing in the season's first rains, in Patuakhali. Then poof! She was gone.'

'After I quit the party,' he went on as if in a reverie, 'I felt empty. And into that vacuum I had let in romantic love. At sixty-five! It sounds ridiculous, I know,' he chuckled defensively, 'this was almost surely on the rebound. Because the party had so flogged this sort of thing as a bourgeois tic. Anyway, a woman had expressed interest. Have you seen my poems from that time?'

'I have. She seemed quite keen to find out your story.'

'She was. And I wanted to respond. But here's what happened: I became deluged with memories of Noni-di. As if by cracking open that door I had ruptured a dam. My thoughts kept looping back to her. Noni-di was three years older, so then, a die-able age. Where was she? How was she? If alive, I knew she couldn't possibly have forgotten me. All day long I would keep busy, hacking away at the stubborn land. But in those inky nights of rural Bankura, I often sat up alone, raking through my life with a fine-toothed comb. And it slowly came to me, like a crimson dawn: I had done it all for her. The soldiering, the jail, the struggle. Ah, the struggle! All of it. For Noni-di. This simple fact was like the piece that finishes the puzzle. It brought me great peace. And also made me wonder: how many others had been like me? How many foot soldiers of revolutions were similarly fuelled? I knew I had to find her, to tell her this. This is when I wrote that open letter, to whom it may concern, laying out what she meant to me.'

'The one that became the preface of your notebook?'

'Yes, but the notebook happened later. I didn't begin curating the poems for a few more years. I wrote that letter first. I didn't know if I'd ever be able to deliver it. But I thought in case she outlived me and it somehow found her, at least she would know. Then I began to search for her in earnest. Generating leads, hounding them down. My quest began in 1979. I found her in 1991. A dozen years, but I did, didn't I?'

'And did you tell her? That it had all been for her?'

The ghost shook his head. 'I had tried to rehearse it beforehand,' he said with a wan smile, 'but the words didn't sound right. And when I actually saw her, I could scarcely say anything at all.'

Act 4

Ash

When the body becomes ash
O divine flame, remember the work
The work, remember.

—Isha Upanishad, Canto 17

4 June 1991
Serampore, West Bengal
Night

SHISHU CAME BACK FROM HIS evening walk by the river. On his desk was the notebook, waiting. He gazed at it with satisfaction. Yes, it did look worthy of Noni-di. There was a quiet dignity about it, its sleek black cover bare but for an abstract motif embossed on the upper left. That happened to be the company logo—this being a corporate diary—but luckily it wasn't gaudy. And the notebook had a nice heft, with a page a day. Over half of which he had deliberately left empty. As an invitation. Would she fill them? The anticipation warmed him. But at its edges was a curl of chill. What would he look forward to after tomorrow?

He opened the notebook and out came darts of self-doubt. So many epigraphs, was that over the top? Too late to change now. He had left a gap between the epigraphs and the content, three blank leaves, like he'd seen in books. Then the long preface: a copy of his open letter. He had edited it somewhat since first writing it a dozen years ago. This, the final version, was six years old. That's how long he had been curating his poems in this notebook for Noni-di. Scanning the letter now, he felt a tug for his old self, the man who had written it. Eh you, shooting out a space probe with no idea if contact was remotely possible. And here I am about to see her, tomorrow morning! Can you believe it?

In the preface he had made a clean breast of his story with Noni-di. A montage of their shared childhood filled with particulate grain—him sketching for her embroidery, them reading banned books together—up until their parting. Then a gist of his life thereafter and why he was searching for her now. He re-read the ending:

'I am deeply indebted to Noni-di. And I know well that this debt cannot be repaid; it is glib to even consider it. I have been anointed by her endless affection. And empowered by that, here is my earnest call to her: Noni-di, wherever you are, please accept this meagre offering from your Shishu.'

He had signed and dated it, as if it were the original:

'Shishu'
Ramesh Chandra Chatterji
Krishi Niketan
Kanuri village, Bankura
8 October 1979

Overall, it didn't read badly, he thought. Except maybe the end was a bit frantic. Too much of a dry howl, like those in newspaper classifieds for lost relatives: 'Wherever you are, come back, father critical!' Shishu chuckled.

Now onto the main matter: the poems. Surely, Noni-di would not miss that he had woven a bouquet of 108. He had even placed 'Offering' as the opening poem, the letter in verse he had sent her on the eve of leaving for Cellular. The rest he had packed into four sections, the arrangement more thematic than purely chronological. Flipping through them now Shishu was buffeted by a raft of feelings for his prior selves: affection, awe, envy, ridicule even. The boy in the first section, straddling free life and death row, new to words and rhythm, wielding them like a fawn testing out antler buds. The jailed youth in the second, lost and straining to keep love alive, using poetry as a crutch and his only weapon. The cub communist in the third with his fierce Red streak. And in the fourth, a man no longer in jail but hardly free, wizened but wiser? It was all here. See Noni-di, he would tell her, I kept a record, just as you'd asked in that letter inviting me to poetry. Thus he would throw open his life, show her all of his phases. Including when he'd been feverish with her in jail. Or when he let romantic love in, much later. Or sent his sole poetry submission to a newspaper and savoured not hearing back. All of it: the peaks and troughs, the personal and political, the heat and heartache. The arc of life. His life, in which she had been so central in her absence. Like a wax mould that melts away.

The earliest poem he had included was from 1928, his first ever, triggered by her invitation letter. And the latest was from 1981. He hadn't written many in the past decade, none worth keeping anyway. Things had been dimming down lately. A brush with illness six years ago convinced him that he had become too fragile to live alone in the back of the beyond. So he had to leave rural Bankura and move in with his brother's family in Serampore. He rued the loss of independence, but being back in civilization had helped his search for Noni-di. Besides, he had grown fond of Serampore, this sleepy little town on the river, with Calcutta only a short train ride away. All around him were crumbling colonial ruins, utterly resonant with how his life felt right now. For example, those fluted columns of the shuttered church down the street? They resembled his neck in the mirror, tendons strained. And poetry seems to have left him. What had kept him going was the search. The window was closing fast, he knew. Over the past six years he had doggedly worked the fractal lanes and by-lanes of Bangal refugee networks. Until the breakthrough a few months ago, when he found someone who could arrange to deliver her a letter. He had finally heard from her yesterday and in a few hours was going to meet her. After sixty-four years!

He felt far more trepidation at this prospect than thrill, Shishu realized. He had worked so hard to create this moment, to see her and to give her his life's work. Her gift to him—his poetry practice—had been a lifelong companion crucial to his survival. No one knew this, much less cared. He wanted her to be his audience of one, the only one he cared about. But wasn't that hopelessly indulgent? Was this less a tribute to her than him seeking validation? And he dearly wanted to find out how *she* had recorded her life in poetry. But why should she oblige? All of this seemed terribly presumptuous. His guts knotted up like he was about to step off a ledge. It had been so long. What if Noni-di had drifted away? What if she didn't let him in?

No, no, mustn't go there, Shishu swatted away these thoughts. There was no turning back now. He imagined the best case: Noni-di sees what he sees and agrees to include her best poems in the same notebook. And they are together in poetry. What a magnificent *us* that would be!

He began to practice what he would tell her tomorrow.

∽

We know how this tomorrow went. That is where we had begun, at their reunion. But what about thereafter? Did Shishu get his wish?

When he visited Noni a few months later, she returned the notebook to him, with exactly one addition. And he never came back to see her again. These facts I have verified. But here are others I cannot:

I can't keep it, she told him, I am not worthy. She couldn't say more than this; she didn't think he would understand. All I have added is one brief poem, she said. Can you forgive me?

Shishu had steeled himself for this possibility but was still crushed. At least his songs had reached her, he could tell. Now she knew, and that would do. He opened the notebook and found the one poem she had added. It was on the back of the epigraph page, in her large looping scrawl. The poem itself was minuscule: haiku-like, with only sixteen words. Shishu inhaled it in a few seconds. Then re-read it, slower. As he did, his hurt made way for elation. He was soon beaming, like an awestruck student with his teacher's elegant solution to something he had thrashed against for a long time. Ah Noni-di, he wanted to tell her, your poem is like that dove on King Shibi's scale that no amount of flesh can tip. But shushed by her brevity, he didn't.

∽

12 August 1994
Government Hospital
Serampore

On this, their final visit, they exchanged no words. Shishu lay in bed, his wasted frame flat as the sheets. Noni sat on a low stool at his bedside. She didn't speak. And he couldn't. He was taking far too many shallow breaths a minute. Of air tinged with Dettol.

His brother had called with the news that Shishu was dying

and that he had, with great effort, asked for Noni. So Ma and Baba had brought Noni to this bleak state hospital in Serampore. To this grungy and overcrowded ward, with spill-over patients strewn on floor mattresses. Shishu had a cot, though. A metal cot, its headboard crusted with rust, but a cot. And a two-drawer metal chest at his bedside, atop which Ma had arranged the fruits and the jar of Horlicks she had carried for him. There even was a window above his bed. But its grimy pane, lashed today by rain, was practically opaque.

He couldn't speak but Shishu's gaze was trained on Noni, his sunken eyes dim but unwavering. He had taken Noni's hand in his. 'Go on, say something,' Baba urged her, 'you were so eager for this visit. Surely you have much to say!' But she made not a sound. Tears streaming down, Noni sat holding Shishu's hand as he panted for breath. Around them swirled the cacophony of the hospital's visiting hour. Until the clock ran out. And Ma gently pried Noni away.

∽

Shishu passed three days later, on Independence Day, at eighty. He had donated his body to science. Ever meticulous, he had also left an informal will about his meagre possessions. The notebook, he insisted, must reach his Noni-di.

And it did a few months after his death. Upon opening it, Noni saw the additions Shishu had made since she had returned it to him. She saw why he had given it to her a second time.

Just beneath where she had written her haiku, was a heading: 'Verbatim copy of Noni-di's letter of 30 May 1991'. Squeezed within the half page that remained and the next full page, in a dense hand, was her letter reconnecting with him, and a note on its receipt, about a digit being off in the address she had sent him. This last bit made Noni smile despite herself. Then she turned the page, and her chest tightened. There, centred on the final leaf before his preface, Shishu had firmly pasted a neon green sticky note with a poem in her hand, signed and dated 5 June 1991. Noni couldn't believe it. This was on the gift wrap of a book she had given him that day, written on the eve of seeing him. Who was this man emerging from the mists of time? Unsure, she had played it safe with these stiff lines. She read them now, blinded by tears:

> You've sacrificed much
> For the nation
> O, valiant soldier
> You've taunted death
> On a perilous path
> Fearless forever.

How wrenching it was to see her trifling note occupy pride of place! But she now understood. What could he have done? These had been her only words to him—the letter, this note, the haiku. So he enshrined them, within the three blank leaves between the epigraphs and his preface. He gave her words the right of way before any of his. He composed the *us* in poetry that he had wanted, with the scraps he had. Noni's insides felt like a furnace. She understood why Shishu had never come back. What was left to say that he hadn't already said in the notebook and she couldn't?

But she hadn't been able to tell him why she had failed. That the notebook had felt to her like a giant mocking mirror. A strident reminder of what she had not, could not, become. She couldn't bear to look at it nor look away. She had to give it back. But now, receiving it the second time, she saw not the mirror but the shrine Shishu had built. He had tended to it lovingly until he could not. It was her turn now to honour it.

Noni held on to the notebook for six more years before passing with the century, at eighty-nine. Even a week before her death, Ma had seen her flip through it, caressing the pages.

༄

12 June 1991
New Alipore
Calcutta

The dog days of summer. The air soupy and the monsoons about to break. For the past week Noni had felt the steam rise within her, as if in rhyme with the outside. That's how long it had been since Shishu had left her his notebook. She had read all of it, all 108 poems. Some multiple times.

She understood what he was asking and was petrified. She saw with painful clarity the Noni-di Shishu thought he had met last week: the resplendent paragon he knew as a child, grown only more sublime in absentia. How would she live up to that? She hadn't been able to make existential choices like he had. No, all her cards had been picked for her. How could she tell him that her poetry life had withered? That she had not been able to keep her self whole. That she had not created a poetic record of her life. That her tribe—of children, grandchildren, great-grandchildren, now nearly fifty strong—was her only record. She had seen Shishu's flame last week, still marvellously blue. Had she kindled it? Perhaps. A lifetime ago. But it was he who had kept it fuelled and shielded. And where was her flame? In Shishu's earnest gaze, eager even, she saw the cinders of her own promise. She saw a dead volcano, whose ashes had made rich soil in other valleys.

Late that afternoon, she heard what she'd been waiting for. The deafening crash of thunder. She rushed out to the balcony for the spectacle. Jostling dark clouds had dimmed the day to a greenish hue. A moment of stillness, portentous. Then the flaccid sky ruptured, unleashing sheets of rain. Unbridled at first, the rain whipped streets to a smoky whiteout, mussing trees every which way. An assault much-awaited, life-giving. Gradually, as if with both parties sated, the rain calmed to a steady hiss. Noni stood buffeted by the spray, cooled inside and out. How many times had she watched the monsoons arrive? Yet each time it felt new. She took deep drags of the petrichor the parched earth had released. It brought back memories of another arrival. In Patuakhali. She could smell the scent of that time. The last time Shishu had seen Noni. Maybe the last time Noni had seen Noni. How they loved getting drenched in the season's first shower! The fat drops striking skin like lead shot. She remembered it all, her tears mingling with the new rain.

The rain lulled to a patter in the evening. Glistening leaves, rinsed of summer's dust, drip-dripped. Noni opened the notebook, turned the epigraph page and on its back wrote:

> Seeing you after so long
> So much I want to say
> Words clamour, they
> Muzzle me.